My Choice

My Choice

Brandy Blackmon

Published by Push Power Boss Enterprise

ISBN: 979-8-9892995-7-7

Cover Design by Sandra Rzeczya

Interior Design by Brandy Blackmon

This is a work of fiction. Names, characters, places, and incidents are either products of the author's imagination or used fictitiously. Any resemblance to actual events, locales, or persons, living or dead, is entirely coincidental.

First Edition: October 2024

Printed in the United States of America

For permissions or inquiries, contact:

Brandy Blackmon; blackmonbrandy27@gmail.com

Why My Choice?

Misa Macky is a sixteen-year-old girl navigating the complexities of high school, a journey that resonates deeply with my own. At that age, I too was Misa Macky, yearning to fit in and experience the thrill of young love. Like many teenagers, I dreamt of being a typical girl with a crush, but the reality of approaching that crush often felt overwhelming. I found myself wishing for the confidence to say something as simple as, "Hi."

This story unfolds through Misa's eyes, capturing her experiences as she enters unfamiliar territory—dating. We'll follow her emotional roller coaster as she faces the challenges and triumphs of a new chapter in her life, illuminating the often-tumultuous journey of adolescence.

Brandy Blackmon

1

This is it. This has got to be the perfect turnout for today. Walking here on the path that circles around the best park in town along with the greatest guy in the world on such a gorgeous sunny day. The wind is gently blowing, making the grass dance around us as we walk hand in hand along the trail. The afternoon sun is shining so bright, it's like we have the spotlight on us. There aren't many people around to bother us either. It feels like a scene out of a movie. Sano and I were just about to pass the swings when he slowed to a stop.

"Sano?" I called him. He glanced around bringing his focus back to me. I hope he's not considering getting on the swings. This skirt is not long enough for that.

As I got more anxious, I noticed a smile growing on his face. That only heightened the anxiety. Sano doesn't always smile. Is he really considering the swings?

"Misa," he started, "we've been hanging out for a while now, and I called you out today to ask if we can make this official. I really would like you to be my girlfriend." His words were as serious as his gaze was on me. I was speechless. Did he really ask to be official? With me?

"Yes, Sano, I would love to be your girlfriend!" I didn't hesitate to answer. I waited so long to say those words, years in fact. I couldn't hide my happiness as I was smiling ear to ear. This was the happiest day of my life!

"You've made me the happiest guy in the world." The sun was hitting his beautiful hazel eyes perfectly as his warm smile shined just as bright. It couldn't get any better than this.

"Oh, Sano, just kiss me already." I wanted to seal this moment to know it was real. I didn't want this movie to end.

I leaned in as he did the same with his eyes closed and lips puckered. But I stopped short of his face as I noticed it began to change.

"Misa!" I heard a voice and backed away from him as I watched his face turn into a girl's face.

"Misa!" He called me again. His voice was a pitch higher.

"Sano? What's happening to your face?" I asked. I reached out to touch it, but my hand didn't make contact in time before it disappeared.

Suddenly, the perfect bright and sunny day in the park became gloomy. The world around me was getting darker, and Sano was completely gone.

"Misa! Will you wake up?" The voice made me jolt in my seat. When I lifted my head from my desk, I saw my best friend staring at me.

"W-what? Katie?" I was still half asleep.

"What are you doing dreaming? Class is over," she said, pointing to the clock on the wall. I slept straight through the bell.

"I was asleep? I was sure I was just talking with Sano." Still a bit dazed, I looked around for him.

"What are you talking about? He's already at track practice."

"Really? It felt so real this time." The disappointment that filled me was nothing new. That's the third time I had a dream like that in the past week...

"You're so delusional. Come on let's go." Katie just shook her head and turned toward the door. I gathered my things in sadness and walked out of the classroom behind her.

What does it take to get the guy of literally your dreams? Is it because of my looks? I'm not particularly short; around five foot seven on a good day. I have long curly light brown hair, and brown eyes. And I think I can dress pretty well if you ask me. That is, if you consider your wardrobe that consists mostly of skinny jeans and fitted T-shirts, along with the occasional skirt for special occasions dressing pretty well. But I guess Sano doesn't like average height, long brown hair and brown-eyed girls who wear a lot of skinny jeans. Although, I don't really know that for sure since I don't talk to him. Like, at all.

I've had this crush on him since we were freshmen, and I'm still too shy to talk to him two years later. The only things I know about him are his incredible features. He's about six feet tall with the greatest dark brown hair, and the prettiest hazel eyes I've ever seen. He's on the track team and has been since freshman year. He's kind of quiet, but still popular in our school despite not being the average loudmouth jock. I think that's enough to know about someone you've been crushing on for two years.

"You know, Misa, you shouldn't sleep so much in class." Katie started her lectures again as I was finishing up at my locker, "Your grades are going to continue to drop, and you'll never make it out of high school with us."

"Gee, thanks Katie, that helps a lot."

"I'm just saying that you're holding on to a crush that probably won't get anywhere. You're going to waste your whole life on someone you won't get, and you'll be forever alone, still believing and hoping for—"

"Katie!" I didn't want to hear such negativity anymore. "You're not helping me here! Besides, you never know, he might come around one day."

Just as I said that we left the school building and had to pass the track field. The track coach was strict. They were already in uniform standing together as the coach was talking to them.

"Now you guys know we can't leave it all up to Sano again. I need you all to shape up." I could hear the coach speaking to them.

I spotted Sano instantly standing next to the coach as he continued praising him. Sano is the best runner on the team and has been since he started freshman year. His legs are small but strong and firm. I don't know how he can be so fast, but running must be his calling.

Watching him as he held his head low listening to the coach made me think of my dream earlier. My heart sank as I still try to hold on to the slim chance of that dream one day coming true. I must have been staring because Katie had to come and pull me away from my trance.

"Look, I'm your best friend Misa. I'm just trying to stop you now before you go and get yourself hurt."

"You're being overprotective. I won't get hurt. Plus, I'm already sixteen and going to be seventeen this year. I'm probably the only girl who has yet to have a boyfriend in this school. Probably the whole city. You should be encouraging me to go for it," I tell her.

"I understand what you're saying, but this situation isn't something you should be trying for. I've been down this road before. I was all alone, watching everyone else have fun and be all lovey-dovey while I sat back just looking at my crush go out with another woman. She put her dirty little spell on him. That backstabbing, short skirt wearing whore." Her sympathizing with me turned into anger just like that.

"Whoa, Katie. Calm down. That was like, eighth grade when that happened. We're in high school now. And she was a cheerleader, so yeah, her skirt was short. Plus, you have a boyfriend now." I had to remind her.

"Yeah, I know. But did it make you feel any better?" she asked, genuinely thinking that would make me feel better. But it didn't. I wanted to react more to that statement, but we saw the only person that could make Katie's bright blue eyes glow right after calling someone a whore. Her boyfriend, Eden.

"Hey, Katie." He walked up to us.

"Eden," Katie called as they greeted each other with a kiss.

Eden is one of the few in our school who can surprisingly put up with her like I can. Most people steer clear of her in fear of getting on her bad side. And not only was he up for the challenge, he's also been with her for almost three years. He's on the quiet side too, which is totally opposite of Katie.

"So, Katie, what time were you able to go today?" He asked her.

"Around maybe five or so? I have to help Misa get the last of her things from my place."

"Where are you guys going?" I asked a bit surprised seeing as I was not informed on couple plans today.

"What, I didn't tell you? We were just going to hang out after you left since you said you had to be home by a certain time. I mean, you can come with if you don't have to get home. We were just going to the mall."

I could hear a little guilt in her tone. She had no problem inviting me along when she thought she was cutting time with me short.

"No, it's cool. My mom was pretty clear on getting home early." Even if that weren't the case, I would rather go home than third wheel after today.

We set off for Katie's place. We both live a few blocks from the school so riding the bus hasn't been a thing since middle school. I was on the left side of Katie and Eden was on the right of her. No sense in him leaving and coming back in a couple hours, so he's coming along with us.

I kind of trailed back a bit and watched them walking hand in hand making small talk about his classes. I doubt either of them really noticed I'm not next to them. Their relationship makes me jealous sometimes, but I know Katie would never let a guy get in the way of our friendship. We've been friends since first grade. When we got into high school, she cut her hair to a short brown to do that 'reinvent myself' thing. She's also known for her blue eyes, which could be used for beauty and for bad.

We've always had classes with each other, and she's the one who always looks out for me in my time of need. Even though she's been with Eden a lot lately, she'd drop any plans she had in a second if I needed help. We even lived together for a while due to my parents' job being far away, and I didn't want to move away. Recently, they've been using a lot of their vacation time and coming back home, so I've been there. Yesterday, my mom told me to stay home for something she has arranged, so I'm getting the last of my important items from Katie's place.

"Speaking of parents, Misa, do you really not know what your mom wants?" Katie looked over to me and stopped after seeing I wasn't on the side of her anymore.

"No, I don't," I said catching up to them. "She told me it's something we've talked about before, but she goes on and on about everything, it's hard to remember exactly what she's referring to."

"That really doesn't explain anything. Maybe it has something to do with her being able to come home so much now. You think she might be getting fired?"

"Please, that's the last thing to consider. You know my mom did everything to get into that Masidone Company. She would never do anything to risk getting fired from the biggest company in the country. She'd do anything to stay there."

"I guess you're right. Your parents even act like strangers to avoid having in-office relationship problems. This Masidone Corp. must really be top notch for them to go that far just to keep bragging rights." Katie said.

"They only hire the best. You have to pass like four different interviews to get in there, and they apparently have amazing benefits along with amazing pay. My mom said they even had meetings with some famous people." I sighed wishing I could know more about that part, but they aren't allowed to talk about the people they meet with.

"Let's not forget the special apartment rates for employees at the complex he owns which is what sealed the deal for them. You know I would've been long gone if your mom hadn't been cool with me staying with you."

"My mom applied once. Didn't make it past the second interview. She said it felt like she was being interrogated and couldn't handle the pressure. I bet it wasn't that bad." Katie said with a straight face. This is coming from a girl who stared down the principle who almost suspended her after she threatened another girl with her own notebook.

"You probably would have scared the interviewers." I laughed at the thought.

"I would not! I'm perfectly capable of being nice when I need to be. Right Eden?" She turned to him, and he looked away.

"Of course, Kay, you're always sweet."

"See?" Katie said.

"Well, aside from the other day when you yelled at a girl for bumping into you in the hallway, and last week when you weren't feeling well and told Mr. Hallen's he was talking too much when he went off subject again. There was also that day when I was coming to get you, you were about to yell at someone else who accidentally stepped on your book you had on the floor. Not to mention—"

"Basically, he agrees with me." I stopped him before he ended up single. Even though none of that was a lie.

"I can't believe either of you. I'm the nicest person ever and could pass any interview with no problem. Besides, I'm sure you'd want to give that place a try when you get old enough since your mom and dad got in." She said.

"No thanks, I don't want anything to do with that place. It's making them crazy, so I don't need to be a part of that. I'm perfectly fine with living my normal life without being a part of the Masidone company cult." Even if I wanted to, someone with my grades would be laughed at for applying, but I don't need to remind her of that…

We finally reached Katie's house, and I went straight for my already packed bag I left on the floor next to her dresser. I hadn't forgotten about these couple's plans and didn't want to stop them from being together by adding me in.

"Misa, you really don't have to hurry. We still have all evening to do stuff."

"No, it's really okay. Plus, I told you, my mom wants me home. I'm surprised she hasn't called me yet. Let's plan something for this weekend if you two don't already have plans."

"That works. He has a family thing, so it'll just be you and me."

"Sounds good." I told her. I grabbed my bag and said bye to everyone and headed to my house that was only two blocks over.

Leaving Katie like that happens sometimes. That's what happens when your best friend has a boyfriend and you're stuck dreaming about a boy who probably doesn't even know you exist. I guess I can only dream until it's my turn for cupid to shoot his love arrow. Someone like Sano doesn't come around often. One of these days I have to work up the courage to talk to him. I mean, what's the worst that could happen?

With each step I took, I found myself thinking of all the ways it could go wrong when I found myself walking in my house. Something was different.

"Mom, I'm home! Do we have company over?" I yelled to her seeing an unfamiliar coat lying neatly on the couch.

"Misa, if you know we have a guest, why do you feel the need to yell?" she asked, coming from the kitchen. I suppose I could've been a bit calmer about it, but I was still lost in thought about Sano.

"What took you so long? I said to come straight home after school today so you can meet Ken."

We both stood face to face in the living room as I looked at her wondering why I was supposed to know that name.

"And who's that?" I finally asked. "Your fiancé." She told me.

If I didn't know any better, I swear the world stopped spinning in that moment. There was a sting in my eyes from how wide I was staring.

"My fian— what?" I asked after she didn't crack a smile or burst into laughter about the joke that is apparently not a joke. "When and where did a fiancé come from? I don't even know anybody that could be a fiancé and way too young to get married to someone I don't know!"

She just sighed, "Misa, we've talked about this already. No one is getting married now, but it was decided that you got to know Ken for that possibility. Don't you remember?"

I traced my memory of a possible conversation about this. Then a short conversation from last week about the idea of love and marriage and "how would you like to marry into a successful family?" played over in my mind.

"You mean you were serious about that? Mom, I'm not marrying some guy you just found for me. What are we, village people?"

"We didn't just find him. He's the son of the Masidone family. You know, the people we work for? You know, some of the richest people in the country? And he is as sweet as can be, I have high hopes for you both. He just had to go to the bathroom. You'll see him in a minute."

I can see the hope glowing in her eyes as she completely believes this is something I should be a part of. I don't know if I accidentally fell asleep again at Katie's place, but I wanted out of this dream.

"B-but, Mom, I have someone I like already," I blurted out to her.

"Hmm, are you talking about that Sano person? I'm sure you don't need to worry about him, honey."

"How do you know about him? You looked in my journal, didn't you? How could you?!"

"It's not like you got anything good in it," she said, almost disappointed.

"Why do you always invade my privacy!?" Anger started rising in me.

"Ah, so noisy down here," Just as quickly as my anger rose, it faded being replaced with shock hearing a deep voice coming from upstairs.

I couldn't help but stare. Coming down the stairs and joining the family quarrel was a tall, nicely dressed guy that looked as custom-made as his clothes. His hair was dark and styled up with fresh finger waves. He was wearing a white and black button up with a black shirt underneath. I don't know why, but I was pretty sure it was personally customized to fit his broad shoulders. He was rubbing his ear as he continued walking toward us.

"Oh, Ken, you're back," my mom says as if there's nothing wrong when everything is, "This is my daughter, Misa. And Misa, this is Ken Masidone," she introduced us. I'm pretty sure I was still staring at him.

"Ah, so we finally meet. It's so nice to meet a vocalist such as this one. I was under the impression someone was talking through a megaphone," he said jokingly. His comment snapped me back to reality.

"And you expect me to like a guy like this? That is not happening." I crossed my arms and turned away from him. I know I'm a bit loud at times, but he didn't have to make that the first thing he says to me. Talk about a bad first impression.

I was about to walk away when my mother said, "Now Misa, show our guest some respect. He came all the way from the comfort of his home to see you."

"Yeah, I came all the way here to see miss temper head," he said still making fun of me with a grin as if he's having fun.

"You'll have to excuse her. Misa gets a little excited sometimes. Now, I'll leave you kids alone. I'm sure you'll get along just fine. I'm going to finish making dinner while you two start getting better acquainted," my mom said winking at me, and leaving the both of us standing alone in our living room.

Our living room was a little spacious. We had a recliner, a love seat, and a couch in the middle of the room with a small coffee table and TV in front of it. But as we stood face to face between the couch and table I could swear the room was closing in on us. He just stared at me for a minute and started to smile again.

"Wh-what?" I asked a little creeped out.

"So, Misa, is it? Can I call you Mimi?"

"No! I don't like people giving me nicknames."

"Aw, you're no fun."

"How long is this meeting supposed to last?" I asked flat out.

"Well, since I came out here for this little matchmaking game my father is having me play, I'll be staying here for a little while, so we can get to know more about one another."

"Wait, staying here, as in my house? Like, living here? You're joking, right?" I didn't bother to hide my shock. Now I know I have to be dreaming.

"Yes, how else will we get to know each other? I live in another city 120 miles away. Not particularly a walk around the corner if you ask me." He tried to make sense of this nightmare. What else could be the reason for letting a complete stranger live in my house?

"Maybe you should find yourself another girl a little closer to you and tell your parents they made a mistake." My mom really has gone crazy to want a total stranger living in her house.

He looked at me and thought for a moment before he replied, "Mm, nah, I think I'll stay here with you. You're kind of cute when you're angry," he said with a smile that struck me harder than it should have.

I felt the heat go straight to my face. "Do what you like. I have nothing to do with this and I have homework to do."

I ran off into my bedroom upstairs and shut the door and left it at that. My room was my safe place. The only thing I was missing was a lock to my door that both my mom and dad had said no to at least fifty times. If he's telling the truth and really is staying here, I need to ask a fifty first time for that lock. I know my mom loves the place she works, but to go this far and bring the son of the people she works for to our house to hook us up is crazy. I mean, I'd be lying if I said he wasn't cute and all, but his personality is anything but.

"I'm sorry, Ken. You'll just have to give her a little time to warm up to this," I cracked my door back open and heard my mom talking.

"It's understandable. Having a stranger come into your home is something anyone would need to get used to," he said so smoothly to her, "I've become very excited with this new little adventure."

'New adventure' he says. Is this what rich people call a hobby? Moving into people's homes and hoping to find their marriage partner? I don't like

this whole arrangement situation they've got me in. I already have someone I like anyway, so shouldn't this game be over already? A little over an hour ago, I was dreaming about Sano. Never once have I ever dreamed of this happening. I want absolutely nothing to do with him. And I definitely do not need this following me to school. I've managed to make half of my junior year rumor free. I don't need one started because of him.

2

My simple dreams of Sano and I walking through the park holding hands aren't real. But waking up and remembering that a strange rich kid moved into my house is. How exactly did I get in the Masidone lineup of marriage candidates? I feel my mom is behind all of this since I know my dad wouldn't let a boy stay in our house and get close enough with me to possibly form a relationship. He doesn't even like the idea of me dating, so I know my mom did something to get him on board with this. She must have found out about their son and this 'match making game' and jumped on the band wagon.

I would've thought if I didn't agree, or if I had someone else, they'd let me off the hook with this, but sadly, that isn't the case since he's still here. That won't stop me from trying to get rid of him though. I've already started the ignoring process; giving him the cold shoulder long enough should have him rethink things. I don't have time for people who will insult others on their first meeting.

Surprisingly, I'm glad I have school today. Hard times call for 'time to talk to Sano' plans to take place seeing as simply stating I like someone isn't enough to get Ken to leave. I could see the sun coming in through the cracks of my curtains letting me know it was just about time to get ready. I turned over in my bed and heard a voice oddly close to my ear.

"Wake up, sleepyhead!" Ken sang. He was there beside my bed, in my room. I nearly fell to the floor from shock.

"Ken!? What's your deal coming in my room like that?!" I asked.

"Well, your mother has been calling you for twenty minutes now. You're going to be late for school," he says, pointing to my clock. I had all of thirty minutes to be in my classroom chair.

"Oh no! I overslept again!" I jumped out of bed and started getting myself together.

"Ohh, so you wear that to bed," Ken said looking at me, nodding in approval. I didn't know what he was talking about until I realized I was wearing just a shirt and my underwear.

"G-get out you pervert!" I quickly tried to cover myself with my covers.

"Alright, alright, I'll see you downstairs, pinky," he said leaving out. I made sure my door was closed really, really wishing I had that lock.

"Oh my gosh!" I said exhaling. He just saw me in my underwear! He hasn't even been here a full day, and this has already happened. I don't think I've ever been this embarrassed in my own house before.

I listened for him to go downstairs and made a mad dash for the bathroom. I didn't exactly have time to sit in embarrassment as I've been late twice this week already. After I got dressed, I had no time to eat breakfast. I paid no attention to Ken and just kept going. He's already seen too much of me for one day anyway. I was running like mad to get to school on time. I went straight in and headed for my classroom, setting foot in the door just as the bell rang.

"Made it!" I say, finally able to breathe again. Luckily, Mr. Hallens is hardly ever in his class early, so he didn't catch me this time. As I was catching my breath, I felt someone looking at me. I looked up and saw it was Katie. Once I got my breathing under control, I went over to her.

"This doesn't seem like a regular overslept face. Something happened?" She asked. Katie, my best friend, can tell everything about me even if it's a slight change in expression.

"It's a long story. I'll have to tell you later."

"All right, class, take your seats." The teacher finally came strolling in holding his morning cup of coffee he didn't seem to have had enough of yet.

"We have a new student coming in and I need to see what seats are opened." The cold chill I'm getting is a sign that makes me hope this is all but a terrible coincidence. I repeated that to myself over and over until I saw Ken walking through the door.

"Alright everyone, this is Ken and he's yet another body in this small room."

Why this class? Why this school!?

"I'll try not to take up much room. Hey, it's pretty in pink!" He looked over after I accidentally made eye contact.

"Miss Macky, do you know our new student?" Mr. Hallens asked.

"I-I have no idea who that is Mr. Hallens."

"Is that really how you're going to treat your fiancé?"

"What!?" My eyes could've fallen out of my face from how wide they got.

"Well, well then. If that's the case, why don't we sit you next to her then?" Mr. Hallens chuckled.

"Sure, I'll sit there. You don't mind do you, pinky?" He actually came and sat next to me.

I was pretty sure Mr. Hallens was only joking. And first period so happens to be the one class Sano and I share! He sits two rows over. I can never look at him again after this. He'll probably never take me seriously now. Still less than twenty-four hours have passed since Ken came here, and he's ruining everything!

Ken took his seat and leaned over to me. "You know, you didn't have to run. Your mom was kind enough to drop me off just as you left out. Would have saved you some energy." He whispered and grinned like he was having a good time. I turned away from him resisting the urge to hit him.

That made getting through the first half of the school day brutal. Lunch time couldn't have come sooner. I just needed to survive this and get through the rest of school, and my life, without seeing anyone. The topic of new student romance has already gotten through the school like wildfire. Rumors spread faster than the plague at this place. I just knew it would happen. And it did. I was going quickly in the hallways to the lunchroom, not paying attention to my path ahead when I ran into someone.

"S-sorry!" I blurted before even seeing who it was. I backed up to let them pass when I noticed it was none other than Sano that I was standing in front of. "S-Sano. Uh, sorry, are you all right?"

"Yeah, I'm fine," he answered.

"That's good. Well, I-I should go then." I started to walk away. I didn't know what else to say. My plan to talk to him didn't involve a hallway attack!

"Oh hey," he suddenly called out to me, "good luck, and congrats with that fiancé of yours." Then he continued to walk away.

"Wait! He's not..." I tried calling back out to him, but there was no use. His fast legs put him through a huge crowd of students shuffling around. I can feel the panic begin to develop. Yet another bad first impression. All still within twenty-four hours of this storm starting.

I took the walk of shame to the lunchroom and found a table in the corner. The lunchroom is large. Round tables, long tables, and short tables all filled the center while outside there were all different food options. Katie and I normally sit at a small table with other friends, but today I went back by the vending machines to try and hide. However, Katie came and found me with little to no effort.

"Misa, what happened?" She asked as I kept my head on the table. "Does it have something to do with that guy whom you still haven't fully explained?"

"That guy showed up out of nowhere. And according to my mom, he's supposed to be my '*fiancé*.'" I lifted my head adding air quotes since I refuse to accept this.

"So, what, you're in like some marriage arrangement type thing?" Just as I was about to say no, I felt someone come up behind me.

"Yeah, we'll be together forever!" I looked behind me and saw it was Ken with his arm wrapped around my shoulder.

"What are you doing over here?" I said moving him off me.

"Oh, there's that angry face again! What's got you so upset, Mimi?"

"I told you not to call me that! Why did you tell the whole class about this situation?"

"I had too! If I didn't, who knows who would try to take you from me?" He put his hand to his chest. Ken is having way too much fun with this.

"Do you really have to bother me right now?"

"As much as I'd like to, I have to stop by the office again. Just saw you here and wanted to say hi. See you later, Mimi!" He smiled and walked away.

"Ah, so you guys are together?" Katie asked observing the situation.

"No! We aren't!"

"You sure? He sees otherwise."

"It's not what he makes it."

"And here I thought you wanted Sano this whole time. You know, you really had me fooled." She kept going.

"Katie, you don't understand, this is my parents doing. I had no part in this."

"I don't know about that. I saw the way you were looking at him. Outside you had a fierce and a harsh aura, but inside you were warm and at peace."

"That's not true. I don't even know the guy."

"It could be love at first sight. That's how it was for me and Eden," she said looking off into the distance as if remembering it all. I remembered it perfectly. Katie's temper was a lot less controlled before she got with him.

Back then— We were at the freshmen assembly looking for seats when someone bumped into her. As if she knew it would happen, she quickly reached out to them and yelled, "Am I invisible? How about looking before moving!" Then she walked passed, brushing against them returning the favor. I found the closest seats to where we were, so we could avoid any possible expulsion on the first day of high school. The assembly was held in the gym, and we sat on the fourth row of the bleachers.

As we sat down, someone was taking a seat on the other side of Katie. I watched as he was sitting down and bumped into her. I saw instant trouble again, but as I noticed her face grow angry again, the person quickly said,

ickly turned her head, making her fresh
e wind. I saw the anger she wanted to
ed at the stranger. "Yes, I'm fine."
eard before. I think…it was a shy

relief in his voice. He smiled
ngers through her hair, tucking it
n it was shoulder length because her
as slightly weird and unnatural. Never
with a new face. Suddenly, the two of them
ded to introduce himself. His name was Eden.
ne Katie whisperer.

Ken was nothing like that. I couldn't like someone like
mean, how can I like someone who came in my room and
ny underwear and said I was as loud as a megaphone? Plus, I
o anyway. He might think Ken and I are together, but I could just
im that he misunderstood.

"I just want to wake up from this nightmare." I said.

"Maybe it won't be that bad." Katie tried to comfort me.

I looked towards the direction Ken walked out. Two tables in front of
us sat a bunch of girls. They had also been looking in the direction he had
left. One of the girls looked back to me. I was certain she was one of the
girls from the gymnastics team that used to try and talk to Sano.

Recently, not as many girls have been talking about him. It may have
something to do with how he's been even more antisocial than usual.
Something about the way she looked back to the hall Ken disappeared down
makes me think Sano may soon be yesterday's news.

Of course, that just may work out in my favor. I just need to get rid of
this uneasy feeling.

I leaned against Katie, and I just exhaled heavily for the third time
today. "I hope you're right."

3

The good thing about getting through the rest of the day was kno[w]
I had no other classes with Ken, and I didn't even see him after he left
lunchroom. Part of me hopes his sudden transfer wasn't actually accept[ed]
and they sent him back home. The last bell had already rung, and everyon[e]
was flooding the hallways. The sports teams headed to the locker rooms. I
passed the small theatre classroom and saw some club members sitting
around on the tables and stage. Others were headed out of the side exits to
head to the buses.

My usual walk around the school to leave out the main entrance
seemed as if something was added. And that something was eyes. I felt the
eyes of everyone staring at me as I walked through the halls. I didn't try to
make eye contact with anyone until I looked and found Katie at her locker.

"Katie, what's going on around here?" I asked her.

"What do you mean?"

"I feel like everyone is looking at me."

"Really? What gives you that idea?"

"Just look around." I told her. She wasn't really discreet about it as she
looked up and down the hallways.

"I don't see anything out of the ordinary. You sure you aren't just being
a bit paranoid today because-"

"Misa!" A distressed voice cut her off. We both turned around already
knowing who that voice belonged to. John. If there was anyone in this
school that was good at making his appearance known, it was John.

"Misa! Is it true? Say it's not true!" He asked skidding to a stop in
front of me.

"What are you talking about, John?"

"Are you really marrying some new kid?" You could hear the hurt in
his tone.

"What? How do you know about that?"

"What do you mean how do I know? Everyone knows! That's all
anyone can talk about. How could you not tell me? You were supposed to

take my hand in marriage!" His eyes were focused on me as he spoke nonsense.

"I've already told you a million times John, we're just friends."

"And I know you're just saying that. You know we were meant to be together!" It's like he didn't even hear what I said.

"So, it's really around the whole school already?"

"Yeah, I found out from my good friend, Mr. Powell." He said.

Mr. Powell, if I remember correctly, is one of the janitors. If it's gone that far already, it'll be even harder to change Sano's mind with everyone reminding him about it. That's probably why he congratulated me in the hallway. He may really think this is real. I need to do something and do something quick to stop this before it gets even more out of hand.

"You know, I think you got it wrong," I told him.

"What? You mean you will be my girlfriend?"

"No, not that. What I meant was, I'm not with anyone. Ken is known to be a jokester and just likes messing with people. So, you should go tell everyone that it's not true."

John may be a little thick-headed, but he is the gossip king around here. If anyone could start, change, or end a rumor, it was him.

"So, what you're telling me is, you're not getting married, and I still have a chance?" He asked.

"Uh, yeah, something like that." I couldn't really say no again and hurt my chances at such a crucial moment.

"Alright, you can count on me!" He said, giving me an 'ok' sign and a wink.

John was only an inch or two taller than me. He still had growing acne on his forehead that he tries to hide with his hair. Plain T-Shirts and jeans were his usual dress code. Although he seemed plain, his nice eyes and dimply smile kept him from ranking bottom of the charts.

For some reason, he has this weird liking toward me. I don't know when his fascination towards me started. I always thought of him like a brother and nothing more. But since he is willing to do anything for me, having him around comes in handy sometimes.

"Misa, are you sure that this is a good idea? This is John we're talking about." Katie asked after he left.

"Don't worry Katie. You know he's good at what he does. If this works, then maybe I'll be able to talk to Sano easier."

"And what about that Ken guy?"

"He'll be fine. We're not together, and I'm not interested, so it's not like I'm doing anything wrong. He'll easily be able to find someone else."

"But Misa..." She wanted to continue. I've already made up my mind and she saw that. I want this to end before anything starts.

Katie and I parted ways, so I took a nice quiet walk home. Or at least what I thought could have been a nice quiet walk home.

"There you are!" This confirmed my theory of Ken getting kicked out being false as I heard him following me.

"What are you doing here?" I asked a bit bothered.

"That's not a very happy greeting. Something like, 'I've been waiting all day to see you' or 'I was just thinking about you' or maybe, 'I was hoping we could go home together' would have been better." He said while acting out his lines.

"And why would I say any of that?"

"Because now that I'm around, those are phrases you should want to use."

"Now that you're around, there are some phrases I want to use, but those aren't it." I told him.

"Aww, what's wrong Mimi? You don't sound too thrilled about me being here."

"Gee, how'd you figure that out?" I said and turned to him. "No offense, but I was perfectly fine before you came around talking about matchmaking." I didn't want to be mean about it, but I couldn't find a better way to express how perfectly fine I was before some random guy came into my life.

"Anyone would need time to adjust to someone new. How else would you make friends without talking to a stranger first?" He just looked at me and smiled. That was probably the first normal thing he's said to me.

"For us, that stranger phase will be a little different given the circumstances of how we came together. Sure, living together isn't exactly conventional, but should you really dismiss it when you haven't even given it a chance yet?"

If it had been under normal circumstances like meeting at school, or a store somewhere, things would be different, but this guy isn't here just to find another friend. His purpose is to seek a wife. I don't know if it's a rich person thing, but regular sixteen-year-olds aren't looking for such a thing.

"There's nothing you can say that'll make me change my mind." I told him and continued walking.

"Don't worry, I'm sure I can change that unchangeable mind." He smiled with brimming confidence.

He's so sure of himself. Of course, a guy like him has high confidence. How else could he have made it far enough to transfer to a new school and into someone else's home?

He continued to walk with me. To walk home alone with a guy I hardly know was strange. I didn't say anything else and kept it a long awkward walk with this three-foot distance between us. I occasionally looked his way and saw he was looking around as if to make note of where he was going. We were going down a neighborhood, so there wasn't much to see other than houses and cars.

He isn't as flashy as he was yesterday. He wore a grey top, some nice blue jeans, and dark grey high-top shoes. He walks with his head held high, and without a care in the world. The more I look at him, the more he doesn't seem like the 'arranged married' type. Maybe my mom just wants another kid around. She had always wanted another one, but it just never happened. Whatever the case may be, I just need to know what's going to happen next.

"Well, aren't you two looking cute already." My mom greeted us when we came home. I ignored her comment and headed for my room.

"It was a bit of a long day today." I heard Ken tell her before I closed my door. A long day was an understatement. And *he's* the reason for it.

If he intends on staying here, I'll definitely have to change my regular routine. Starting with how I sleep. I cannot let what happened this morning happen again.

"Misa?" I heard someone knocking on my door. It sounded like Ken. Reflexively, I checked to make sure I hadn't stripped into something more comfortable yet and luckily, I was still fully clothed. I stood behind my door and cracked it in case he tried to storm in.

"No need to be alarmed. I actually came to apologize for this morning for coming into your room without your consent. In my defense, your mom said it was okay since you sleep like the dead." I couldn't deny I was a heavy sleeper. Katie once pushed me out of bed to wake me up and I was still out...

"I suppose since you know you were at fault; I'll forgive you this time." I told him. It was actually kind of nice of him to apologize. I didn't think he would.

"This time? So, what you're saying is, next time it'll be more acceptable? I hadn't planned to do it again but if you want me to, I would be happy to oblige." He gave me his grin I've seen far too much already.

"You're such a perv!" I closed the door in his face. I heard his footsteps going back down the hallway and into his room. My parents' room was downstairs. I had the whole upstairs to myself, so I had nothing to worry about.

Now Ken is here, sharing the same space as me with no one to stop him from whatever he's planning. I looked at my clock and saw the time. It had officially been twenty-four hours since he showed up before me. If I want to get out of this arrangement, I'll have to do it as quickly as possible.

Day two of mystery man Ken started much like day one ended. I ate dinner in my room and barely said a word to him the rest of the night. I made sure to sleep decently, only I didn't actually get to sleep well. And because of that, I woke up to my alarm going off twenty minutes later.

No one bothered to wake me up this time, so I was rushing again. I didn't check on the status of Ken and his whereabouts either. I just wanted to make it to school without getting another tardy slip. I wasn't as late as yesterday, so when I made it, I was able to take my time. The halls seemed more covered in social groups than normal at this hour. Once again, it felt as if they were all staring at me.

"Misa!" Katie shouted coming towards me.

"What's wrong? What's going on around here?"

"Do you know what people are saying now, thanks to that *brilliant* plan of yours? Everyone is thinking that you and John are together now."

"What!?"

"Misa! My beloved, you're here!" I turned and heard John singing as he came down the hall.

"John! I told you to stop the rumors about Ken and me, not start one about you and me!"

"But I had to! No one was going to believe me if I didn't."

"And you figured you could stop it like this?"

"Yep! And it worked out great! Now everyone believes that we're the ones together. Let's try making it as believable as possible!" He wrapped his arm around my shoulder. My plan completely backfired on me.

"This is all on you." Katie shook her head.

It couldn't get worse than this. At this point, transferring out of school would be a better option. Maybe this is the universe trying to tell me my simple plans are not the answers to this type of problem. Ken is the son of a billionaire. My strategies will take more planning to get someone like him out of here. With this in mind, I'll have to let him slide for a while until I can figure out a better way to handle this. He has won this round, but I am far from out.

4

The days passed on. Every day I woke up, Ken was still here. I lost count of how many days it's been when I concluded that he isn't going anywhere. It's like we rented out the room to someone who's simply living here while it's convenient. He did go back to his house a couple of times but came back here again. My mom only said that it's better to take things slowly. But like this, nothing is really happening.

On top of that, her vacation time was up last week, and it has become even more awkward now that she's not around. Imagine the rumors if it came out that two teenagers were living alone. What happened to parents believing in no dating before marriage? She's actually having me, at sixteen, try to date to marry!

Ken's still trying to get too close to me, but I tell him to leave. So far, I don't see anything in the love field. I've gotten used to a few of his creepy advances. That's just more of a reason I stay away from him.

Walking into school today reminds me now is not the time for Ken drama, but a real-life crisis. Midterms are coming up way too fast, and I'm freaking out! I wouldn't call myself an A+ student. I wouldn't even call myself a B student. I'm somewhere on the borderline of acceptable…

"Katie! I need your help! Please, this is a huge crisis!" I ran to my best friend when I saw her at her locker.

"Whoa, what's wrong Misa? Where's the fire?" she asked concerned.

"These tests are what's happening. If I don't pass them, I won't pass the class, and I'll have to retake it!"

"Oh, is that it? Calm down, it's just a test." She said, lessoning her concern.

"You know I'm horrible when it comes to test taking. Last time I left almost the whole thing blank. Something like that cannot happen again."

"Something like that happened because you fell asleep when you got your test paper." She reminded me.

"I couldn't help it. I was up late trying to study and then I had a terrible migraine trying to figure out all the questions."

"Why don't you just study more so you won't have to think about it so much with last minute cram sessions?" She asked.

"It's not like I don't study, I do. But when I go to study, I somehow end up doing something else." The face Katie is giving me is telling me I didn't exactly help my case.

"Well, that's your problem, Misa, you're just distracted too easily. You need to stay focused and not get off topic so fast."

"That's easier said than done."

"Okay, well why don't I just come over today then. I'll help you study so you can actually study."

"That sounds great, but I can't today."

"Why not?"

"Well, see there's this show that I like, and the new episode comes out today, and I can't take the chance of missing what happens after the girl woke up from the c—"

"Misa!" She snapped at me, "That right there is your problem. TV can wait. If you're really serious about trying to pass midterms, that I remind you is in a few days, then you need to stop messing around like, yesterday, and get to it!"

Katie was right. If I don't get it together, then who knows where I'll end up. In our second semester of junior year, I was still not taking my studies seriously enough. Next year, we'll be seniors, and I have to shape up now. Katie is the smartest person I know. Having her help me study will help me a lot.

We went straight to my house after school, sat in the kitchen, and got to it. She wasn't going to let me out of this one. And after last semester's scare of almost repeating biology, I didn't want her to. If I didn't know any better, I swear she had a side job as a teacher. She had worksheets and pages marked and even had notes of what she's going to help me with. Is this how an A+ student works?

"Here," she said handing me a paper, "Let's start with some math, your second weakest subject. I'm going to time you, so you can work just as quickly during the real thing."

"Aren't you supposed to be helping me? Not pre-testing me?"

"This is helping you. By timing you, I can see how long you spend on one problem helping with time management, and then go over the ones you get wrong. Killing two birds with one stone." She said very proud of herself with this plan.

I went along with it since she thought it would work. I should gain something from working with her when it's all over. I took the paper and was given twenty minutes. That was probably the fastest twenty minutes I've ever experienced in my life.

"Let's see what you have." Katie stopped her stopwatch. She examined my answers closely and started shaking her head as she went through all the problems.

"Misa, out of the twenty minutes I gave you to answer fifteen questions, you answered ten and only got six of those right."

"Well, it's your fault. These questions were hard!"

"All you had to do was simplify these numbers and multiply. My thirteen-year-old sister can answer these without a problem."

"Didn't your sister skip a grade and test into some fancy private school? Of course she's really smart. Cut me some slack!"

"You asked me to help you study and you should know how I am about studying. Let me see the easiest way to explain this to you."

"There is no easy way. Math sucks. Let's move to something without numbers."

"Alright then, how about your next bad subject. History." Katie said, pulling out the thick textbook and study guide.

"I hate history the most!" I said losing my motivation by the second.

"You know, I bet Sano likes smart girls," Katie muttered while flipping through the book.

"W-what?"

"He just seems like a guy that doesn't like simple and uneducated women." She continued.

History is the one class we share. I don't know all his classes, but the times he had to answer questions in class, he would get them right with no problem. He's probably an A+ student who likes other A+ students. I really need to work harder to show him what I'm made of.

"So, about that study guide." I perked up a bit.

"I knew that'd get you," she smirked.

If I want to avoid looking like an idiot again when we get our test results back, I have to put aside my will to slack off and put on my thinking cap. We continued to study for another hour and a half. I'm pretty sure my brain melted about forty-five minutes ago, but I didn't tell her that.

"Alright, Misa, we'll stop for today. Even though midterms are right around the corner, I won't overload you with too much. I hope with this, you've got a better idea of everything and see that studying isn't so bad."

"I feel like I've gained so much just from today." I tried smiling.

"Are you sure? You don't really look it." She said, seeing past my lie.

"I did, really! Now go on. It's late and I should do some double checking before hitting the sac."

"Alright then, see you tomorrow." Katie grabbed her things and left.

"Geez, I have such a headache! I should've asked somebody else for help!" I was able to finally say it now that she's gone. I didn't have the heart to tell her, her way of teaching was way too hard to understand.

"I can help you!" I nearly had a heart attack as I saw Ken peeking down the stairs.

"K-ken. When did you get here?"

"I've been here the whole time. Listening to you struggle with simple problems was very entertaining." Since I always leave school without him, sometimes I never know when he's here or not since he's so quiet.

"So, you think you're smarter than me?"

"I mean, I have been making straight A's all my life."

"Really now? If that's the case, then why haven't you advanced any grades or even graduated by now?"

"What's the fun in that? I've been asked that quite a few times at my other school, but I rather stay and have the school life experience." He explained. He had the option to be done with school but chose to stay. What kind of guy is he?

"Since you think you're so smart, why not answer these Algebra II questions I did earlier. It's only fifteen questions, so it should be a cinch. I'll give you twenty minutes," I said handing him the paper like Katie, "Show all work." He looked at the paper and examined the problems.

"I'll have this for you in ten." He went to the table in the kitchen and started. He couldn't possibly do them that fast. Could he? I watched him as he continuously wrote on the paper like it all came to him so naturally. Even Katie didn't work this fast.

"Here," I looked at the clock when he showed me the paper. Only ten minutes passed. "I even double checked my work," he said, leaning back in his chair. All the questions were right according to the answer sheet. And there aren't any signs of erasing either. I had it wrong. This is an A+ student.

"Math is my specialty." He said as if reading my mind.

"Okay then, I guess you can help me with the problems I don't understand in my work packet." I headed back to the living room to get my things.

"Whoa, whoa, whoa," he said getting up. "Who said I was doing this for free?"

"What do you mean?"

"I think I should get something in return for my services."

"Something in return? Like what?" I asked. He couldn't possibly want money.

"Hm, how about a kiss?"

"A what? No way!"

"Alright then. My services are closed," he put his pencil down, and headed towards the stairs.

"Wait, can't you come up with something else? A handshake maybe?" I asked.

"Nope! I want a kiss from you as payment," Ken likes to joke, and he's trying to be funny at a crucial time.

"Fine. If you help me on this packet, and I learn something, I'll do it." I'm praying he isn't serious; he's a jokester after all. But the huge grin that grew on his face is telling me otherwise.

I feel as if I just sold my soul.

He came back to the table and started writing stuff down on a sheet of paper. I looked over his shoulder trying to see what he was doing.

"Alright, now to dumb down what your friend was saying for these problems, you should use this formula to solve them. To know when just determines on what you are given." He started explaining it all to me using the formulas he just wrote down. And the crazy part was, I was actually understanding what he's telling me. It's so simple and way less complicated than how Katie was going on about it.

"Wow, Ken, I actually get this. Is this right?" I showed him my work.

"Yes, it is. Good job. Now when you go over these in class tomorrow, you'll be able to answer some of the questions instead of looking so perplexed."

"I could've done without that last comment, but thanks anyway for the help." I started gathering my papers.

"I'm officially studied out for one day, so I'll be headed off to bed."

"No, no, no," he said stretching his arm out in front of me, cutting me off as I tried to make my quick escape.

"You surely haven't forgotten our deal in only a half hour of working. I sacrificed my time to assist you. I deserve a little compensation."

"H-how about money?" I tried offering an alternative.

"Does it really seem like I need more of that? I told you, there's only one form of payment for this. Now we can settle it the easy way or the fun way."

I'm afraid to ask what the fun way is. But I had no time anyway as he was moving closer to me. "Alright, fine. Close your eyes first!" I told him. Like a dog, he did what I said.

Throughout all the time Ken has been here, I've never really let him get too close to me. And now that it's just the two of us, I made it a point not to be left alone in any room with him. Now here we are, face to face with the intention of me kissing him because he wants me to pay him simply for helping me with a little homework. I felt my heart rate increasing. With our height difference, I would have to stand on my tip toes to even reach his lips. Is it because this is my first kiss that I felt so nervous? I couldn't tell him that at my age, I still hadn't kissed anyone, but my body wouldn't move. He stood there, eyes closed and waiting, and I was frozen.

"Are you nervous? Could this perhaps be your first kiss?"

Without much thought, he figured it out. My heart was going to pound out of my chest from embarrassment. He opened his eyes and looked at me. We were only inches apart. I could feel his body heat by him being so close. I could even smell the body spray he uses. My body reacted before I could think and pushed past him. I went upstairs into the bathroom. In complete embarrassment, I ran away from him and hid like a little kid.

It was just a kiss. It's not like I like him, so why is my heart pounding so much? The second most embarrassing thing happened in my house. Both are the cause of Ken. The bathroom is the one door inside the house with a lock. Needless to say, I used it in fear of him coming to find me in this shameful state. If there really was ever a time I could disappear, now would totally be it.

5

Not only was last night the most embarrassing night of my life, but this morning is also the most confusing one of my life. I don't know how, but I ended up falling asleep in the bathroom. The confusing part is the fact that I'm now waking up in my room. I was pretty sure I locked the door. Did Ken get in and bring me to my room?

Not only did I run away from him, but I also had to be broken out of the bathroom. I really can't show my face to him now. I rolled over, reaching for my phone and shot out of bed. The confusion left as I noticed the time. I had twenty minutes to make it to class. There was no way I could make it to school on time. It's no surprise Ken didn't try to wake me up after last night. I ran for class after getting ready. I was still ten minutes late, and Mr. Hallens wasn't happy.

"Miss Macky, your tardiness has been high recently, go wait for me in the hallway. I want to have a word with you." He told me. There wasn't anything I could say to explain myself. Or rather *want* to explain.

"You too, Masidone. If you're having some lovers spat, do it when it doesn't concern my class!" I looked and saw Ken had been right behind me.

"No, Mr. Hallens, you got it wrong," I told him.

"Whatever the case may be, you need to get to my class on time, now go!" He put both Ken and I in the hall in total awkward silence.

I had no idea he was still home. I figured he was going to ignore me after I ran away from him. I watched the clock down the hall as the numbers didn't change. It felt like forever already standing out here with him waiting for Mr. Hallens to talk to us. Should I say something? What's the appropriate thing to say?

"I see you're late huh? Guys like you should learn to be on time." I tried to stay cool.

"I could say the same thing about girls like you." he said back to me. I just kept my head down not saying anything else.

When we got back into the classroom after Mr. Hallens gave us a "why it's important to be on time" speech, all eyes were on us. Even Sano had been looking. Everyone has been so confused on what's going on between us after the mess that started when he first got here, so this'll still cause another hot topic at the lunch tables.

"Today is your last chance for questions. Speak now or forever hope you'll do fine tomorrow on your midterm," Mr. Hallens officially started class. "For some of you, this can make or break you. Test and quizzes count for the biggest part of your overall grade. If you have a B average and do poorly tomorrow, it could knock you all the way down to a C or lower depending on your percentage. So, I'll ask one more time, any last-minute questions over the study guide before we move on?" A few hands went in the air.

I spent most of my time studying my math last night. I spent little time on history even though that is my worst class. I didn't want to draw any more attention to myself, so I hoped someone had a question about the whole packet. That was wishful thinking, but we did go over most of the study guide during class. The bell rang and Katie flew over to my desk as I was packing up.

"What was that this morning?" She wasted no time asking.

"Absolutely nothing. I just overslept," I said a little too quickly.

"Ah, must have been because you were finishing that packet for our next class, right?"

"Uh, yeah."

"That doesn't sound too convincing." Katie knew something was off.

"It is convincing. Ken even helped me with it."

"Really? He helped you when I left?"

"It was just a few problems I didn't understand, so he showed me how to do them." I gave her the short version.

"Is that why the both of you showed up late? Staying up studying all night? You prefer his help over mine?"

"No, it's just that I got confused and he said he'd show me. But I don't think it was worth it."

"What do you mean it wasn't worth it?" She asked.

"Well, he only helped me under a condition."

"A condition? What kind of condition?" I could see the glow in

her eyes as she wanted to know this condition I haven't fulfilled yet.

"W-well, in order for him to help me, he wanted me to repay him by giving him a kiss." I was nearly at a whisper as I spoke. But unfortunately, Katie has good hearing.

"He did? Did you?"

"No, I didn't. I ran like a little girl and now I can't even face him."

"I think that's because you're starting to like him." She said with an evil smile.

"I do not! I just couldn't do something like that with him. He had no right to ask me to do that."

Flashbacks of the feeling of him so close to me went through my head. I kept quiet, wanting to forget the subject as we walked to our next class. I looked back noticing Ken took off in the opposite direction to his next class. I'm probably making a big deal out of nothing. He didn't say anything about it earlier. Maybe he's over it and won't ask again. This is really making me crazy. I walked into my class and saw that the teacher wrote the answers on the board to the problems we had to solve so we could check them ourselves.

"I'm sure they're all right since I helped you," Katie said.

"No, actually they aren't. At least the ones you tried to help me with."

"How is that so? If you followed my steps and instruction, you should have gotten them no problem."

"Your instructions might as well have been in another language. You didn't even check to see if I did them right or not."

"I had to have you do something on your own."

"Yeah, well it's a good thing this isn't being graded."

"Okay, so what, the help you received from Ken paid off?" she asked. I flipped the page and checked the last few problems.

"Actually, it did." I said a bit shocked.

"Humph, just couldn't accept the guidance from a female mind."

"I can't believe all it took was a little of Ken's help and tips."

"You know, you should probably give him more credit than you have been. Or does your pride not let you?" Katie asked.

"What's that supposed to mean?"

"It means that if you don't get your act together, you'll end up blowing a good thing."

"I hope your future career isn't a therapist." I said to her. Sometimes she doesn't make any sense. But I think I understand what she was trying to say.

I tried not to think about it too much during the day, and before I knew it, school was over. I have to do some more serious cramming to make sure I pass tomorrow. I can't very well ask Ken for help again. He may still want his payment for yesterday. Katie has a study date with Eden. My parents are always away for work. I seriously can't ask anyone other than Ken.

I took the long way home to have some time to myself. It's still a bit hard to believe I went from a lonely crush to living with a rich son looking for a wife. The idea of marriage was far from my mind, but the idea of dating wasn't.

I still don't know much about Ken though. Granted, I still don't know a lot about Sano either, but the time in which I've known Sano is longer and I still have more of an interest in him than I do Ken. Judging by the way he was looking at us in class today, he probably believes that we are together. My plan to try and change his mind is taking longer than I thought.

My long walk came to an end when I was suddenly at my front door. I slowly opened it to walk in the house and saw Ken already home and out cold on the couch. He must have fallen asleep there. Looking at him like this, he actually looks like a normal guy sleeping on the couch after a long day, and not the usual pervert looking for advances. Seeing this soft resting face, I guess he's kind of cute with the way his hair falls on his face. He also has surprisingly long eyelashes.

I think his pervy nature is rubbing off on me. I shouldn't be watching him sleep, but maybe I should take this chance to pay him, so he won't come after me later. It should still count even if he's asleep. The agreement didn't mention anything about being awake or not.

I went to the front of the couch and slowly faced him. My heart rate began increasing. I can't believe I'm going to do this. I began my decent to his face. Even though he's sleeping and can't see me, I shut my eyes not trying to witness this. I could hear his slow breathing from his slightly parted lips. Being this close to his face, I could smell the shampoo he uses in his hair. I know I was closing the gap between us, but I still hadn't landed. I peeked to see I was just half an inch away from his lips. Then I looked up and noticed him looking back at me.

"Attacking someone while sleeping is foul play you know," he spoke softly.

"Uh, Ken! I was uh, j-just seeing what color your hair was. It's actually brown up close."

"Yes, I'm aware of that," he said.

Silence filled the air as we were both still staring at each other. Before the moment got more awkward, I tried to back away from him. Ken saw my movements and put his hands on my shoulders to hold me still. My eyes widened, not expecting him to stop me like this. I was forced back in his line of view. Words couldn't find their way out of my mouth.

But Ken's mouth did find mine. It was official. Ken and I have now kissed.

"Now your debt has been paid," he said, letting go of me.

"Y-you jerk!" I got up and moved back. I had my hand over my mouth.

"Why are we getting all shy now? If it's to my understanding, I was an innocent bystander trying to relax when suddenly, I was about to be attacked." He said sitting upward.

"That doesn't mean you can do what you like!"

"It was simply self-defense." He stretched his arms, not the slightest bit phased by what just happened. I was still in shock feeling the sensation of Ken's lips on mine even though it was only a couple seconds. I didn't know what else to say.

"I should probably mention," Ken started again, "the reason I appeared to be sleeping is because I was waiting for my ride. I got a call right after school from my father, who wants to see me today, and someone should be coming any minute now to get me."

"You're going to miss the midterms tomorrow?" I asked.

"I'll more than likely go to school from home tomorrow morning. Sorry for not giving more notice, but I was just informed myself. I was going to tell you when you came in, but I must have dozed off for a minute due to a late-night locksmith activity I had to do."

My eyes widen. He really did break me out the bathroom. I'm once again at a loss for words. The sound of a horn outside stopped my search for communication.

"That must be my ride." Ken said getting up from the couch. He tossed his book bag over his shoulder and turned to me.

"Don't do anything fun while I'm out." His smirk seemed bigger today.

I just watched him as he left out the door. He got into one of their expensive cars. The tinted windows were too dark to ever catch who was picking him up, but they drove away quickly this time. Once I saw they cleared the block, I went and crumbled to the couch as I was free to let everything out. For the first time in my life, I, Misa Macky, have finally been kissed. And it was with a guy named Ken Masidone.

The night came and the night went. My focus on the test was gone. After all my last- minute cramming, it took one little act to take me off track. I did my best on midterms. I spent most of my time just trying to stay focused. With each class, I got more and more drained. I spent lunch time studying for afternoon classes. By the end of the day, my battery was dead.

I ignored Ken. Not because of what happened, but because it happened, and can't face him right now. And because of that, I don't know how I did because I was too busy thinking about it. The next day, I made it to class on time. I needed to be ready for whatever was going to happen. The bell rang, and Mr. Hallens came into the classroom.

"Time to get your test back." He couldn't wait to humiliate us.

That was his specialty. Along with pretending to be a role model teacher when the principal would stop by. After that, he'd go back to his off-subject conversation. Mr. Hallens turned to the whiteboard and began writing names. He didn't intend to write our scores out publicly like that did he?!

"Alright you all. I have ten of your names here. The five on the left side are the ones that scored the highest on the test. The five on the right are the ones that scored the lowest and will be moved to the front of the class. The five of you on the right can grab your stuff and come to the front. A few of you will need to move to the back."

I saw five people in the front get up to move to another seat while four others around me got up and moved to the front of the class. The fifth person was still processing the fact that they were a part of the bottom five.

"Now, Miss Macky, I know you could have done better than that. Take this seat in front of me and we'll work on changing this." Mr. Hallens said to me as I still didn't move. I can't believe I was in the bottom five. When will the humiliation stop?

"I think you all should do a bit more studying as well," he continued.

I finally decided to get up and go with my failing crew. I studied the top five names. Ken, the A+ student, was first. Sano was number two. As I figured, he was really smart as well. I don't dare look in his direction and show my shame. The seat I took was next to Katie. She was already in the front of the classroom, and the fourth name on the list.

"I thought you prepared for this?" Katie whispered to me after I came over.

"I did. I-I must have been distracted and missed some things," I told her. And that wasn't a lie. I was completely distracted by what Ken did, but I definitely couldn't tell her that. I wouldn't hear the end of it.

"You all made it just barely through the first milestone, it's time to start the second session." Mr. Hallens put us in the center of the class to make sure we could give our full undivided attention.

The only good thing about this was the fact that I didn't have to look at the two distractions up here anymore. The other teachers followed Mr. Hallens' overnight grading trend and had our midterms ready for us to look over. I did better in my other classes in comparison. Since that history grade brought my average lower than it already was, it's almost impossible to bring it back to passing. I should go thank Ken for putting me in this situation.

"I'll see you later." I heard a voice around the corner of the hallway from me.

I was headed to the exit doors when I saw who the familiar tone belonged to. I stopped as I saw it was Sano heading out the main entrance as well. It was rare to see him this soon after school and not at track practice. Either he doesn't have practice, or he wasn't going. I was planning to take my time going home and dwell on my grades, but never thought I'd have this chance to try and talk to Sano. I tried to catch up to him but slowed down as I was gathering what to say.

We were now both outside, and he made a left, going the opposite direction I'd go for home. I didn't know he lived within walking distance. Would it be wrong to just trail behind him a little to see what the actual distance is?

Following him is wrong. I shouldn't do that. But why won't my feet stop moving? After a block, he turned and went another four blocks. He was going further than I thought. And I was still behind him. I kept my head down in case he decided to look back and notice me. The gloomy and cloudy sky made it seem even creepier. He crossed the street and went up to a big brown brick house.

"Hey look, he's home!" Sano opened the front door and kids flooded the entrance.

I was hiding behind a car across the street. I had a clear view through the windows. There were three little ones no older than eight or nine. Those must be his little brothers and sisters. I didn't know he had such young siblings. He greeted them all and told them to stay in. The gray sky showed signs of rain, so outside playing wasn't happening. And neither was me getting home dry. The crackle of thunder came. And it started pouring.

"Crap!" I muttered. I didn't bring my umbrella with me to school, so this is going to be bad getting back.

"You might want to come in until it lets up."

My heart almost stopped at the sound of Sano's voice, which was a bit loud. Loud as if he's talking to someone far away. Someone far, as in me. I peeked from behind the car and saw him standing in the doorway looking my way. He knows I'm here.

6

So, maybe I shouldn't have followed Sano home. I'm not sure why I did, but my legs kept going in his direction. This must be karma's way of saying, "I told you so." Now I'm stuck in the rain far from home hiding behind some random car because he knows I'm here!

"Unless you want to get sick, you should probably come in," he called out again.

I have two options: Pretend he didn't see me and just stay hidden, or humiliated myself by going in. Faking a heart attack seems a bit extreme. My book bag is a really bad umbrella, so I have no choice but to go with option two. I took a deep breath and got up from behind the car. Faking a heart attack might be too much, but dying of embarrassment seemed highly possible as I crossed the street and headed to his front door.

"Uh, h-hey there. I mean, thanks for this nice offer. Sorry for the bother." I kept my head low as I entered his house. He's going to think I'm such a stalker! I went in and he closed the door behind me.

"Wait here a minute." He said. He disappeared down a hall on the right.

I was standing in the living room. The inside was a lot bigger than it seemed on the outside. They had black furniture that stood out against the eggshell white on the walls and polished hardwood floors. Sano returned quickly with a towel in his hand.

"Here, you can use this to wipe off." He handed me the towel.

"T-thank you." I took it and wiped my face trying to hide my embarrassment. I can't believe I followed him home and now in his house using his towels!

"Would you like something to drink?" He offered.

"Uh, sure, thanks." He went to the kitchen, which was over to the

back of the house. The few minutes felt like hours until he came back with a glass of water. I took it, not saying much else and started drinking to drown out this awkward meeting.

"Did you have fun following me?" I nearly choked when he asked that.

"I-I wasn't following you! You just so happened to be going in the same direction as I was, is all. And I got caught in the rain," I obviously lied.

"Oh, so it was my misunderstanding then?"

"Y-yeah, it's a small world. Who knew you lived around here in this nice house with such young siblings." I drifted as I heard them playing in another room.

"My parents adopted those kids." he said.

"Really?"

"Yeah. It was a few years ago. My mother wanted a big family, but was only able to have me, so they decided on adoption."

I couldn't help but be a bit surprised. "Well, it looks like everything turned out for the better."

"It did. They were really quiet when we first took them in. But now they're very active and lively." He said.

Just as he did, one of them came in the living room with us and went straight to Sano. I think she's the youngest of the three. I'd say around six.

"Sano, Sano!" She shouted while playfully pulling on his hand.

"What is it, Cindy?"

"When are you going to play with us?"

"Sano has a guest right now, so he can't play. Say hi to Misa," he told her.

"Hi!" She said, waving to me.

"Hi," I replied. She was little and cute with her light brown hair in two pigtails that swung around as she moved.

"You'll play with us later then?" Cindy asked.

"Without a doubt. Now go on and go play with the others for now." He told her and she ran off to the other room.

"It must take a lot of energy for you all to take care of them."

"Well, it's actually just me right now watching them."

"Where are your parents?" I asked suddenly.

"My mom is in the hospital, and my dad is out of the country for business."

I had to gasp. "S-so you mean you're here taking care of all three of them by yourself?"

"Well, they're usually well behaved, and it's only three of them. A boy and two girls. It's not that bad." He said so calmly, like taking care of three kids was nothing at all.

"Is your mother getting out of the hospital soon?"

"She's been there for a month now. She hasn't told me much about her condition, so I don't know if she'll be released soon or not," he said, looking off into the distance.

"Oh, sorry if I asked too much."

"No, it's fine. I'm fine," he assured me.

"But do you get help at all?"

"My dad sends money, so I manage. And I have an aunt who lives down the street who watches them if I'm not home or if I have somewhere to go."

"So that's it? No other assistance?"

"Are you worried that I'm not able to handle things on my own?" He asked.

"No! It's not that. It's just, I'm a bit shocked since you go to school and have track and stuff. It must be a lot for you. I was just wondering if you were doing this all by yourself and needed help at all."

"Are you offering?" he asked. I'm not sure if I actually was offering, but to help and get to spend time with Sano sounds like the start of my long-awaited plan.

"I don't have any little siblings, but I'm sure things could be easier if you had another hand to help you lessen the work on yourself. Just until your mother gets better."

"I guess having someone else around would make things easier to get done, but wouldn't Ken be upset if you were to start hanging around me?"

I didn't expect him to ask that so suddenly. Being here, I nearly forgot about him. "Oh, I'm sure he won't mind. Maybe it can just be the days you have track practice. That way, I could watch them while you relax from all the running and stuff you do." He paused for a moment like he was thinking about it. Maybe I shouldn't have asked. I did just follow him home. That walking in the same direction story was hardly buyable.

"Why not?" he finally responded.

I was ready to hear a "No, you creep!" So, hearing him give the okay was very unexpected.

"If it's you, then I think it should be okay," he said.

"Really?! I um, don't get to hang around kids a lot so I'm sure this could be fun." I tried to keep my cool while mentally jumping in joy.

"It'll be a change for sure." He said. Not sure what he meant by change but agreeing to letting me over must be another dream.

"It looks like the rain has stopped." I said after glancing out the window seeing the sudden downpour gone. "I should probably get going before it starts again." Leaving sooner than later in this case is best before he changes his mind.

"I guess I'll be back Monday." It was Friday, so this little dream wouldn't start until after the weekend. I got up and stumbled over myself trying to head to the door. I felt something falling from my bag doing so.

"Misa, you dropped something," he said. He picked it up, looking at it as he was handing it to me.

"Oh, that's my friendship bracelet. I can't afford to lose this. I've had it for a long time. I can't exactly remember when or where I got it because I had an accident, and my memory is a bit fuzzy from back then." I explained to him. It got a little too small for me to wear, so I keep it in my bag.

"Oh, I see. You were always a klutz, but you try your best," he said with a little smile. I could tell I was blushing, so I turned away.

"Yeah, I can be a bit clumsy at times," I replied with a dry laugh, "So uh, I guess I'll be leaving now." I didn't want to use all my luck up in one visit, so I wanted to save some for next time.

It felt as if I was floating when I left his house. Never in my wildest dreams did I think stalking would turn out for the better! He talked as if he knew me. We have had a class together since freshmen year. We don't have to talk to know each other exists since we've seen each other practically every day.

Now, we'll see each other in school and outside of school. With that, it'll be a lot easier to get to know him without the trouble of others around us. With him having the kids around, I should probably bring something for them. They seem really close.

If I get the kids respect, I'm sure Sano will start to like me too. I don't know what kids would like, but if I kept it simple like bringing them cookies or something, they would love that. No kid can refuse a good cookie.

I'm not a cook, but I can spend the weekend trying to make them some. I stayed on cloud nine all the way home. When I got in, I went straight to the kitchen to see if we had ingredients for cookies. The only problem is, I don't know exactly what all goes into a cookie.

"Welcome home." I looked past the cabinet I was in and saw Ken standing at the entry way of the kitchen. "Looking for something specific?"

"I was looking for something to make."

"Oh, so you cook now?" He asked a bit shocked and suspicious. Considering I haven't touched the stove since he's been here, I wouldn't put it past him that it sounds odd.

When my mom is home, she cooks every day. But when she's gone, it's whatever we have that doesn't involve the stove. Somehow, I burn or make something explode in some way or another when I cook. My mom doesn't trust me with the stove alone and neither do I.

"So, what are you making? A special meal for me?"

"Um, no."

"And here I thought you were finally trying to be a wife fit for someone of my caliber." He said feeling high and mighty. I can't exactly tell him I'm looking to make something for another guy.

"Let me guess, you know how to cook too?

"I've dabbled with it." He said. I would've thought maids, or a hired cook would take care of things like that. What kind of rich person cooks for themselves?

"Whatever you're making, we can make it together." If there's one thing I've learned about Ken, is to never trust anything he says while giving me that mischievous smile he's showing me right now.

"Actually, why not order a pizza instead?" I was still sensitive to him and couldn't risk something like what happened the other day happening again now that I'm finally getting involved with Sano.

"Aww, you're no fun." He pouted. He didn't press on after that. Maybe he knows I'm still watching him. Trying to bake with him hovering around would be difficult anyway. It would be better to try again tomorrow when he isn't paying as close attention.

Ken gave me space for the rest the night, which was both nice and odd since he's never left me alone without a fight before. I woke up the next day to find him closed away in his room working on something.

I wanted to ask what it was, but I took the alone time to try to figure out what makes a cookie become a cookie, so I'll have them ready for Monday. I've seen my mom make cookies before. If I can just do what she did, this shouldn't be too difficult. I stepped into the kitchen and went to the sink to wash my hands, and for the next hour and a half, I hoped for the best.

"Which class are you practicing fire safety in?" Ken asked when he came into the kitchen, fanning away the smoke that was coming from the oven.

"It's not fire safety, it's called baking." I was trying to make that sound believable as I was scraping the mess off the pan.

"You mean you were actually attempting to make something someone was supposed to consume?" Ken was looking around at the ingredients I had out. I had pretty much everything on the counter.

"Is this vinegar?"

"I'm not a cook, okay? I've never been good at cooking. And I thought it was something I saw my mom using before."

"Maybe it was water, or something used for a different dish, not... What were you making exactly?"

"Cookies." When I said that, his face really went to shock. I know they didn't come out right, but he could've made a different face.

"First off, were you using a recipe, and second, did you follow it correctly?" He asked.

"Well, I didn't think I needed one. I was trying to go off what I've seen my mom make. But I guess that wasn't the greatest idea I've had."

"Since you know you aren't the best cook out there, it's probably better to start with a recipe. I'm sure they would have come out a lot better, or at least edible that way." I'm not sure if that was supposed to cheer me up or not, but I did know I needed to try again.

"How about I guide you before you put the house at stake," he said, pulling out the flour from the cabinet. I figured it's something I should've used.

I avoided it once, but if I don't want to poison anyone, it's probably a good idea if I got some assistance. It's going to be weird having him with me in the kitchen baking, but what other choice do I have?

"Maybe that's for the best," I said. He smiled and I felt a hint of excitement in him as he started laying out things we'd be using.

He started showing me some recipes he knew and used all the time. He seemed like another person as he was cracking eggs and mixing them with butter and sugar and stuff, showing me what to do. It took almost no time for them to come out and actually look edible.

"Ah, another job well done, if I do say so myself," he said giving himself praise. "After living together for a while now, you'd think some of my genius would have rubbed off on you."

"There's only so much you can say before you start sounding a little too conceited," I said packing away some of the cookies.

"You know, I should charge you for this." He continued on.

"Wait a minute, I never actually asked you for help. You did this all on your own," I told him.

"Still no fun. I took the time out to help you make these for... Actually, why are you making cookies?" he finally asked. I was hoping he wasn't going to. I can't tell him I made them for Sano.

"I was making them for Katie. She wanted something sweet, and I told her I'd make her cookies."

"That was nice of you. Good thing I was here because the poor thing wouldn't have been able to move for a week if you were going to try to give her what you had earlier, but good try though."

"Thanks." I added much sarcasm. I felt a little bad that I had to lie to him after he helped me, but with these great tasting cookies, I'll be able to win over those kids and start a good relationship with Sano.

"Thanks for the little break. Now I must return to my work."

"What work? You mean you have homework you didn't finish right after it was given to you?"

"I appreciate the compliment, but that's not the type of work I was referring to. It's not really work either, more like studying. My father wants me to start understanding the business more, so he wants me to look into things about marketing and management."

"Don't you think it's a bit too soon for that? You're still in high school." I said.

"It's never too soon for him. 'The sooner the better' he says. He figures by the time he steps down, I'll know and understand everything there is to know and more." He said. Hearing that makes this arrangement seem all the more serious. I should probably end this before it's too late. "I don't mind it much," he continued. "But it is limiting our time together." He put his hand to his chest as if he were heartbroken.

"I'm sure you'll survive." I told him. To be young, smart, and perverted must lead an interesting life.

Just like he said, he went back to his room to 'work.' His father must have asked him to do this when he went to see him a few days ago. I've never met his dad. I wonder what kind man he is. If he's anything like Ken, I hope I don't have to meet him anytime soon.

Since Ken stayed busy, the rest of the weekend went by smoothly. Monday rolled around before I knew it and I was up running for class again. Ken said he tried waking me up, but it didn't work. I ended up late and had to stay after school.

Luckily, Sano and I arranged to meet at his house and not when school was over. So, I needed to kill time until practice was done anyway. I told him I'd help him with the kids, but I was actually hoping to spend more time with him. I feel I have so much to learn about Sano. Hopefully, I'll be able to get to know him more by doing this…

"Alright, you're all free to go," the teacher told us. I gathered my things and headed out to the beginning of hopefully something new.

"Misa." I was walking out of the classroom when I heard Katie call my name.

"What are you still doing here?"

"Eden had to stay after to make up an important test he missed the other day, and I was waiting on him. I knew you had detention, so I came here to ask why you were late this time since I didn't ask you earlier."

"I don't know. I went to bed on time after I made sure I had the cookies I baked-" I froze not intending to tell her about the baking. Katie froze in shock as well.

"Wait, you were baking something? Misa? Misa Macky did? You can't even make ice, why are you baking?"

"Your kind words are so touching," I said in sarcasm.

"Sorry, it just took me by surprise. Who exactly were you trying to bake for?"

"Why does it have to be who? Why couldn't I be making them for myself?"

"Misa, we all know you can't cook. You yourself said you'd never cook again after that time you blew up the cooking lab."

"Almost blew up, thank you. How was I supposed to know you can't microwave aluminum foil?"

"So again, who are they for?"

"I told you, m-myself. Now can you stop the hounding? I have to get going." I tried walking off. I can't exactly tell Katie about this yet.

"Alright, Misa. You can keep your little secrets. But remember who you're dealing with. Don't go around doing things on your own," she said. I know she'll find out. That's why there's no need to mention it now.

Katie hates secrets, but she'll have to wait for now. I need to establish a safe zone with me and Sano before I tell her the tale of my stalking adventure.

7

When I imagined finally going to hang out with Sano, I thought that when I arrived, I would give the little ones the cookies, they would get excited about the kind gift and tell Sano I'm the best. Then, they would go on about their day. The rest of the time could be me, Sano, and the moments I've been waiting for. But I was sorely mistaken by that. I'm not even here twenty minutes, and I'm completely overtaken by them.

"Misa, let's play this!" One of them shouted while holding up a board game.

"No, no, play tag with me!"

"I want to play too!"

I was surrounded.

"Misa, do you have more cookies?"

"Yeah, yeah, they were great!" The two younger ones jumped around me. I think Ken might've put extra sugar in them. They're so hyper. How does Sano put up with this? There's only three of them, but they have the energy of ten.

"Hey, you guys, give Misa some space." Sano came into the playroom and saved the day. "She's only one person so she can't do all the different things you want her to do. How about you guys go play outside for a little while? Then I'll play with you all after I make dinner." Sano suggested.

"Okay!" They all scurried out the room and into the backyard. I don't know what spell he used to get them to listen so well, but I need to learn it!

"Sorry about that. They get a little excited when they meet new people, plus they don't handle a lot of sugar well. And I guess they really loved your nice offering," he said, looking at the empty bag I had that once held at least a dozen cookies.

"Sorry, I didn't know they weren't supposed to have them."

"It's all right. I've never seen them so energized. They must've taken a real liking to you."

Winning over the kids, *check*!

"It was fun. And um, did you say you were about to make dinner? I can help you if you'd like." Now's my chance to spend some real time with him.

"Sure, can you make hamburgers?" He asked.

"Of course. That's an easy one." Telling him I can't cook isn't the best move right now.

"Okay, good. I thought you didn't enjoy cooking. I heard you say once that you'd never want to cook anymore after that incident you had in the cooking lab."

I gasped, "Y-you know about that?"

"I was coming from the bathroom when I heard the explosions happening, I got curious and went to see what was happening, and I saw you out in the hallway on the floor, trying to put out your apron that caught fire."

I can't believe he saw the most embarrassing thing I could've done at school. The fire alarms went off, everyone was evacuated, the fire department and police showed up, and there I was the cause of the commotion with half my shirt burnt and wet from someone throwing water on me.

"That was like two years ago, and a really bad mistake, which shouldn't happen here." I told him. No wonder he thinks I'm a klutz. He didn't just hear about that terrible day; he saw it happen.

"Can you handle seasoning and shaping the meat? I'll cut up some potatoes and make some fries," he said as we entered the kitchen.

"Yeah, no problem." But what do I use is the question. I don't watch cooking shows or watch everything my mom makes. What kind of these seasonings does he mean? Salt? Sugar?

"I already pulled out the things I was going to use," he said, as if reading my mind. The choosing part is now over then. Next question is how much? Since there's a lot of meat, I guess I should put in a lot. That makes sense to me. I shook a lot out of each bottle first and went to mix it all in.

"Misa wait!" Sano blurted, "I think you used a bit too much." He looked down at the mountain of seasoning I had sitting on top of the meat. Apparently, that's too much.

"Oh! I did? Sorry, I'll take some out." I should've known that I wouldn't need that much. My thoughts became cluttered, and I rushed for the garbage to take out some of the salts when I stumbled. Everything went flying into the trash can.

"Oh my gosh! Sano, I'm so sorry! I wasn't trying to. All the meat is now..."

"It's okay. Don't worry about it, we can make something else," he went to the freezer to look at what else he had.

"No! I'll go to the store and get some more. There's a store down the street. It should only take me twenty minutes. I'll be back quickly." I rushed out of the house in total embarrassment.

This time was supposed to be used to get closer to Sano. It's day one and I've already shown a reason to stay away. This is my first strike. He said don't worry about it. If I strike out, then there'll be something to worry about.

The store actually was around the corner. It took me almost ten minutes to get there. I went straight to the food section and began searching. I should have brought the packaging with me because I had no clue what kind of meat he had. I need to give my mom a lot more credit and to all cooks in the world. I didn't think it was this difficult. Why are there so many different kinds of meat?

"Misa! Are you buying this to cook for me?" A voice close behind me made me nearly jump out of my skin. And to my surprise, I turned and saw someone I hadn't seen in days.

"John? What are you doing here?"

"I was getting throat medicine. I've been sick as a dog the past couple days and happened to notice you in here. I thought you were finally seeing the truth and was buying stuff to make a big dinner to finally say you'll go out with me!"

He must really have been sick. I'll never understand the things that go on through his head.

"John, don't you think it's about time you gave up on this?" I tried pleading with him.

"No way!" His delusions must get worse when he's not well. "By the way, what brings you to this side of town?" he asked me.

"I'm um, visiting a friend." Which hopefully isn't a lie. We kind of just jumped into things.

"Crap, I'm late," his question reminded me of the time. Twenty minutes have passed already, and I'm still here in the store.

"Sorry, can't really talk right now. Good to see you're alive. I have to go," I told him.

Before he got the chance to reply, I picked up a package of meat, went to check out, and hoped for the best. I ran back to save on time.

"Sorry I'm late returning," I said out of breath. But from the smell of things, I could tell I had already taken too much time.

"It's fine. I actually should be saying sorry. I found out Mia didn't eat at school today and wasn't feeling too well. I wanted her to eat, so I started making something else."

Mia was the oldest of the three. She was sitting at the table in the kitchen. She had a lot of energy before I left. No food plus cookies must have given her a stomachache.

"I see. I wouldn't want anyone to go hungry because of me, so, it's fine." I tried not to sound disappointed. So much for quality time together in the kitchen.

"You can use this for another day," I handed the meat to him.

"Thanks, I'll use this tomorrow. Maybe you can help me with that."

I stared wide-eyed, "You'll let me help again, even though I ruined today?"

He let out a small laugh. "It would've been odd without some excitement coming from you."

"I'll be sure to do better tomorrow," I said. I wasn't sure if I should take that as a compliment, or something meaning I only mess things up. I totally need to figure out how to change his mind if that's even possible.

He finished the new meal he was making and asked me would I like some. It took everything in me not to say yes and eat with him and the kids like a big happy family, but with the way the sun was starting to set, I realized I should probably get home.

I didn't want Ken trying to figure out where I've been late at night. Leaving his house, I got to understand a lot more about Sano than I ever knew. One thing for sure, he's a great cook. Of course, he would have to be since he is taking care of his siblings.

To think a calm guy like him leads such a busy life. He doesn't seem bothered by it at all. I'd go crazy if I had to do everything he does on my own. When I finally arrived home, the first thing I saw was Ken moving around like he was searching for something.

"Playing a game of hide and seek?" I asked. He was on the couch when he stopped moving and looked at me.

"Why yes, yes I am, and I finally found you!" he said like I was the thing he seemed to be looking for.

"I really doubt I could fit under the couch."

"That may be true, but you never know. There could be a trap door or something underneath."

"If there are any trap doors in this house, they got put there by you."

"I can have one added if you'd like." There goes that look again. I went from a nice evening to a pervert looking to add trap doors in my house.

"Since you're wondering," he went on after seeing I didn't take the joke, "I seemed to have misplaced a pen that was specially engraved. But the search is over," he said reaching between the couch cushions and holding up a glossy silver pen with black writing I couldn't make out from my distance.

"That must be a really special pen for you to search so hard for it."

"My mother gave it to me a while back. She had some made for my father and decided to get me a matching set."

"Well, aren't you all just a cute family." I said a bit jokingly. Although, the idea was kind of cute. The closest thing we've done was my dad buying me a "daddy's girl" shirt that I ended up staining at a carnival.

"I wonder about that." He said softly after a long pause. Was calling them a cute family a bad thing? It's just a pen but getting matching sets for a father and son was nice of his mother. "I know what is cute. That facial expression of yours. Are you thinking about me?"

"N-not at all." I told him. It amazes me how he can tell what I'm thinking.

It's just that comment felt like there was more to it. Maybe he has something going on? He hasn't even asked me where I've been this whole time. That's probably for the best though. If he's finally losing interest, then I can get back to my life before he showed up. Only this time Sano will be in it.

8

Everything was going so much better after that first day disaster. I could not afford to let that happen again. The kids are loving me more and more. I haven't set fire to Sano's house yet, and getting this past Ken wasn't as hard as I thought. He hasn't asked me what I've been doing or why I was coming in late. Has he started losing interest?

This morning, he didn't come to wake me up for school like he always does. I wonder, did he find me out? Would it really matter if he did? It's not like I agreed to him being here, so I'm not really doing anything wrong. But why do I feel a bit guilty all of a sudden?

"Hey, Misa, you do realize that school has been out for over ten minutes now." My thought was broken when I heard Katie speaking.

"What? What's going on?" I said in confusion.

"Class was over forever ago. I didn't get you because I thought you had another detention or something. But then I realized there was no detention today, so I came back to see if you were still here. Why are you still here?"

"I must have been daydreaming again."

"You're doing a lot more of that these days. Is something going on?"

"No, I was just thinking about something that happened earlier."

"What happened earlier?" She asked.

"Oh, not much. Just something I may be overthinking."

"If it's about Sano again, then you probably should just let it go. You've been acting strange in first period with him. You haven't even talked with him yet, so don't stress yourself about him." she said. I hesitated for a minute. I've been acting strangely because I want to talk to him in class, but with Ken here, doing that would cause trouble.

"What if I have talked to him?" That made her eyebrow raise in suspicion.

"You actually talked to him earlier? What did he say?"

"I think we should get going, shouldn't we? You said it yourself; school has been over; we should probably go." I completely avoided her question and walked away.

She called after me, but I kept going. I don't want to keep this from her, but I don't want to tell her and take the chance of jinxing things. I still haven't really redeemed myself to Sano, so I still need to show him my good side. I don't want to be known as 'the girl who always screws up.' I must show him there's more to me than that, but I'm not sure how.

"You were always a klutz, but you try your best." Sano's words echo in my head; some of the first words he said to me. I cannot let it stay that way. I felt my pocket vibrating. I looked and saw it was the man of the hour calling.

"Hello?" I asked answering the phone. This is the first time he's called me.

"Hey Misa, were you still planning to come over today?" He asked.

"Yeah, I was actually on my way now." Even though, looking at the time, he should still be in practice.

"Okay, well, something suddenly came up and I was going to be late getting home." He started. The line was quiet for a minute before he spoke again. "I know this is something I should not be asking you, so feel free to say no. It's perfectly understandable if you do, but do you think you can watch the kids for a little while for me? I would've just asked my aunt, but I know they took a real liking to you." His voice was steady as he spoke, but I could tell there was something he wasn't telling me. Is he really asking me to go to his house alone to watch the kids for him?

"Yeah, sure I can. It's no problem. I'll be happy to help."

"Are you sure? This is a huge favor."

"Oh, don't worry about it. I'll get there right away so they won't be alone."

I hung up the phone and rushed to his house. They should be getting off the bus soon. My nerves were on edge not knowing what was going on. For him to suddenly call me to watch the kids must mean something happened. He called me first. For him to do that, he must trust me. This can be my chance to show him I'm more capable than I've been leading him to believe. I arrived at the house and knocked on the door. They must have been looking out of the window because they knew it was me.

"It's Misa!" I was greeted with a stampede. "Are you here to play with us?"

"Yeah, you're playing with us again today?" They were all talking at once. I didn't know where to start.

"Where's Sano?" Mia asked.

"Sano has something to do before he gets home. I'll be here until he gets done taking care of his business."

"Oh, so does that mean we won't have to go to Auntie Fay's house then?" Mia wasn't afraid to ask questions. She was almost eleven, but Sano told me she is usually the one that knows the most and likes to take charge of the others when he's not around.

"You'll get to stay here since I'll be here to with you."

"Yay, fun time with Misa!" The two younger ones started running around.

"Hey, remember, we can't be bad. Otherwise, Sano will get upset," Mia said. They both stopped yelling and ran into the other room. They don't hate him, but I guess even Sano has to get strict with them sometimes.

They were all at an orphanage before. They were left alone, but his family came and got them and took them in as their own. Now Sano is the only parent to them, and he doesn't show the slightest bit of regret of having them. I just knew he was a good guy.

It's been over an hour, and I've finally managed to get the hang of these little guys. I can even help them with their homework. I still haven't heard from Sano, and he didn't say when he's supposed to get here. I was hoping he wouldn't be too long so he could make dinner.

It was getting late, so I may have to make something myself. He has frozen pizzas in the freezer. I don't want to chance anything bigger than that, and I say that's better than nothing. I went ahead and popped one of them in the oven after turning it on. So far so good.

"Misa, could you help me with another question?" Brian came in and asked. He was the middle kid and two years younger than Mia.

"Sure." He was a smart little guy. I don't think he really needs help with anything. You only get so much homework as a first grader anyway. I still went to see what he wanted. He had been going through Mia's book and doing question from it.

"Why are you going through Mia's book?" I asked him.

"If I want to be smart like Sano and help my sisters when he's not around, I need to be smarter," he said. I couldn't believe at his age he was already thinking like that.

I went ahead and tried to help him with the problems he wanted to do. I'm not a tutor by any means, so I did my best to explain the questions in a way he would understand. The way he looked as he tried solving the problems kind of reminded me of Sano. He was so focused and tried to understand the third-grade questions. If Sano made it in the top of the class for midterms, he must study a lot. Brian will be just like him at this rate.

"The pizza!" I had been working with Brian for so long, I had forgotten I put it in. I could smell it coming down the hallway. I rushed into the kitchen and saw smoke coming out of the stove. I quickly grabbed an oven mitt to pull it out. I accidentally set the oven too high. Why am I screwing this up now?

"Misa, I'm here." I heard a voice coming in at the worst possible time.

"What's that smell? Did something happen?" Sano came in smelling well overcooked pizza.

"Sano! I'm so sorry. I was helping Brian with homework and left this in too long. I didn't know how long you were going to be, so I just put this in for them since I didn't want to chance messing up a real meal."

"Sano, Sano! You're home!" Cindy came running in and hugged him. His shocked expression softened as he saw her happy face.

"Well, it looks like nothing happened to anyone which is the good thing."

"I'm sorry, Sano. I said I wouldn't mess up again, but I did, and I swear this time it won't happen again."

"It's all right, Misa. I understand you didn't mean to do it. I can make something else. This is no big deal." He assured me it was okay, but always messing up isn't all right for me. I'm at my second strike. I know he won't keep saying that if I do this again.

We all stood in the kitchen for what felt like forever. That's when I felt my phone vibrate. I looked and noticed two missed calls and two texts from Ken. He's been trying to contact me the whole time. The sun was starting to set. He must be wondering where I am finally.

"Was that from Ken?" Sano asked me. I didn't want to answer, but from my hesitation, he figured out the answer himself.

"I'm sorry again for asking you to stay for me."

"Really, it's no problem," This time I'm assuring him. We've only recently started hanging out and he trusts me enough to stay at his house with his little siblings. I can feel the progress growing. I don't want to lose this. "It seems I should be getting back though."

I didn't want to go so soon after he got home. I want to talk more with him, but Ken might put out a search party if I don't get going. I said goodbye to him and the kids, and he thanked me for staying. Sano is so nice and considerate. Any other person would be put off by the constant screw ups. 'Misa the klutz' cannot be around forever. Maybe if I worked on my cooking skills or something, I could minimize a lot of errors since that's what I keep messing up the most here.

As I got closer to home, I shifted my thoughts back to what I was going to walk in to. When I got to the door, I opened it slowly, hoping Ken was upstairs and couldn't hear me.

"Misa! Where have you been and why do you keep coming home so late!? You can't keep your husband to be wondering all day." I almost thought my parents were home the way Ken came at me.

"Geez, you sound worse than my dad. I was doing something that's none of your business." I went in and sat on the couch to where I was finally able to breathe easily again.

"Hmm, you have that cute, worried expression on. Something wrong, Mimi?"

"I told you, don't call me that. And it's nothing that concerns you."

"Aw, why you have to be like that? We're in this together. The least we can do is make the most of it," he said, giving me the idea I was looking for.

"Well, if you want to make the most of it, why don't we start doing something together then?" I shouldn't use him like this, but maybe I can get him to help me learn what I need to know about cooking.

"That's more like it. We can do anything. Take baths together, go skinny-dipping, draw each other n—"

"That's not what I meant you pervert! I was thinking something more along the lines of you teaching me how to cook." His face changed when I said that.

"Well, that's unexpected," he said.

"How is that unexpected? Cooking is fun. It's a good way to bond. There's nothing like making your favorite meals together, right?"

"I guess we could do that. Of course, if you want to go the teaching rout, it has a fee that has to be paid."

I was hoping he wouldn't mention that. "Can't we discuss that afterwards? I'm really interested in learning." I didn't want to think about his whole payment thing.

"Have I inspired you from before to be a master chef especially for me?" He said, thinking high of himself again.

"I wouldn't say that exactly. I just want to learn how so I won't be seen as someone who can't even make a simple meal for herself. I want to be able to do something right." I was already sixteen. The least a young woman like me should be able to do is make a grilled cheese without burning it.

"I see. So, you want to start after school then?" he asked.

"Uh, it would have to be around this time in the evening. I can't right after school."

"What's gotten you so tied up after school all of the sudden?"

"I um… I'm doing something for someone after school so that won't work." I started walking to the kitchen, "We could start now. There's no time like the present!" The sooner I can work on this, the sooner I'm able to show a new side to me.

"I don't have much else to do today, so I suppose we could start now," he said following me into the kitchen and going to the cabinet.

"Since the last time you tried making something for someone, you were going to poison them, let's start off with something simple such as Kool-Aid," he pulled out the Kool-Aid powder and sat it on the table. I looked at him and he looked at me. He was serious.

"Are you making fun of me?" I asked.

"Sadly, I'm not. You asked me to teach you, so, this is the first project I'll have you work on since it's late." He wasn't just serious; he was completely serious.

"Now, it shouldn't take you too long. I've laid out what you'll be using. I'll give you ten minutes to do this." He put the pitcher, sugar, Kool Aid mix, and stirring spoon out for me. I just looked at it. "You'll have to use water from the faucet," he said, assuming I was wondering about the water. Of all the things to be wondering about at this moment, that's what he thought to mention.

"You seriously think it'll take me ten minutes to make Kool-Aid? Just give me a minute, I'll have this ready for you." Just because I burned a couple cookies the last time, he thinks I can't even do something as simple as this.

"Ok Ms. Chef, I'll be back in three then." He walked out leaving me with this. I started adding the Kool-Aid to the pitcher and sugar. I never did put enough sugar in my Kool-Aid, so I added a bit more in, so he won't have anything to say about it, and stirred. I know I'm not the best in the kitchen, but this is a little insulting.

"Have you finished my tasty beverage?" Ken came back three minutes later exactly. I don't understand how he can be the son of the Masidone company, and his *tasty beverage* is a child's drink.

"Here, I think you'll see your misjudgment and move on to something better." I handed him a cup and he drank some.

"Are you trying to give me a sugar rush at this hour? There's way too much in here. And I even put out how much to use."

"Well, I thought it needed more."

"Did you even taste it?"

"No."

"You have to understand that there are measurements for a reason. You have to go by them until you're skilled enough to know by just taking a look. But you won't know that unless you sample your work, even just a little. Let's try this again." He couldn't be more serious.

"Use what you see," he said. If I knew he'd be like this, I wouldn't have asked. He was a lot easier to work with when it was my schoolwork.

"Now isn't the time for distractions. You must focus."

"Ken, it's just Kool-Aid! Chill out," I told him.

"What do you mean 'just Kool-Aid'? It's the foundation and fundamentals of drinks. If you can't take making this seriously, and whole heartedly put your all into it, then you'll never make anything great!" Ken went on a rant.

Was he for real about this? Getting so serious over flavored water? I know I don't know him well yet, but something has to be going on in his head. I quickly made his drink, so it would be over.

"Alright here. Your wholehearted Kool-Aid, pre-tasted and everything." He took the cup again and drank some.

"Now that's what I call a cup of juice! You've passed the first trial."

"Now that that's done, can we try something more taste bud satisfying than a sugary drink?" I asked.

"Only one new thing a day. You shouldn't overwork yourself."

"Explain to me how it's possible to overwork myself from making Kool-Aid?"

"Oh, it's possible," he answered. Sometimes, this guy makes me wonder exactly who he is. He's obviously not the average high-class guy you'd see on TV.

"So tomorrow, since there's no school, maybe we can work with breakfast."

"What?" I asked.

"Yeah, first you started with a drink, now for the appetizer or breakfast in this case."

"No, I mean we don't have school tomorrow?"

"Didn't you hear the reminder over the intercom in fifth period?" With my Sano concern, I must have forgotten about that. With this, I can practice making little things. I should be getting better at my skills in no time. I'll be able to impress Sano and show my mom he wasn't just some kid I wrote about. I can see my dream finally becoming a reality!

"You seem awful happy over a little day off," he said watching me.

"Oh, I um, was just thinking about how much time I have to catch up on some work I have to do." I lied.

"Are you lying to me, Mimi?"

"Again, with this name? And no, I'm not." I tried to sound believable, but he moved closer to me. I backed into the counter and had nowhere else to go.

"You, saying you're happy for a day from school to do work is like saying I'm able to blend oil and water. You're coming home late, and now want to suddenly learn to cook? That's not the Misa I know."

"What do you mean? You don't even know me," I protested.

"Oh, but I do. You can't hide secrets from me. I will find out."

"Geez you sound like Katie. Do you all really think I'm that easy to read?"

"Indeed," he replied with no hesitation.

"Well sorry for being predictable."

"But I never said it was a bad thing." He got even closer to me. "See, with predictable people, they're easier to read and understand than those who are complicated and hide what they are feeling." He had his whole body around me. I had no way around him.

"Hey, you're getting kind of close here," He was inches away from my face. His dark brown eyes were staring at me so intensely I had to look away. He seemed closer than he did when he kissed me.

"Am I getting close? Or is this what you really want?" I could feel his breath on the side of my face as he spoke in a low tone.

"Y-you're such an animal. Get away from me!" The temperature in my face was doubling along with my heart rate as I pushed him away.

He started laughing. "Oh Mimi, you're so cute when you're being shy. You're paid and full for this."

"What?"

"I never said what kind of payment I wanted this time now did I?"

"You sick perv. I'll never ask for your help again!" I walked out of the kitchen.

"Oh, but Misa, you need me!"

"As if!" I'm better off buying a cookbook and using the internet. I can teach myself. Ken is just too much. His being here has lessened the burden of a lot of things, and also me being here alone, but some things just don't add up with him. And I doubt they ever will.

9

I thought the rain would be gone today, but this heavy downpour beating on the windows means it's still around. Even though there's no school, all sports still had practices, but the outdoor sports like soccer and track are probably canceled. Sano must be relieved about that. I messaged him to make sure he knows I won't be there since practices were canceled and going that far in this rain would be bad. I'll have to hold off on that cookbook today as well.

"Misa!" I heard an unusually happy Ken coming down the stairs toward me. "Misa, hug me!"

"Whoa, Ken, are you drunk or something? Don't just come out of nowhere asking for random hugs."

"But I'm about to leave for the day."

"You are? Weren't you supposed to help me with my cooking?"

"I thought you didn't want my help anymore?" He said confused. I did say that. Why did I just ask?

"If you want me to stay, I'll gladly stay here with you all day." He said sitting a little too close to me on the couch.

"Um, no, that's alright, I mean, where are you going this early?" It was only after nine in the morning. I'm not even sure why I'm up this early.

"Some place my parents are taking me."

"You don't know where they're taking you?"

"I have a feeling they're not even sure yet. Either way, I won't know since it's a birthday surprise."

"Birthday surprise? Today is your birthday. When did that happen?"

"Well, I'd say seventeen years ago today is when my birthdays started happening. Around three in the morning to be exact."

I guess I deserve that smart remark since I never asked him this. He could have at least said today was his birthday though. That's usually something people like to mention.

"My parents always take me somewhere. Usually somewhere out of state or out of the country."

"What?!"

"But since it's raining outside, they'll probably keep it local."

"You go out of state and country every year? How?"

"You forget, our name is worldwide," he said with his high and mighty tone. I almost forgot that he was not just rich, but incredible wealthy. That is why my parents, mainly my mom, were so pushy about this arrangement.

"So, back to my original reason for coming down here now, hug me!" He threw his arms out and leaned toward me.

"Whoa there, you pushy perv. Just because it's your birthday doesn't mean you'll get special treatment." I said moving over.

"So, mean. I don't ask for much often."

"Yeah, *ask* is the magic word. You don't often ask because you act on your own."

"Okay fine, I'll start asking before I do. So, I'm going to ask, could you at least wish me a happy birthday?" He asked like he really wanted to hear that from me.

"Fine. Happy birthday to you, Ken. I um, wish you a good day."

"Oh, thank you!" He suddenly launched toward me, closing me in a tight hug. "You even added 'wish you a good day' in it. Thank you." "Okay, okay, that's enough, you're welcome, now let go." There was the sound of a horn outside. I was able to keep my cool even though that was a bit of a surprise. He actually hugged me.

"Well, it seems my ride is here. If only I could stay with you all day, but sadly, this is something that is looked forward to every year, so I have to go. Don't miss me too much, 'kay?" He smiled widely as he got his bag and headed out the door.

He can be so happy-go-lucky sometimes. He gets so overjoyed with just the little things I do. And no matter what I do or say, he keeps coming back. I have been so wrapped up with Sano lately, I guess I haven't been around him as much. But what does it matter if I've been around him or not? I like things perfectly the way they are now. I felt my phone vibrating in my pocket. It was Katie calling.

"Hey," I answered.

"Hey, what are you up to today?"

"Oh nothing. I was um, going to work on becoming the master chef I know I can be."

"What's with this cooking thing all of a sudden? You've never once seriously thought about cooking, let alone doing it since the incident."

"Well, I'll need to start eventually, won't I? So why not now?"

"Misa, I've known you since first grade. I know your patterns, and this surely isn't one of them."

"Change is a good thing." I tried telling her.

"I'm going to come over and see what's up," she said.

"But it's raining."

"You think that's going to stop me from getting information?" She almost sounded insulted. If I know Katie, she'll come around in ten feet of snow.

"Fine, come if you like." She was already out the door when I hung up. It was going to happen eventually, so I guess now is as good a time to tell her since Ken is out for the day. Ten minutes later, I heard a knock at door.

"That was fast," I said letting her in.

"I'm around the corner and already dressed, so all I needed to do was leave." She said closing her umbrella.

"I'm surprised you're not trying to go to Eden's house."

"He's super sick, so I wanted him to rest up. And more importantly, I wanted to see what's up with you. You've been different lately."

"How so?"

"Your new interest in cooking, always hanging around school when it's over, you avoid answering me when I asked you what you were doing, you even got Ken wondering about you. I wasn't going to say anything, but yesterday after school, he asked me if I knew where you were. I couldn't tell him if I wanted to because I didn't know either."

"Did he really ask you that?"

"I was surprised too. I figured it had to do with whatever you weren't telling me, so I didn't ask him anything. I just want to know what's new trying to be processed in that head of yours."

"Geez, why can't I try something new without the world tuning it into a federal crime?"

"Because Misa Macky doesn't change her habits often, especially in secret. Although, you've only started acting differently since Ken came about. Does he have something to do with this?"

"Please, he's just a freeloading pervert living in my house."

"I think he actually likes you," she said.

"I doubt it. He's only here because of our parents."

"He really doesn't seem like a bad guy. You should give him a chance." Katie really seems to want me to be with Ken.

"Why should I be forced to like someone I don't know? At least with Sano I've known him…"

"Sano?" She repeated. I got frustrated and mentioned him.

"You know, you brought him up before saying you talked with him. Are you really letting a little encounter change how you're feeling?"

"If it was just a little encounter, then I wouldn't have been to his house." I finally admitted.

"What? You've been to his house?!" She exclaimed.

"Yeah."

"When?"

"Well, you know. I've been going there since last week." I didn't look at her when I told her. When I glanced in her direction, she just shook her head.

"Ah, so the mystery has finally revealed itself. You've been going to his house and what? Cooking for him? You two secretly going out or something?"

"No, it's not like that. I um, kind of followed him home one day." Saying it like that made it sound just as bad as it was.

"Oh, Misa, don't tell me you were stalking him?"

I couldn't really deny it, so I kept going. "So, after that, he found me and invited me into his house, and we started talking. Now we hang out at his place. I found out he has a lot going on at home and asked if he needed help."

"Really?"

"Yeah, there's more to him then he lets on."

"So, you're leading a secret life with him now? Won't you be messing up something with this thing you got with Ken?" She asked. "That's why I was trying to keep quiet about it."

"Why can't you just tell your parents you really don't want to deal with this? I'm sure they'd understand."

"Well, I guess I could try talking to them again but..." I trailed off.

"But what? Do you like Ken now? Are you trying to keep both? Just a two timer, huh? I thought I knew you better than this, Misa." She started shaking her with judgment.

"Katie, you've got it wrong. I like Sano, and Ken is kind of annoying at times, but somehow..."

"So, you're just going to lead them on and break hearts when it's over with?"

"That wasn't my intention. You're confusing me. I just wanted to get closer to Sano. The chance only seemed to have come when Ken happened to come around and twisted things."

"Well, Misa, you have to figure out what you want to do before something bad happens. Whatever you do with Sano should be kept on a friend level while Ken is still here. But if you're not getting rid of Ken, then that has to mean you have some kind of interest in him. And if that's the case, you need to figure out what kind exactly and if they'll grow into something more."

"What?" I got a bit confused.

"All I'm saying is that I don't want anybody hurt and this is all riding on you. In the end it's all up to you. Ken already seems cool about this agreement. When it comes time for it, you're the one that will be answering yes or no."

"Let's not look that far ahead in the future." Could I really see myself going ahead with this marriage arrangement with Ken?

"Misa? You here?"

I was startled at the sound of my own mother's voice coming through the door. Both Katie and I turned from the couch as she came in shaking off her umbrella.

"Mom? You didn't tell me you were coming today?"

"I wanted to surprise you. Hello, Katie," she said.

"Hi, Mrs. Macky."

"Where's Ken?" my mom asked.

"He's with his parents."

"What? They've come for him already? I told them to wait a little

longer." Disappointment filled her tone.

"Why? You had something to give him for his birthday or something?"

"His birthday? Oh, that's right. That is today. So that means they're just taking him out?"

"Yeah, was there something else?"

"I thought they decided to take him back." She said.

"Why would they take him back?" I was a bit surprised.

"Well, I heard from his father there was another young lady that he feels is a better fit for Ken. I told him to give you a little more time to come around first. I just hope they intend to bring him back. This could've finally been our chance." I didn't know his dad had started to reconsider this. And there's been another girl too?

"Have you ever met her?" I suddenly asked.

"No, I haven't. He just called me in the other day and told me they have other options."

"Wow, he's not playing around, is he?" Katie asked. Thinking back to when Ken said his father told him, "It's never too soon," he isn't playing around.

"We can only keep our fingers crossed for now. How about I make you both something since I'm here."

She was worried about this possible change in events but went on to the kitchen. I couldn't be more confused about the news and happy for my mom's food at the same time.

"Well, Misa, here's your chance," Katie said.

"My chance for what?"

"Your chance to give Ken the boot and let him go to the other girl."

"With Ken being here, I didn't think there'd be others."

"And who knows, she might be the more possessive or aggressive type. You have to watch out for those girls in these situations." Knowing Katie for as long as I have, I'm pretty good at handling aggressive people.

"I think you've been watching too many TV shows. For all we know, she may not even show up."

"I guess we'll only know that in time," Katie said.

I'm curious to know who this other girl is, and what made her come in now? Ken must have told his dad I wasn't interested and they're going with another plan. I can't help but feel this sort of anxiousness. This is going according to plan, so why the nervous feeling? I don't have any special feelings for Ken, but he does keep things livelier.

I do like Sano, but at the rate I'm going, he's going to hate me by the end of it and I'll never get him to like me back. He never seems to get upset when I do mess up. Maybe he actually likes me too. Still, even though he has conditions, Ken always helps me if I need it and it's helpful to me. The more I think about those two, the bigger headache I get. It's going to take forever to figure out this situation I've gotten myself in.

"You poor thing. Just say the word and I'll get rid of the both of them for making you have to worry so much." Katie saw my frustration and put her arm around me, assuring me she would get rid of them. And the scary part is I know she would try.

"Please do. That sounds a lot easier right now." I rested my head on her.

There's a first for everything. And with firsts comes the difficulties of understanding exactly what the new thing is. I may be a little late experiencing this love field, but at this rate, I would rather stay in the outfield a little longer now.

My mom cooked and made food to last a couple days. Turns out she came by partly to check on me, but mostly to check on the situation. She couldn't stay too long with her long drive back to the city. She headed out shortly after cooking. I didn't want to tell her I'll soon be able to cook like her because she may never leave me alone again from fear. Katie left a little while after her, leaving me to myself and my thoughts.

Night was setting in and it was still raining outside. It almost felt kind of lonely. The day went by a lot different than I had planned. The only thing left to do was to head to bed and hope to wake up with everything back on track.

"Misa! It's time to wake up!" The high spirit and cheerful call of my name seemed to echo louder than it really was. I didn't have to open my eyes to know it was morning. That's the only time I hear Ken in such high spirits.

Wait...

"Ken? When did you get back?" I rolled over in my bed and saw Ken standing in front of me.

"I got back about two hours ago." I looked at the clock and it was 7AM.

"Two hours? Where did you go?"

"Well, my parents were so undecided, we ended up going out of state and saw a theater show. It was very nice."

"You traveled for a theater show?"

"Yesterday was the last showing of it, so we decided to catch it while we could. We even did a little shopping. Here, I brought you back a souvenir." He handed me a bag. They did so much in just one day. They really are something else.

"Come on, you have to get up. You don't want to be late after a relaxing day off," he said. The only relaxing thing about yesterday was sleeping.

Thinking back to what happened, I remembered what my mom told me about another girl. Ken isn't acting like there's someone else. Maybe she wasn't a serious thing. The time was ticking. I needed to forget about that and get ready, so I won't have to run to beat the bell.

"Oh, I see you're wearing pink again." he said, looking at me after I got up.

"What, g-get out!" I reverted to my alone days, not expecting him to greet me first thing in the morning.

"I'll be waiting for you! Let's walk to school together."

"As if!" I yelled.

"You know you want to." He sang as he walked out. Though he's acting really upbeat, I couldn't help but feel like there was something off about him.

We ended up walking to school together since he left when I did. The whole walk felt a bit distant. The closer we got to the school, the quieter he seemed. I wanted to ask about his sudden change in emotion, but I couldn't bring myself to ask. Something about a quiet Ken made me uneasy. After we got to school, he went to his locker, and I went to mine. We went to class separately.

"Something wrong?" Katie was already in the room and saw the confusion on my face.

"I don't know. I thought today was going to be a good day, but I have a feeling something isn't right."

"What do you mean by that?" She asked.

"Alright, I need everyone to their seats." Mr. Hallens suddenly appeared right before the bell rang. "We'll be having another new student, so I have to see where I can put her."

Another student in our class. We already had a full room. I didn't think we could fit more in here.

"Jennifer should be coming in any minute now. And she'll have the seat behind you Miss Macky," Mr. Hallens said. I used that desk for my book bag which meant I could no longer use that desk. When I turned to grab my bag, I saw Ken with a distressed look.

"Hi. Is this Mr. Hallens' first period history class?" A girl walked in. She looked unbelievably polished and dolled up. I even heard a few guys whispering behind me.

"Yes, you must be Jennifer, please have a seat behind Misa over there. Raise your hand for me Miss Macky." I raised my hand so she could see where she was going.

"Misa? Oh, that's a fun name. I hope we can become friends," she says with a glowing smile. "Nice to meet you Misa." She stuck out her hand as she was going to sit.

"S-same here," I said taking it.

Her nails were painted purple like her skin-tight shirt that I'm pretty sure was against school policy. Her freshly bleached blond hair was in loose curls that went past her shoulders. Part of me didn't believe she was a high schooler as she batted her eyes with long lashes and eyeliner, but her light voice and small face kept the idea alive. Once she sat down, she looked back to her right, which is where Ken was, and winked.

"Don't look so overjoyed," she whispered sarcastically to him.

"You two know each other?" I found myself asking.

"Yeah, we know each other, we're good friends, isn't that right Kenny?" Ken didn't answer her.

Could this be the other girl my mom was talking about? She turned out to be the real thing. It couldn't be. Ken doesn't seem at all happy that she's here.

"Well, isn't that nice to know a friend on the first day," I said.

"Yep. But too bad you guys won't be friends much longer."

"What?"

"Jennifer, don't start," I heard Ken finally speak, but she ignored him.

"It took me a little longer to get here, but now that I am, you guys won't be a thing much longer, kay? So, to make things easier for everyone, it's best that you stop getting closer to each other," that glowing smile turned into an evil smirk. She has to be the other girl. Where does she get off threatening me like that? Are his parents really considering her a better option? What exactly about that attitude is great?

10

"I can already see you guys don't seem compatible. So, let's drop the act, okay? It'll be easier on everyone that way."

This Jennifer girl is serious. Is she really the other fiancé? How could someone like her? I haven't known her for a minute and she's already attacking me. People were already staring because of her doll-like beauty, but that little introduction really sparked the interest of some that were able to hear her. She didn't say anything else and pretended to be a good student the rest of the class period. My concentration was gone the minute I saw her. Before I knew it, class was over, and we were handed our homework.

"So, Misa, all things aside from the other matter, why don't we work on this together later since I don't have a book yet?"

Jennifer asked like I was going to easily overlook that threat earlier.

"Sorry, I can't. I have other plans," I said without sounding the least bit sorry.

"Oh, you and Ken have better plans today?"

"Um, no, I have something else to do."

"You mean you don't spend all your time together? Some relationship you two have," she said with obvious sarcasm. "If it were me, we would do things all the time." She flicked her hair back while smiling a smile only a pampered princess would have.

"Well, Jennifer, I think my relationship with Ken is none of your business. So, if you'll excuse me, I have a class to get to." The bell rang and I got up to go to my next class. I've never let anyone get to me so easily, but with that behavior, it's hard not to.

"Misa!" I turned and saw Katie catching up to me.

"Oh Katie, just who I needed."

"Who's that Jennifer girl? What exactly was that this morning?"

"It's the other girl. The one my mom mentioned."

"Wow, really? She showed up a lot sooner than I thought. And to go through the trouble of transferring this late in the school year. I would think it's safe to say she's the clingy type?" She asked.

"More like twisted type. The first thing out her mouth was her telling me not to get closer to Ken."

"Maybe it's a good thing. If you want to get rid of him, then tell the girl here you go." She gestured handing him over.

"I mean I guess, but would she really have gone through the trouble of coming here if it were that simple? Ken's not going to go away that easily. I'll just see how this plays out for a few days. If I can even last that long."

"I hope you can make it through this. You know if you need any help, I'll be there to help rid the issue. You know I'm there for you."

"Thanks Katie, but that's kind of why I want you to stay out of this. You might do something drastic like last time." I said reminding her of the last time she 'helped' get rid of an issue.

"I did nothing of the sort. That girl had it coming." She said playing innocent.

"We had a minor disagreement; she accidentally ripped my bag, and you purposely cut almost six inches of her hair."

"In my defense, I was aiming for three. Not my fault she moved. Plus, she deserved it. She ruined your bag and made you have to buy a new one. I gave her a free haircut, which by the way, she needed."

She said it like she did her a favor. Katie will definitely act first and think second, so I really couldn't have her dealing with someone from Ken's side of the world. That look and style Jennifer has is like Ken, so I know she's no regular girl.

Turns out, I have two other classes with Jennifer. She seemed completely different since Ken wasn't there. She didn't say anything to me and barely glanced in my direction. It was relieving actually, but somewhat suspicious after the way she acted when she first came in.

There was something else suspicious. I hadn't seen Sano at all today. He must not have come to school, which is rare for him. I wonder if I should still go to his house today. He hasn't messaged me or anything.

If he got sick or something, he can't really take care of the kids like that. I should go to his house anyway just to make sure everything is all right. With Jennifer showing up suddenly, I feel I shouldn't go, but I've come this far with Sano. I'm not going to let her interfere now, but to stay on the safe side, I took the back exit out of school and headed to his house.

I tried calling him as I headed there, and it went straight to voicemail. I got an uneasy feeling, not sure what to think could be going on. When I finally made it to his house, I quickly knocked on the door, but I didn't get a response. It was quiet so no one must be in. I waited another minute in case he might've been coming from upstairs when I heard kids' voices.

"Hello? It's me, Misa." I yelled at the door.

The door opened slightly. "Oh! It is Misa! You're here to hang out with us again?" It was Mia who opened the door.

"Yeah, I am. Um, is Sano here?" I asked.

"Sano isn't home. I think he's still at the hospital. He told us he was going there after we went to school this morning. He told me that if he wasn't back by the time we got home to go to Auntie Fay's house.

But if you're here again then we don't have to go." She said.

"Why is Sano at the hospital?"

"It's probably because of mom." Brian said. I almost forgot that his mother was in the hospital. Something must have happened for him to be there all day. I hope that isn't the case.

It was weird being at Sano's house without him knowing. I called again to see if he'd answer but got the voicemail again. I stayed with them for a while before I felt the need to get worried again.

It's been over an hour now. Just the other day he couldn't make it in until it was late. Was he at the hospital then too? I never did get around to asking about that. I think we should call this Auntie Fay anyway to see if she knows his whereabouts. When I went to ask Mia about his aunt, I got a call. It was from Sano. I quickly answered, already relieved to hear from him.

"Hey, Misa, you didn't by chance go by the house today, did you?" He asked. He sounds a bit stressed.

"Yeah, I came here because you weren't at school, and I wanted to know if everything was okay." I told him. I could hear a sigh of relief from his end.

"Yeah, everything is okay now. I had to do some things for my mother, and I didn't get the notice until this morning. I had no idea how long I was going to take. My phone died and I couldn't get in touch with my aunt, so I was just wondering if you were there. I'll be home shortly. I'll explain it better when I get back. I can't thank you enough. I'm really sorry for this. You're really the best."

"It's no problem, really." I tried not to react to that last comment, and we just ended the call after that. He's been out all day with his mother. I was relieved to know nothing happened to him, but for him to have been gone all day with his mom, something must have happened. Not too much time passed when I heard the door open.

"Hey, Misa," I heard Sano coming in, "Is everything alright here?" He asked. I came out of the other room with the kids when he came in.

"Yep. No smoke or burned food," I said a little too proud of that.

"That's good. I'm really sorry this happened again." I've never seen him look so stressed. He took a moment to gather himself. "The whole time I was gone, I was actually hoping you'd come here, and you did, which was really great."

So, he was hoping I would come over. I made the right choice in coming then. Otherwise, the kids would've been here by themselves without knowing what was going on.

"Well, you don't miss school often, so I wanted to make sure nothing had happened," I told him.

"My mom has been having some complications, so I've been visiting her a lot."

"Is she okay?"

"Yeah, she's doing all right for now. She doesn't want me to worry, but I know her treatments aren't going too well." I felt my heart sink. I wanted to ask what exactly was wrong, but from the tension on his face, I couldn't bring myself to.

"Will you be going to see your mom more often now?"

"It's better she doesn't have visitors every day, but I will be going a few times a week."

"W-would you like me to be here when you go?" I offered.

"I couldn't ask you to do something like that," he said.

"You're not asking, I'm offering. It wouldn't be a problem. If it's to help you Sano, I'd be more than happy to do it." I almost felt a bit embarrassed saying that.

He thought about it before responding. There's plenty of people my age babysitting, so it's not unheard of. It's just a matter of him being okay with me doing it.

"Alright then. Thanks, Misa. I never thought I'd have such a kindhearted friend," he said. Then, without skipping a beat, he reached out to me and grabbed me into a hug. My eyes got wide as I was taken aback by the sudden embrace. I was in Sano's arms.

"Oh, sorry," he said quickly letting me go. "I'm sure Ken doesn't want other guys hugging you."

"Um, n-no, it's fine. It's just a hug, nothing wrong with that," I said, a little flustered.

"Speaking of Ken, I've been wondering, why does he always let you come here? I was assuming he was the jealous type, but he's letting you come to another guy's house." The question was a bit unexpected. He doesn't know I never told him.

"Well... I kind of never told him where I was." I admitted.

"So, you've been lying to him?" He asked.

I don't know how to answer that without sounding guilty of it. "Um no, he hasn't exactly asked where I'm at." So now I'm lying to him again.

"So, you just come over here without telling him anything?" he asked with the appropriate amount of suspicion. I was blanking out, not sure what to say. I can't just come out and tell him, '*You're the one I wanted to get to know, so of course I wouldn't tell Ken about this.*'

"Well, Ken and I aren't together anyway, so it's not like it's a huge deal, but-"

"Hey, Sano really is home!" The kids stampeded into the living room with us. They couldn't have come at a better time. I wasn't sure what I was going to say next.

"Where have you been, you've missed all the fun we had with Misa."

"Sorry I'm late. I'll play with you guys in a minute," Sano hugged them all and sent them back. He really does care for them. But with his mother being important too, it must be hard to balance them both.

"I um, I should probably get going." It's a little earlier than usual, but if he's getting interested in Ken all of a sudden, it's better to go before I say something that'll get me in trouble with either him or Ken.

"Well, alright then." he said. I may be going crazy, but he sounded a little disappointed. Did he want me to stay? If he wants me to stay, could that mean he's coming around? That hug just now was a little too tight for it to just be nothing. Maybe he is, or I'm thinking too much.

I said bye to the kids and Sano and took off for home. If he's really starting to get an interest, I should just tell him how I feel. I know he'll get upset if I keep lying to him. I mean, I'm sure he knows I like him. It'd just be better if I came out and told him instead of these excuses. But with him being so concerned for his mother, I don't want to put him in an awkward spot. I'll have to wait for the right moment. If I can get one.

11

"Misa! Where have you been? You've left me here all by my lonesome again." I was almost sure I entered the wrong house hearing Ken so energetic like he was this morning.

"Well, it seems your spirit has been lifted."

"What do you mean?"

"You didn't seem too pleased with our new transfer student today." I reminded him.

"Oh, her." I must have killed his buzz because his mood almost changed completely. "You should probably watch out for her Misa. I'll do what I can to get her out of here."

"Why? Who is she?"

"She's an acquaintance of mine." He said. Is he trying to hide who she really is?

"You don't like her?"

"Do you want me to like her?" He countered.

"No. I mean she seems fond of you. And she's not that bad looking."

"Oh, but Misa, she doesn't have that cute upset face you have."

"Even so," I said overlooking that last comment, "it seems she came a long way to be with you. You should be happy that someone came all this way to see you," I said, feeling that I've heard these words somewhere else before.

"Misa, you're so mean. Do you really want me to leave you?"

"At least with you gone, I won't have to worry about my space being invaded."

"Well, at least your space is invaded. Can't say I can relate. You never invade mine, or even here long enough to. Where have you been going? You disappear so quickly after school without anyone knowing where you are."

"Do you really care where I am?" I asked.

"Of course, I do. I always want to know where my beloved Misa is."

"I really don't understand how you can like a person so much without even knowing them."

"But I told you, Misa, I do know about you. Do you really believe I would come here without knowing anything?"

"So, what, you've been watching me or something?"

Ken paused for a moment. "I was given information about you. You should have had some about me too, but it seems you didn't get it or just didn't look at it," he said. That could probably be what my mom was trying to show me a while back. I didn't take her seriously at the time, so I didn't bother.

"Besides all those details," Ken went on, "we should really spend more time together. If you keep disappearing all the time, Jennifer will have more of a reason to stick around."

"Sorry, Ken, but I've already got things to do after school and I can't let them down."

"And that would be?"

"Um, something for a friend. Their parent is in the hospital, and I said I'd help them out." I figured saying that much wouldn't reveal who it was.

"Such a kind thing for you to do," he said, but his tone didn't really sound exactly nice.

"What, you got a problem with that?" I asked.

"No, not at all. But I've gotten curious, is this person you're helping a girl or guy?"

"And what if it was a guy?" I asked, curious if Sano was right about the jealous thing. Ken walked toward me, and I walked back, getting stuck between him and the wall again.

"And if it is a guy, why are you always with him? I have no problem with you being the nice, kindhearted person you are, but you have me here waiting and wondering where you are and if you really are with a guy or not. I don't think that's fair for me."

His eyes were steady as he spoke. I could almost hear a bit of a hurt in his voice. Ken was serious, and seriously close to me. I think he might be taking this to heart. I know I'm new to this, but could someone like him really be interested in me? This whole time I've been trying to move forward with Sano and left him here never really considering his feelings.

"Ken, are you, perhaps, getting jealous about this?" I tried pushing my luck a bit more and asked him with an innocent look.

I guess I pushed too far. Ken threw his arm against the wall and angled my face up to him with his other hand. I couldn't tell if he was getting upset or just being him when he grew an evil grin.

"And what if I am? Who wouldn't knowing you've been at a guy's house doing who knows what all this time." he said. Suddenly I got a bit angry and pushed him back.

"I'm not a pervert like you! Nothing is happening." I walked off toward the stairs. "And I'm sorry, but I just can't stop going. I said I'd help, so you'll have to endure it for a little while longer."

I quickly got to my room and dropped to my bed. I don't know what it is with him putting me in such a tight position. He went from happy to sad to—that so quickly. The look he was giving me looked like he wanted to kiss me again. Is that how someone who's jealous acts? Was he really that upset about me being around another guy? I didn't think he'd be that much of a jealous type.

And I'd like to know exactly how much he knows about me. It's not like there is much to know. He makes it as if he knows my whole life. I want to ask, but that'll be saved for another day…

The weekend came and Ken went home Saturday morning. I was actually a little happy to have some time to myself over the weekend. But that lead to a really strange dream about Ken and Sano having a confrontation about everything. I hope something like that doesn't really happen.

Maybe it's telling me to make a choice. I didn't take Ken seriously at first, so I didn't think I had a choice to make, so maybe I should start being nicer to him and paying more attention. At least that way, I could properly say no. I just don't want to add to Sano's problems by ending our time together.

I rolled over in my bed and saw my clock. I had thirty-three minutes left before the school bell would ring for class. I jumped out of bed in a panic. When I got up, I saw a piece of paper next to my clock. It was a note from Ken.

-Misa! Why do you sleep so hard? I tried waking you up, but you didn't budge.

I had to go. Please forgive me! XOXO

-Ken

Ken must have returned this morning. After reading it, something inside my chest tightened. I don't know what it was about receiving this, but it was the first time I've ever gotten a note from a guy before. I looked at it again, but then threw it down. I didn't have time to look at a little note that couldn't mean anything. I made it into the classroom a few minutes after the bell rang. Mr. Hallens hadn't shown up yet, and people were still talking and out of seat.

"Oh great, you're here! I was afraid you weren't coming, leaving me with no one to share books with." The first person I ran into was Jennifer. She was just as dolled up as she was before, but in hot pink.

"As much as I'd love to share books with you, Jennifer, I think the teacher will be giving you one today." I tried adding as much polite sarcasm as I could.

"But sharing with you would be more fun." She looked at me with her sparkly eyes. She's already captivated half the guys in our class with those eyes, but all I saw was a lie. She isn't who she's pretending to be.

"Wouldn't you rather share with Ken anyways?" I say looking to him already here and seated. It must be because he went home that he was wearing one of his 'fresh out of the store' blue plaid shirts and matching color high top shoes. He usually comes back after going home 'dressed to impress.'

"Gee that's a nifty idea too. We'd probably work better together anyway. What do you say?" She threw her head around to him.

"Sorry, I left my book at home. I was hoping to look off your book, Misa."

"If you had enough time to leave notes, then you should have had time to get your book."

"Aw, he leaves you little love notes. That's so cute! Do you leave him notes also?" She asked me.

"Why do you care?"

"Because, love notes are cute. Maybe I should start leaving you lovey-dovey notes too, Kenny. I'm sure mine would be more interesting than hers." She smiled. Mr. Hallens finally came into the room. Meaning this conversation was over, so I didn't have to answer her lovey-dovey talk.

"Sorry, got held up with someone. What's this? Oh, Jennifer, I have a textbook for you," he was still sipping his coffee as he went to his desk and saw the book lying there, "Bring it every day to class as we use it all the time." He handed it over to her.

"I'll be sure to bring it every day as I plan to do very well in your class, Mr. Hallens," she said in her most innocent, perfect schoolgirl voice. She played the roll well. She's more cunning than Ken. She could probably con a con artist. I can't be bought in by her games though.

"Kenny, what page are we on?" I heard her ask.

"Don't know. I thought it was established that I didn't have a book," he said with much needed sarcasm.

"Oh, that's right. Well, Misa, you should share your book with him," she said, still talking to me.

"I'm too far away. You have a book now. Wouldn't it be easier for you two to share?" Ken was two seats behind and one over away from me.

"You mean you don't mind? And I wanted to see how lovey-dovey you could be in class, but I'll go ahead and show you what that's like." I had to keep telling myself to hang in there. I feel like Ken must have been getting annoyed too from the way he acts toward her.

"Shouldn't you be paying attention?" He asked her.

"Oh, right, I almost forgot about this." She ignored him and reached into her bag and pulled out an envelope. "Jenny told me to give this to you." She extended her arm.

"I don't want it," Ken said without even looking to see what it was.

"But she'll be sad if you don't take it." Jennifer said. I was confused since I didn't know who they were talking about. Who was Jenny?

"Mr. Hallens, may I be excused to the restroom?" Ken suddenly raised his hand and asked.

"Sure, just be back in five minutes." Mr. Hallens gave him the okay. He got up and hurried out.

"Well, well, looks like it's just us," Jennifer said. Her enthusiasm was fading quickly. "And I told Jenny I'd give this to him."

"Who's Jenny?" I asked as the curiosity was beginning to be too much.

"Who's Jenny? You really don't know, do you? Ha, of course you wouldn't. Jenny is Ken's real fiancé."

My eyes bulged, "His real fiancé? So, then who are you supposed to be?"

"Me? I'm her sister. Jenny goes to a private school, but I came here in her place because she didn't want to change schools. You thought I was his fiancé? Ha. Ken's a nice guy and all, but that's Jenny's guy. You really are a dumb little girl that knows nothing."

"Enough of the chit chat you two, class has started," Mr. Hallens said from behind his desk. I turned around and we both got quiet.

I can't believe she isn't the right one. And there's another one sharing a direct blood line that I have to watch out for. Are they clones? Jennifer and Jenny? Would that not be the same person? Ken never mentioned a Jenny before. Was he trying to hide her from me?

A whole new ocean of questions rolled in my mind with the new information. I looked over to Katie who was looking at me with her eyebrow raised. I can almost read the questions in her brain just from looking at her. But she'll have to wait since I don't have answers either.

The time ticked away, and class was just about done.

"Alright that's it for today. No homework tonight." Mr. Hallens told us. Just about everyone sighed in relief. Except me. I still wasn't over the new discovery.

"Hey Ken, how about you come to the house and help me catch up on what I wasn't here for," Jennifer said.

"Sorry, but you won't be able to swindle me into whatever it is you two have planned," he told her.

"Aww, but you'll be bored hanging around her all the time. She probably doesn't even know how to have fun." She tried to whisper that to him, but it was fail since I heard her clearly.

"Actually, Misa and I are going out this weekend." He suddenly told her.

"You are?"

"We are?" I looked over and asked.

"Yep!" He said bringing out his usual smile. The bell rang and he stood up. "Well, have to get going. See yah, Mimi." He walked out the classroom.

"Wait, Ken, I still need you to take this letter!" Jennifer got up and chased after Ken. And I was left there in confusion. When did Ken and I agree to go anywhere? First the notes, a clone, and now this? What a way to start the morning.

12

The first day off the weekend is typically the hardest and the longest trying to get back into the weekday routine. This was definitely one of the longest days following one of the most confusing mornings. I can't get this date thing out of my mind. Not only that, what Jennifer said has already gotten around. Someone actually said to me, "it must be hard for you right now." Do people not have anything better to do than to spread rumors and gossip?

Heading out of the school around my scheduled time in the opposite direction of my home and to Sano's house, I prepared for what he could possibly say or ask. He has to know about what happened in class. Last time he asked about Ken and if he knew I was here.

Anyone would wonder knowing my situation with him. Part of me just wonders if it could mean anything else since he asked so suddenly. I had just reached his house when I saw the kids out playing by the garage.

"Look, it's Misa!" I got the usual greeting from the little ones. They were surrounding me again. Every time I see the road before me covered in kids, I always wonder what Sano practices to have so much patience being able to deal with this all the time on his own.

"You're here again to see us?" Cindy asked.

"Yeah, I'll play with you guys, but did Sano make it home?" I asked just to make sure he's here.

"Yeah, he's been here. He's in the kitchen," Mia said.

"He has? Well, I'll be back to play with you guys after I let him know I'm here," I told them as I walked through the garage and to the door that led to the kitchen. I knocked and went in when I saw him.

"Hey, Misa, you're here," he said.

"Yeah, just got here. Oh, what happened?" The first thing I noticed was Sano's ankle wrapped up.

"It's nothing really, just a little sprain. I cut a turn too sharp, but I should be fine. I just can't do any running for the next few days.

"Just a few days? Are you sure you should rush back into it? I know you're like, the team's best, but I think you should take it easy."

"Maybe. Thanks for your concern. I'll be more careful in the future," he said.

"Do you need any help with something? You should rest your ankle, so it'll heal better."

"Thanks for worrying about me, Misa, but I'll be fine."

"But…" I started to say something, but I didn't know what else to say.

"From what I heard in class this morning, I think you should be more worried about other things."

"Huh?"

"You know, with that new girl and something about another fiancé," he said.

"So, you heard that conversation?"

"I wasn't intending to eavesdrop, but I overheard it." He wasn't at school the other day when Jennifer first came, so not only did he not know who she was, he hears what she said.

"That's another matter. I think you being able to walk and run is more important right now."

"I said I'll be okay." He chuckled over my concern.

"At least let me help make dinner or something." I suggested.

"Alright, if you want, you can-"

"Misa, are you going to play with us?" Sano was interrupted by Brian and Cindy coming in.

"Well, it seems you're needed elsewhere," he said.

"I did say I was going to play. I guess I'll keep an eye on them outside and you can focus on what you were doing."

"Sounds like a plan," he said.

Maybe it was for the better I left out of there. It feels like it's getting harder and harder to talk to him. If he heard all that 'lovey-dovey' stuff Jennifer kept talking about, he's going to get the wrong idea.

"Ow!" As soon as I walked outside, I heard Sano shout in pain and something falling.

"What happened?" I asked running right back in.

"What's wrong Sano?" The kids ran in after me. Sano was leaning over with his wrapped foot in the air. He went to pick up a pan he dropped.

"I'm fine. I…"

"No, you're not fine. It doesn't look good at all! You should go to a doctor to get that checked out," I said. He put the pan back on the stove leaning on the counter.

"I don't think I need to go to a doctor. I'm sure just icing it will be good."

"Well, do you have an ice pack?" I started looking in the freezer.

"Oh, we were playing doctor with it and lost it," Cindy told us.

"You lost it?" Sano asked.

"I'm sorry Sano."

"If that's the case, I'll go get one." I suggested. I didn't even give him time to protest before I left. I've never seen him in pain like that. He's been really out of it lately. I wonder if he has something serious on his mind. He does have a lot on his plate—his mother, the kids, his grades, track, just a lot.

As soon as I got in the store, I was able to find the ice pack easier than when I was looking for the meat.

"Misa!" I was in the checkout line when I heard someone call my name.

"Misa, Misa!" I turned and saw John approaching me. He must live in the area for him to keep finding me here.

"John, you're around again?"

"I live down the street, so I frequently come here. Sorry I wasn't at school. The virus I had was terrible. But now I'm as healthy as a man in love! Did you come here because you sensed I was out and coming around? And you wanted to meet up and talk about our love?" I don't think that virus is completely out his system with that question. "So, are you finally going to take me for a spin?" He continued.

"What makes you ask that?"

"Well, I had this feeling that you were having problems with Ken, so I managed to crawl out of bed and ask my reliable sources and was informed about another girl that's come back to take him. So, if he's gone and you're all alone, you were brought here by fate because we were meant to be together!" I can't believe it reached John like that already.

"John, I think you're a little off," I said.

"What do you mean?"

"Well, it's not what you think. But overall, we are not getting together."

"You mean you and Ken?"

"No, I meant you and me. But I need to get going. It's nice knowing you're better though," I said walking off after I checked out. "Misa, where are you going? I thought you lived in the other direction," he called.

"Going to a friend's house, and I really need to get back," I said as I kept going.

Even John, who hasn't been to school, knows. And from the way he said it, it sounds as if they think me and Ken are actually done. I wonder if Ken knows about that and how he's handling the news.

Right now, I'm holding an ice pack to bring back to Sano at his house to help him. That's how I wanted it to be. Just me and Sano. So why is a little school gossip bothering me so much?

While the ice pack was freezing, I put ice in a bag wrapped in a towel for him to use.

"How's your leg feeling?"

"It's feeling a lot better since putting the ice on it," he said.

"That's good. Just keep icing it with the other one when it's ready, and it'll get better in no time," I said with a smile, feeling like his personal nurse. I even managed to help him get dinner started.

"I feel like I've said this a lot, but thanks for doing this for me," he said.

"It's no problem, really."

"I'll admit spraining my ankle isn't the best feeling in the world. But I'll get through it."

Just take it easy and keep resting. You seem like you have a lot on your mind." I told him.

"My mind might have been elsewhere when this happened." He admitted.

"If you have something you want to talk about, you can talk to me if you want." This could be a chance to start really getting to know him if he's willing to talk to me.

He sat quietly and didn't say anything like he was thinking. Maybe I asked too much.

"Sano," Cindy came running in toward him, "it looks like it's going to rain so we came inside." I went to the window and saw the partly cloudy sky was covered in dark grey clouds.

"Maybe I should go before it gets bad outside."

"You sure you want to chance getting caught in the rain?" Sano asked.

"I'll be all right. It's just rain." I still wanted to know what was bothering him, but I don't think he wanted to talk about it.

"I'll still come by tomorrow if it's not a problem. To see how you're doing," I said on a whim.

"Sure, that'd be nice, Misa." He replied quicker this time. He didn't seem like he wanted to tell me what was wrong, but he still doesn't mind me coming around. I guess that's a start.

I quickly tried getting home, but my quick wasn't quick enough when halfway, a loud rumble of thunder came with pouring rain. I didn't have an umbrella, so I had to run the rest of the way home. I could probably take Sano's place on the team with all the sprinting I've been doing.

"Well, I guess it started raining." When I made it home, I was greeted with Ken's sarcasm. I was completely soaked.

"Really? Thanks, Ken, I didn't notice one bit."

"I'm joking."

"Yeah ha-ha, you should be a comedian," I wasn't completely in the mood to joke around with him as I took off my completely soaked shoes. Ken had disappeared suddenly up the stairs while I was still trying to avoid creating a pool in the house.

"Here." He came back down and handed me a towel.

"Th-thanks." I took it and started wiping off. I feel like a similar scene happened before.

"So, are you coming back from that *guy* friend's house of yours?" I could hear emphasis on guy.

"I told you, it's not like what you're thinking."

"And how do I know it's not like that?"

"Because I told you, I'm not a pervert like you. Why can't you trust that?"

"It's not that I don't trust you, it's just that it's beast out there Misa! And it's mating season! They can attack at any time."

"I think you're just the lonely wolf."

"I wouldn't have to be so lonely if you spent some time with me." He said like it was my fault.

"I wasn't the one that told you to come here. Don't blame me-"

"Earlier, when I said we'd be going out this weekend, I was serious. I want to go out somewhere with you," he told me.

"Huh?" It took me by surprise that he'd mention that again so suddenly.

"It doesn't have to be anywhere fancy. It can be just a trip to the park or something. I just want us to try getting closer before you completely reject me. So, how about it? After this rain, it's supposed to be a nice weekend, and you don't have anything to do either right?"

I hesitated before answering. "No, I don't."

"Well then, it's settled! We can go Saturday, probably around three! That'll give you enough time to sleep in and get ready. Find something nice to wear. I can't wait. Just you and me, us together, out there in the world." Ken, with his energy boost, went merrily up to his room.

"Hey! I never exactly said yes!" I shouted to him.

Of course, he didn't respond to me. I know I said I should pay a little more attention to him, but to schedule a date with him. I've grown anxious. Going out somewhere with Ken? This should be interesting.

13

I don't think any amount of time could prepare me for this. The week flew by and in just a couple hours, I'll be out in the world alone with Ken. Not only that, after seeing Sano again, we agreed that I should wait until he starts practice again to come by so often. Just as I thought he wanted me around; he gets rid of me.

He's really been out of it these days. Maybe he wasn't interested after all. Either way, I won't be seeing him after school for a while, and I have to prepare to go out with Ken. I kept asking him where we would be going, but he only said it was a secret.

I woke to a quarter to one on this fated day after tossing and turning half of the night. He said to look nice and be ready at three, so I'll need more time to get ready. He's rich, so we could end up going anywhere for all I know. Not to mention, this would be my first date. How am I supposed to act?

Do I act the girly type or just throw on jeans on and rough it? What if we went somewhere fancy? I'd just embarrass myself and Ken dressing like that. But this is Ken we're talking about. Why should I have to get all dolled up for him? I guess with his history, it's better to try and look somewhat presentable.

"Misa, you ready?" I heard Ken's voice coming from downstairs as I was trying to finish straightening my hair. I grabbed my small purse and headed downstairs.

"Are you still not going to tell me where we're going?" I asked.

"I told you it's a—whoa" He stopped as he saw me.

"W-what?"

"Nothing, you look nice," he said looking at me. I had on my favorite black skirt with my navy-blue shirt that split on the sleeves.

"Well, you said look nice. And with your background, you could be taking me anywhere."

"Right, when I said that I just meant look nice since it'll be a memory of our first date! But that'll do just fine as well." he said all smiles.

I'll have to remind myself to kill him later for making me go through all this trouble. He didn't look too bad himself though. He had on a grey button up with a black design on the front with a white shirt underneath along with some dark jeans and grey shoes.

"Alright, off we go," Ken said as we headed out toward a black matte car that I didn't know was out here. I didn't think about exactly how we were going to get to where we were going. He opened my door to let me in. After closing it, he went around to the driver's side to get in.

"So, is this your car? Since when can you drive?" I asked a bit nervously as he started up the engine, getting ready to pull off.

"I got this car last year when I got my license after turning sixteen. My father just limits how much I can use it. You haven't gotten your license?"

"No. My parents haven't had the chance to teach me."

"I could teach you. It's not so hard once you start doing it."

"You haven't had your license that long. You can't go out teaching people how to drive."

"I taught my brother how to drive back when we were still like, thirteen," he said like it was completely normal to be driving around at the age of like twelve.

"You have a brother?"

"You really don't know about me, do you?"

"Okay then, since you think you know so much about me, tell me something about myself." I challenged him.

"Well, I know your full name is Misa Noir Macky," he said.

"Anybody can know that."

And when you were younger, people use to call you 'MNM' like the candy because of your initials." I gasped. That one took me by surprise. I stopped telling people my middle name to get rid of that name a long time ago. Leave it to my family to pick something like that.

He stopped and thought for a moment. "Oh, when you were in middle school, you fell down three flights of stairs and was in the hospital for a week." He continued.

Maybe I shouldn't have asked what he knew. How in the world does he know that? My mother doesn't even know it was three flights I fell down; I told her it was two! I couldn't help but feel a bit creeped out as he kept going, mentioning my klutzy ways and the incident at school.

"Whoa, Ken, don't you think it's just a tad bit strange that you know all this without ever meeting me before?"

"Oh, but we have met," he said.

"What do you mean we have?"

"Ah, we're here!" He said, not paying attention to me.

I looked and saw where we were. "The outdoor mall?" I said, "That's where we're going?"

"Yeah, come on. Let's shop around, my treat!" He said getting out of the car.

He came around and opened my door before I got the chance to. He may have been taught proper manners, but I'm still stuck on everything he just told me. Typically, a person would know your favorite color or what foods you like. Not the things that happened to me in my life.

"Let's go look around in this store first!" He said pointing to a clothing store. He's awful happy about being here. There were a lot of people going in and out of stores with bags shopping around and enjoying their Saturday. And here I am confused and feel unsettled about this.

"Oh, this shirt looks like it would be great on you. And these shoes with it would be even better." Ken was going around looking at designer clothes. He held up a white and black shoulder cut-out shirt with some nice black small heels with a rhinestone belt. His sense of fashion is great, which only made my suspicion meter go even higher. "Oh, I like this hoodie. We should get matching hoodies like these. And maybe get this also."

"Whoa, wait, Ken, you can't just buy the whole store. Why not look around first and then decide later what you want." I suggest before he ends up buying everything including the mannequins.

"Is that how you do things?"

"Um, yeah, it's how us regular people with allowances do things."

"I have one of those too. I can't go over two thousand a week," he said as if that were a completely normal thing. That's like, two years' worth of my allowances!

"Well, Ken, people who maybe get fifty dollars a week usually only buy what they really want. Not just everything they like."

"Alright, so what do you normally do when you're out at the mall with your friends?" He asked.

"Um, well, we normally just hang out, and try on clothes. Maybe buy one or two things. Oh, and we like taking pictures in the photo booth."

"Oh, photos sound fun. Let's take pictures of this momentous occasion." Ken got really excited about taking pictures together. I probably shouldn't have mentioned that part. "The picture booth is over there." Ken dragged me to the booth and pulled me in. "I've never used one of these before, how do you do it?" He studied the machine.

"Do we really have to do this?" I asked not as interested as he was.

"You don't want to have pictures of me to look at always?"

"I believe I can survive without that."

"So, mean. Just go along with it. It won't kill you to be this close for a minute," he said with his pity me face. I couldn't help but give in after that.

"Okay fine, I'll do it."

"Yay! This button, right? On three!" He said. Our faces showed up on the screen before it took.

"Come on, Misa, smile!"

"I'm not in the mood."

"Hmm, maybe if I tickle you that'll help." Ken suddenly started attacking my sides.

"No, Ken, stop!" I couldn't control my laughter. I was really ticklish on my sides. The machine took multiple shots of us. After we were done, we each got a copy to keep.

"That was fun! And the pictures came out great. You're all smiles. I like your cute upset face, but this one is better." Ken was looking over the pictures. Being tickled against my will wasn't necessarily fun for me. But I suppose I didn't hate it.

"Come on, let's go look around some more," he said looking to find another store. I've never seen Ken like this before. He's like a kid in the candy store for the first time.

"Let's go here." He pointed to a place that didn't help that cause.

"The toy town?"

"Yeah, it looks interesting. Let's go in." He's going around as if he's never been outside before.

"Hey, Misa, do you like this?" He held up a little animal plushy.

"Uh, yeah sure, it's a cute little thing."

"Okay, I'll get it."

"Wait what?"

"You said you liked it, so I was going to get it."

"I thought we just had this conversation. You don't have to get everything you see."

"Oh, right, I thought that only applied for clothes."

"Don't you know how to go out and *not* buy the whole place?"

I don't go out often, and I haven't been here in years. This was the first outlet mall I've ever been to. It's changed a bit since I first came years ago, and I've always enjoyed this kind of mall since it doesn't have you cooped up in doors the whole time." He told me.

Hearing Ken say that made me think. "Well, since you haven't been here in a long time, I guess I can show you around. I'll show you the way of us average Joes and how we do things."

"Really? That'd be great!" Ken perked up again. I don't know why I offered to do this. He sounds as if he's normally trapped inside somewhere. If he doesn't get to go out much, I guess this is the least I could do for now.

We continued going in stores and stopped by the booths that were set up selling small items. I hadn't been here in a while either, so it was kind of fun to go in old stores again. There were actually many things I wanted. But I couldn't tell Ken that.

Ken and I split up shortly when I went to the bathroom. I passed a mirror heading for a stall and noticed something. I look like I had been enjoying myself. I had been trying so hard not to, I hadn't noticed. I have to admit, seeing Ken like that was nice. Even though he tried to buy the whole place, he still seemed like your average regular guy here, and not so much one of the richest kids in probably the whole country. I finished up in the bathroom and walked out and saw Ken standing against the wall by the jewelry store.

"This place changed more than I thought. Let's get something to eat now. I've gotten kind of hungry," Ken said when I went over.

"Sure." We went over to the food court and went to a burger place and ordered there. We found seats in the middle of the seating area. I couldn't help noticing a few eyes were watching us. I wonder if they thought he was my boyfriend. What would I say if someone were to ask me that?

"So, Misa, was being with me that bad?" He asked after we got situated.

"No, it wasn't actually. Even though you were acting like a kid in the candy store for the first time, you weren't your usual perverted self."

"Oh, so you like that side of me more?"

"No, that's not what I meant."

"What did you mean?" He asked.

"I just meant, I actually got to know a little more about you."

"Ah, I see. I believe that to be a good thing," he said throwing some fries in his mouth.

"Some of the stores changed since I was last here too, so it was nice seeing the new shops. I think me and Katie use to like coming to this mall when we were younger. But it was just a bit too far for us to go to all of the time, so we just stuck with the regular mall." I told him.

"I think it was after an incident here Katie and I agreed coming here wasn't that great and went back to hanging out at other places." I tried to remember, but the details were a bit fuzzy.

Ken looked down at his food. It made me stop sipping my drink watching him. It looked like he took a deep breath and looked back to me.

"What?" I asked unsure of this behavior change.

"You said not to get everything I saw, but I really liked this, so I got it for you when you went to the bathroom." He wiped his hands and reached into his pocket and pulled out a little box that he put on the table. My blood ran a little cold as the first thing that came to mind was a ring in that box. He couldn't possibly think after one date it was time for this, could he? Like him or not, I'm pretty sure it's not even legal to marry at this age...

"Don't worry, this isn't a proposal." He said reading my mind.

"What is it then?" I asked with a bit of relief.

"Just open it." Slowly, I opened the little box up. Coming to my senses, I realized it couldn't have been a ring. The box was white and bigger than a regular ring box. I took the lid off and saw a small silver panda charm. It was so cute. Did he know my favorite animal was a panda?

"A charm?"

"It's for your charm bracelet." He told me. My eyes went wide in shock. Was he talking about my friendship bracelet I got years ago?

"Ok, h-how do you know about that?" I couldn't take any more of his knowledge about things he shouldn't know.

"I thought coming here would jog your memory, but I see you don't remember still."

"Remember what?"

"It's not the same store, but that's where you and your friend got your best friend charm bracelets." He pointed back over to the jewelry store he was standing next to when I found him.

"How do you..." my words trailed off. I was officially creeped out.

"The last time I was here, or rather the first time, I was wandering around and went passing by that store and saw this girl with her friend. They were looking at friendship bracelets. I overheard one saying they didn't have the money to get it, and she really wanted to get it for the other girl. It was then I walked up and said I'd help pay, but she was really stubborn and didn't want to do it." He looked over to the store, then back to me. His story sounds familiar.

"But then she said it was okay since she really wanted to get the bracelets for her friend. I gave her the difference of what she needed. The girl was happy she was able to finally get it for her friend and the friend said she'd cherish it always. I said you'd better because I don't help the poor often. Which is something I regret saying by the way, but the girl got upset and tried running off and fell." He took a sip of his drink. I feel like he's talking about me and Katie, but I can't get the complete image in my head.

"This happened before you had your accident, so you may or may not remember it."

"I think I remember this. A boy was making fun of me, and I got embarrassed because what he said was true. That boy, was you? How did you remember it was me?"

"Who could forget a face like that? Plus, that friend of yours. She was the first stranger who dared to touch me, let alone slap me across the face and leaving me red for almost two days. And when I saw you two together again, I was sure it was you. I noticed a little while ago you still had your bracelet letting me know you really cherish the people around you, which is a quality I really admire." he said. I guess that explains why he said we've met before.

"Okay, that explains that part, but that still doesn't explain how you know so much about me. Even if my mom told you stuff about me, she can't tell you what she doesn't know." Ken got quiet for a minute, which made me nervous.

"Well, after I was slapped by your friend, the person I was with saw and wanted to find out who she was and wanted information on her to get in touch with her parents. But instead of finding information on her, they found you."

"So, you're telling me you've been like, spying on my life or something?" I asked.

"It only lasted a short period of time. It wasn't to intrude on your life. But for some reason, I was curious about who you were. Not to mention I wanted to apologize for what I said." He added.

I don't know if I should feel touched that someone found interest in me or feel my privacy was seriously violated.

"But, just because I know some of you, doesn't mean I know all about you. So instead of pushing me away, why not actually give me a chance? Try going out with me instead of sneaking off with some other guy?"

"I don't know, Ken. I'll admit, today wasn't so bad, but you're kind of persistent. And normal people don't find being watched like that a compliment."

"I told you I meant no harm by it."

"Yeah, but how do I know you won't do it again and aren't doing it now and got guys in the bushes?"

"I don't. All the files have been thrown out. No one is looking for either of you anymore."

"Ken! You picked quite a place to go, but I finally found you!" Out of nowhere, some girl who looked almost like Jennifer appeared. And she was not happy.

"Jenny?" He said, confused with her presence. Is this the Jenny they were mentioning before?

"I heard," She started, "Jennifer told me about this little outing, and going out with that girl. I searched everywhere looking for you! And here you are with some weirdo off the street!" She said looking at me. "I thought you were supposed to be with some other girl that was supposed to be better than me."

"That's her. This is Misa," Ken said.

"Misa? This is her!? You're trying to leave me for…" she paused for a second as she looked me up and down, "Her!? How could you!?"

I looked at Ken, then I looked back at her. I was speechless. I mean, is she for real?

14

"Ken, so you're telling me this is the other so-called fiancé?"

"Yes."

"But look at her. She's... not like us." Jenny's talking as if I'm an alien.

"Jenny, you're making a very bad first impression," Ken said.

"Bad impression? I'm not here to impress someone who's brainwashed you!"

She thinks I brainwashed him?!

"Was there a reason you were looking for me?" He asked.

"Yes, I wanted to see for myself the person who's been trying to take you away from me. But all I get is someone who isn't even prettier than me!" She exclaimed.

I don't think I can take much more of this. "Um excuse me, but we were in the middle of a conversation. So could you-"

"Ew!" She suddenly shouted in disgust, "Your voice is as terrible as you look! How did she ever get picked!?"

"Jenny! I think you've said enough. Now you need to apologize to Misa right now," Ken stepped up and spoke.

"W-why should I? She's the one at fault for showing her face!" She said even though she was the one who came to us!

"This is part of the reason why I don't want to be with you. Your jealousy goes beyond normal and gets out of control. Not only are you insulting Misa, but you're also embarrassing yourself for acting like this. Now apologize to her." Ken demanded.

"Fine! *Sorry* for saying anything that could have been offensive to you." She couldn't have been more *not* sorry.

"Good, now leave."

"But I said sorry."

"And I never invited you here anyway. So could you so kindly leave us alone?" Everyone around us was staring. This is like school with the public. They'll have something to talk about at dinner later today.

"I won't leave until you agree to leave her and be with me!"

"Well, I guess you'll be standing there for a while. Come on, Misa." Ken grabbed my hand leading us away from there. That would be for the best, so I don't lose my cool. I didn't even get a good look at her. But she did look like a brown-haired version of Jennifer. Maybe they really are clones. But this one's attitude is a lot worse.

"Misa, I'm sorry about her behavior back there," Ken started once we were far away enough, "I didn't think she'd get that upset. She had no right to say anything to you. After she cools down, I'll have her give you a proper apology."

"As long as I don't have to see here again, I'll be fine," I told him.

"Are you upset?"

"Yeah, I'm upset! I don't think I've ever been this insulted before in my life." My blood was still pumping. I've never felt anger toward someone so fast before.

"I know what she said was bad. Whenever she gets upset, she says whatever she feels and is a very hard person to compromise with."

"So, you're taking up for her?"

"No, it's not that. I've known her for a while now, so I'm kind of used to her behavior," he said.

"How long have you known her?" I asked curiously.

"I first met her when I was in the fifth grade. We didn't talk much until a year or so later. Then about two years ago, my father thought she'd be a good person to be with and would be good enough to be a wife for me in the future. I told my father that it was too soon for me to have something like a wife already, and that I didn't even see her like that, but once she heard about this, she started doing everything she could to get me to like her the way she liked me."

"Well, it seems she likes you a lot since she went through the trouble of finding you. She even listened to you and apologized even though she really didn't want to. Guess you got something between each other."

"Misa, don't think that I like her more than anything other than maybe a friend." He said, trying to reassure me.

"Maybe a friend? You've known her for so long, why choose now to want to unfriend her?" I wanted to know. But Ken hesitated before saying anything.

"You never answered my question back there."

"What question?"

"About giving me a chance."

"Oh yeah, that." Meeting the clone made me forget all about that. "I don't know. That's another issue. You didn't pick the greatest time to ask. I'll think about it, maybe." I added.

"You will?"

"I said maybe. All this stuff that's happened today is a lot to take in at once. It needs some further processing," I told him. And there's also Sano to think about too.

"I know you must feel overwhelmed right now, but you shouldn't let Jenny interfere with what you think. Aside from the past stuff, it hasn't been too bad, right?" I didn't really answer that last question since I was already thinking how it hadn't been extremely bad or anything.

"So, want to go somewhere else?" He tried changing the subject.

"Um, gee that sounds fun and all, but all that has happened has really done a toll on me. I'd like to just go back home."

"Alright then. I can understand that."

"I do have one more question." I wanted to confirm something.

"What's that?"

"Are those two twins?" One was enough and two of them were definitely too many.

"No, Jenny is a year younger."

"And they have the same name?"

"Well, legally, yes, but Jenny just goes by Jenny." I wanted to ask why their parents decided to name them the same, but that really didn't matter at that moment. Those two look enough a like to be twins, clones even. I just wanted nothing to do with either of them.

We got back to the car and drove home in an awkward silence. When we arrived home, I suddenly felt exhausted.

"Misa, I want to apologize again for Jenny's behavior earlier. Because of her, our day was cut short," he said sounding at fault. And to think I thought Jennifer was a lot to handle. She has nothing on this one. How could anyone live with someone like that?

"It's fine. I understand. She's a woman in love and reacted when something was wrong."

"But Misa…" Ken was about to say something when his phone rang. "Oh great. Hello?" He wasn't too pleased with whoever it was he was speaking too.

"Ken! How dare you!?" I heard Jennifer clear as day through his phone. "Jenny just called me crying!"

"Why did you tell her I was out today?" Ken asked.

"She told me to tell her everything that happens at school and that was part of it!"

"It was her own fault for showing up where she wasn't invited."

"You didn't have to make her cry because of that!"

"Look, Jenny was the one insulting Misa. All I wanted her to do was apologize and go back home." Ken seemed like he was getting bothered.

"I don't see why you're out with her anyway! You've known Jenny and I way longer than her! And it's not like she's giving you the time of day like Jenny has been trying too!!"

Jennifer was very upset. If she got any louder the neighbors might call to complain. Ken looked over to me and I looked away. I took my things and headed upstairs. This is something I shouldn't hear. Or rather something I don't want to hear. I got to my room and closed my door.

Today was just full of surprises. I saw Ken acting like a kid going around the stores today. He got angry and upset for me. And also finding out that he knows just a little too much about me and my past. Then that Jenny came. Ken must have incredible patience for her kind. I wasn't sure if I wanted to slap her or award her the best *overdramatic queen* there is. I couldn't handle her on a regular basis.

I can't even imagine Ken and Jenny together. That kind of combination seems like it would be all over the place. I wonder if I should tell Katie about this. I was thinking of texting her when I realized my phone wasn't with me. I must have left it in Ken's car. I guess I have to go back down to get it.

"Hey, Ken, can I go back to your…" I was coming down the stairs and saw he was still on the phone.

"I don't care, whether you know how it happened or not, it's what I chose okay? That's all I have to say on the matter. I'm hanging up now," Ken said, ending the conversation. I feel like I missed something.

"Oh, Misa, were you standing there the whole time?" He hadn't even noticed I left.

"Um no, I went upstairs but came back because I left my phone in your car."

"Oh. Alright, I can go get it for you. Wait here."

"Was there something you didn't want me to hear?" I asked.

"Um, no. Don't worry about that. It was just Jennifer upset about what happened. I'll be right back." Ken walked out the door. This is also a new side of Ken I haven't seen. I've never seen him look so uneasy before.

After Ken got my phone from his car, he seemed strange, and we didn't talk much afterwards. It makes me wonder what they were talking about. I didn't tell Katie in fear she'd appear at that moment and do away with Jenny, so I just ended up turning in early. I was asleep for almost thirteen hours. I hadn't slept that long since summer. All of yesterday just felt like a blur. My little brain can only handle so much.

I got up and headed for the bathroom when I stopped and smelled something delicious coming from downstairs. Somebody was up cooking. I went down to see. It couldn't be my mom. She wouldn't come home this early. It couldn't be my dad. Even if he were here, he cooks like me, so I'd smell the house burning down and not this delicious aroma. That could only leave one person then.

"Oh, Misa, you're up. Happy Sunday! Breakfast will be ready in just a minute," Ken said as I walked in the kitchen and watched him flipping over a pancake.

"Um, Ken, you feeling okay?" I asked wondering about this change in mood from yesterday.

"I'm feeling just peachy. I figured since you don't often get to have breakfast, I'd take the liberty of making a nice Sunday morning meal. Why not start the day off right? I'm sure you're famished after thirteen hours of sleep. I'd say that's a new record for you." I didn't want to tell him my record was close to twenty hours when I pulled two all-nighters in a row with Katie binge watching every show we could until we couldn't take it anymore.

"Okay, well that kind of answers something, but it wasn't what I was really talking about."

"If you're talking about yesterday, then please don't let it get to you. Jenny and Jennifer are two girls that can be a challenge and hard to get rid of once they come around." Sounds like a challenge that I accept. I'll get rid of them one way or another. "It may be easier for me since I have known them for almost seven years." He said. He might be used to them, but that's still seven years too many.

Ken was putting the finishing touches on the sausage, eggs, bacon, and pancakes he made.

"Alright looks like everything is done. Let's eat!" He made us both plates and sat them on the table. "Come on, Misa, dig in! It's delicious, of course, since I made it." That cocky attitude only means that he must be back to normal. I sat down across from him. Somehow it feels kind of weird like this. Just the two of us eating breakfast. Kind of feels like another date.

"Misa, you're not hungry?" He saw I was just picking at my food.

"Um, no it's not that. I was just thinking."

"What about?"

"Um, just that this is the first time we've eaten together like this at home before. It just feels different."

"Are we having improper thoughts?" Ken said with a half-smile.

"No! That's not what I meant," I blurted.

"It's okay. I was thinking the same thing."

"You were?"

"Yeah, I was also thinking we should do it more often," he said, "I've been here this long, and we've never actually eaten together like this. It's not so bad to do every now and then."

"Well, if there's food to eat, then I guess it could happen again."

"Really? That's great." He smiled wide and started eating again. He gets so happy over things I don't even fully agree to. Just yesterday, he told me things that make me wonder about him and if he's really somebody I should trust. But there's still something about him that makes me not want to get rid of him just yet.

There wasn't much chat after that. After we finished breakfast, I got my study material ready because Katie was coming over to study for a test we were having tomorrow. If he didn't have all his conditions, I might have asked Ken. I always get confused when Katie tries to help me study, but I was trying to give her the benefit of the doubt since it was too soon for me to go through whatever it was he might've wanted. By the time Katie came over, Ken was long gone in his room, doing whatever Kens do in their rooms.

"You might be caught up in love, but we can't have you forgetting about your education." Katie said when she got in.

"Of course not. Why would I want to forget about something as important as this?" Even though it was the last thing on my mind.

"Right, we can't have you continuously flunking your tests. You're already at risk of summer school. I can't have you taking classes over again. If you're held back, then you won't be able to graduate with us. Then you'll still be in school while we're in college getting our degrees that could take us far, and by the time you get out of school, we'll be long gone and successful while you'll be here by yourself doing who knows what to survive—"

"Katie! Come back. I understand the importance of studying, let's just actually start." We went into the kitchen with my books and got started on math.

"So, what is it that you don't know?" she asked bluntly.

"I'll have you know, I know everything," I said trying to make that sound as believable as I could.

"If I remember correctly, when we arranged this, you said you weren't prepared. So obviously it's something you don't know."

"That was because, um, I didn't have a pencil. You can't take a test without one, right?"

"Here, I've got plenty of pencils. Since you're so prepared, why not solve some problems?" Katie suggested.

"S-sure. These problems are a piece of cake." I looked at the problems she pointed out for me to solve. Our teacher always gives us a billion practice problems for each chapter. And I hardly understood what to do at all. "I got this, it's so easy," I said, attempting to write something. Five minutes passed. "Almost done, just give me a second." I was confused. I couldn't figure out what method to use. I just put what I thought I saw the teacher explaining before. "Here, finished. It only took like a minute to do," I said showing her.

"Misa, you realize it took you like ten minutes to do three problems. And this isn't the right answer either."

"What? How so? That's what you're supposed to do to solve, isn't it?"

"Not for these problems. We're adding rational expressions. All you did was foil. The only thing you needed to do was convert the fraction to make each denominator common. You can't solve anything without those numbers identical."

"Ah, I see. That's what happened. I didn't get that."

"What do you mean you didn't get that? What's not to get?"

"The fact that-"

"The fact that Misa's nice and simple brain can't handle your terminology." I turned and saw Ken leaning on the wall behind me.

"I couldn't help but overhear your struggle with simple problems again." He looked at my book.

"Hello, Ken. I feel sorry for you to need to put up with this," Katie said.

"Hey, it's not my fault this stuff is hard to understand."

"Come on, my little sister was using this book to study out of."

"Yeah, and again, private school. Like fancy. Isn't she studying to get into Harvard?" I needed to remind her.

"I think maybe if you reword it," Ken started. He pointed to my book, "Like this bottom number here. You need to factor it to make it like this other number to make like terms or the same number. And there's a certain way to do that," Ken explained it to me a lot differently than how Katie did. I was able understand it better the way he said it.

"Do you understand now?" He asked.

"Um, yeah, I do actually. It's not so bad once you look at it this way," I said.

"Humph! That's exactly what I said to do. You just like his help over mine." Katie said.

"Help? Speaking of help, you know what comes of help, don't you, Mimi?" He was referring to the payment he wants for his services.

"Hey, I didn't ask you to help!" I said.

"I'll be in the other room watching TV and waiting," he walked out, ignoring what I said.

"You two seem closer," Katie said.

"It's not what you think. Let's just keep going." Of course, from Katie's point of view, everything between us seems fine when she doesn't know the half of what's really happening.

"I still don't agree with tests first thing off the weekend, but you think you'll be prepared for tomorrow?" Katie asked gathering her things.

"I guess I'm as ready as I can be right now."

"Good, oh shoot! It's already almost nine and I told my mom I'd be home at eight. I got to go, Misa. I'm sure you should be fine this time. Maybe Ken can help you more if need be. I'll see you tomorrow." Katie made sure Ken was able to hear that as she left. I haven't told her yet; this was the guy she slapped when we were younger and kind of the reason why we're here today.

I went back and looked at my work. I guess I should start taking things more seriously. I can't keep slacking off on my schoolwork. But my mind hasn't been right since all of this started. I shouldn't let that get in my way and should stay focused on what's important.

"You know, Katie seems like a good friend. You should keep her around." Ken said out of the blue.

"I didn't plan to lose her. We've been friends for ten years. What makes you think we wouldn't last another ten years or more?"

"I'm just saying. I don't think I've ever had a friend that's lasted that long."

"Well, she's the only one. My other friends to just come and go," I said packing my things away. Ken didn't say anything to that.

"Well would you look at the time. It's getting late. I should get ready for bed." I was trying to avoid being alone with him right now.

"What are you talking about? The night is still young. And you slept so long last night, I'd be up for days if it were me. I just think you're trying to get out of payment," Ken said.

"I never actually asked for your help anyway."

"But you would have if I didn't step in when I did. Let's just say I predicted the future."

"You think you know everything, don't you? Just what math class are you taking anyway?" I asked.

"AP calculus," he answered like it was no big deal.

"Alright then. Since you think you're so smart, answer me, what makes you predict my asking for your help? For all you know, Katie could have explained it again, and I could've understood it meaning you wouldn't have needed to step in. Your future prediction could be wrong," I said.

"Misa, we both know you're kidding yourself. Let's just face the facts, and the reality here. The fact is that you knew I'd ask for this. And the reality is that you knew you were going to need to own up to it. Just admit to it," Ken said, making little of me. I did know that he'd want something for assisting me so I couldn't really argue anything. "Alright fine, fine. What perverted thing do you want?"

"For you to agree to go out with me," he said.

"What? No way! You helped me with a couple problems. You can't win a girl's heart doing math homework!"

"Alright, it couldn't hurt to ask. So how about you have a meal with me every day?"

"Every day? A meal?"

"Yes. Could be breakfast, lunch, or dinner after you get home…" He paused for a second, "From your friend's house." I gasped slightly. I nearly forgot about Sano.

"I know you won't do anything wrong, and I trust that. And I only accept this because you said you're helping them with a bad situation that's upon them. But if you break this deal, I'll have no choice but to think other illogical, or possibly true scenarios, and who knows what that'll have me do." Ken said with danger in his smile. I felt a little threatened by it. "So, do we have deal?"

I had to think for a second. "Fine, but I have a counter deal. Since this is an everyday thing and not just a one-time deal, you have to stop with all the conditions whenever I want help with something, okay?" I asked, not sure if he'd agreed, but it's worth a shot. He looked as if he wasn't expecting that. He thought about it.

"Well, you drive a hard bargain, but all right. I'll stop," he said.

"Great. Now that that's settled, I'll be going. All that studying made me tired." I took my things and left. I didn't think he'd agree to that.

Although I'm glad he's stopping. If all he wants is food, then that should be fine. Breakfast wasn't that bad, so it shouldn't be a problem. I told Sano I'm not going to his house again until he was better anyway. It's been almost a week since he was hurt. I wonder if he'll go back to track. I'll be cutting the time short if I go back over there. I'm pretty sure Sano would get the reason, but he would start to think I would rather spend my time with Ken. I've made a commitment to both of them. Whose would I rather stick with?

The night came and went just as quickly. I woke up on time and managed to make it to school early.

"Whoa, Misa, you're here early. All that studying must have gotten you pumped up for next period, right?" Katie asked me.

"Um, yeah sure, let's go with that." I only actually woke up on time because Ken woke me up with talk of needing a heart healthy breakfast. I was looking around and noticed he wasn't in class yet. I took a side glance and noticed Sano wasn't here either. I know Ken is somewhere in the school, but what about him?

"Oh, look, Misa is here."

Oh no, Jennifer is here…

"Did you have a good weekend? I heard you met my sister."

"Yeah, I did."

"She's a sweet girl, isn't she?" She asked like it wasn't the biggest lie of the century.

"She's definitely your sister, I'll give you that."

"Oh? What do you mean by that? Do you think she's fun to be around? She's more entertaining than you I can tell you that."

"Can I punch this girl, Misa?" Katie whispered to me.

"No, not yet," I told her.

"Jennifer, quit messing around with Misa," Ken showed up behind me.

"I'm only asking her what she thought of Jenny. Oh, and she wants me to give you this." Jennifer pulled an envelope from her bag.

"I don't want it," he said.

"Aw come on, she spends a lot of time writing these."

"That's not really my problem," he said, taking his seat. I don't understand why she kept sending notes like that. It's not like he's in jail or something.

"Misa!" I got a cold shiver in my spine at the sound of my name being called by John. "Misa! Is that how it is now!?" He ran over to me.

"What are you talking about John?"

"I had to wait until after I caught up with all my missed work to ask. But you left Ken for Sano and not me? How could you do that to me!?" He exclaimed.

"What!? W-what are you talking about?" I was shocked. He figured it out. And not only that, everyone also heard him!

15

"Um John, what makes you say that?" John hasn't been here. How could he have possibly figured it out?

"The other day when you were leaving the store, you said you were going to a friend's house. My guy radar started going off, so I followed you to see whose house you were going to, and I saw it was Sano's house. Then it came to me. You said you weren't alone so that must mean you two are together since you're going to his house. It was hard enough letting you go to Ken and now him?"

"Uh, John, I think, once again, you are mistaking the situation." I was blanking out. Jennifer was right next to him. The shocking expression she was showing was exactly how I was feeling.

"But I saw you! And you were probably at his house the first time I saw you at the store buying meat, weren't you? I didn't want to think it was true, but that means you guys are to—."

"Hey, John, why don't I help you to your next class?" Katie said, stopping the madness spilling from his mouth.

"But, Katie, I'm not done talking to Misa!" John said as Katie was dragging him out of the room.

"Oh, I think you've said enough."

"Well, well, well. I guess you're not as dumb as I thought you were. Not only are you playing with Ken, but you're actually playing him for some other guy. I knew you were no good," Jennifer said like she was disgusted.

"Jennifer, I think that's enough," Ken said.

"What do you mean that's enough? Don't you see that she's toying with you? Are you actually fine with that?" Jennifer stared at Ken. Ken didn't say anything. The bell rang and the rest of the class was coming in.

"You all don't look too excited to be here. It's the beginning of the week, it's too soon for the faces," Mr. Hallens came in and we all took our seats and were quiet.

I didn't utter a single word. I didn't dare try looking back at Ken. I did my best to ignore the angry pencil tapping coming from behind me. The one thing I did notice was Sano not showing up, and he managed to miss the beginning of a new war. Neither Jennifer nor Ken said anything else to me during school. I couldn't exactly look him in the eye afterwards anyway. Jennifer came close several times to saying something but decided not to after a long angry stare.

Sano never showed up to school. That was for the better since he managed to miss the action, but now that leaves me wondering why he missed school again. I probably shouldn't go checking on him this time. I've already caused him enough trouble by getting him dragged into this mess. It would be better if I texted him to see if he's all right instead, so he doesn't expect me again. I hope he can manage things since he's injured. It only took a matter of minutes before he replied:

-I went to the doctor's today, which is why I wasn't there. Everything is fine so you don't have to worry about stopping by. I'm home and resting.

He always seems so calm about everything and hardly ever shows too many feelings. I can never tell what he's thinking. Even when I was messing up so much at his house, he still didn't say anything.

"Misa!" I heard Katie coming up behind me.

"What's up?"

"So now the word is 'Misa's messing with three guys. Hot Ken deserves better'," she said. I couldn't help but look uneasy. "Don't let it get to you. You know it's not true. But tomorrow, I'm sure it's going to be worse. It's going to get twisted even more than it is now. You have to get this fixed somehow," she said.

"It's fine. I mean Ken doesn't seem too upset by it. But I am worried about Sano. He's the one people are going to look at. No one expected him to be a part of this."

"Sano's a strong guy, he can handle himself. What you need to do is make sure Ken's all right. How sure are you that he's not bothered by it?"

"Well, he already kind of knew."

"He already knew what you were doing?" She asked.

"Let's just say I'm not as sneaky as I thought. He figured it out almost instantly. I told him I wasn't doing anything wrong, just helping him out. So, he said he'd be fine with it. So long as it stays that way."

"And yet you still give him are hard time." She shook her head.

"What do you mean?"

"He even trusts you around other guys, and you still don't give him a chance. I don't mean to sound mean, but other than crazy John, this is the first time I've seen a guy who's into you like this. I don't know what type of spell you cast over him, but you should try it on yourself."

"Well excuse me for not having people after me or having a boyfriend for three years. In case you haven't been around the past ten years, I'm new to this kind of thing. I just don't know how to handle it all. Let me adjust to this!" My sudden outburst surprised me probably more than her hearing it. "I'm going home. I just got a major headache." I walked away from her without letting her speak.

I blew up just now. I hope I didn't upset her too much. It just wasn't the right time to hear that. I know I should give him a chance. He's not really a bad guy. And it's not every day that someone like him comes around saying they like me. I know I need to talk to him about this. That's what I had planned to do when I saw him. My house was quiet when I got in.

"Ken, are you here?" I waited for a response, but I was met with more silence.

He normally comes straight home after school. Maybe he doesn't want to see me now because he knows that it's someone from our class. If it weren't for John freaking out, Jennifer wouldn't have the wrong idea. According to her, she reports everything to Jenny that happens with me, so who knows what'll happen when she finds out.

I went up to my room when I noticed Ken's door was open. I've never actually been in here since he moved in. Knowing him, I didn't think I'd be safe in here. But since he wasn't home, I took the chance and went in.

You'd think he was neat as a pin the way he dresses, but inside his room there was a different story. I didn't think he was so messy. It wasn't clothes that were everywhere, but papers, books, and other small things. It looks like the storage room it used to be before he moved in. I took a look at the papers that were laying around. They didn't look like regular school assignments, but more like documents for something else. They're probably papers relating to his father's company. I was still looking through some of the papers when I heard the door downstairs open. He must be home.

"Ken is that you?" I rushed out his room and went downstairs.

"Oh, I didn't think you'd be home so early today," he said.

"Yeah, I came straight home."

"I suppose that means I should tell you now before I wait too late."

"Tell me what?" I was confused.

"Well, to put it simply, the word spreads fast, not just in school."

"W-what do you mean?"

"My father has been wondering about you and has heard about everything through a certain source." I was shocked. He has to mean the annoying duo. "So, with that being said, he wants to meet you this weekend."

"H-he wants to meet me. Why?"

"I don't know. I've been around here for a while, and with whatever it was he was told, he figured it was about time to see you. I wanted to tell you now so you wouldn't have to worry last minute."

"Is there a reason I should worry?" I asked already starting to worry.

"He's under a bit of stress right now with some negotiations dealing with some other companies. He's not exactly friendly when something is blocking his workflow."

"What does that mean exactly?" I wondered. Ken hesitated before he spoke again.

"He might feel that you're a distraction to me and is holding me back."

"What?"

"I told him it's not like that. But he gets that way about everything. If I didn't fight him about it, I'd be home schooled right now."

"Wait, so you mean—" My words were cut off by the sound of a loud horn.

"Can we talk later? I'm actually here now because I left something and will be with someone from home for a couple hours. Sorry for only telling you now. I thought you were going to be out." Ken went up to his room and grabbed what he needed and rushed right out the door.

So, he comes and goes just like that and expects me not to worry and be calm when he tells me I shouldn't worry about meeting someone who could probably get rid of me in a second without a trace? Just thinking about it is putting knots in my stomach. Ken's father. Head of the Masidone Company. He wants to meet me because he thinks I'm a distraction to Ken. Ken said don't worry, but that's exactly what I'll be doing.

By the time Ken came home, I was in my room finishing homework trying to avoid him. I don't know why I was avoiding him this time. I said I was going to talk to him about the whole Sano thing. But with the new information of his dad wanting to see me, I couldn't bring myself to talk to him about someone else. I ended up going to bed without speaking to him again. The next morning came, and I was rushing out of my room to get dressed to go. I saw a piece of paper on my door that must have come from Ken.

-Mimi the heavy sleeper. I hope you make it on time. -

If he left this, that meant he tried getting me up. He was already gone so the attempt didn't work. I had to run to school on my own again. Through all that happened yesterday, the one thing I wanted to fix was my yelling at Katie. I had a few minutes before the bell and used them to look for her when I got to school.

"There you are." I managed to catch up to her as she was heading into class. "I want to say sorry for yesterday. I was upset and shouldn't have yelled at you."

"No, it's not your fault. I shouldn't have said what I said, so I should be apologizing." She told me. Katie and I could never stay angry at each other. We always let whatever the problem is go.

"But you look like you didn't get any sleep last night. Did something happen?" She asked me.

"Well, yesterday, Ken told me his father wants to talk to me this weekend."

"Really? That came out of nowhere. What's the problem with that though?"

"What do you mean what's the problem with that? Katie, this man is the top of the top. I'm just a regular girl, that's nothing close to that. What if he tries to take me away never to be heard from again?"

"And why exactly would he want to do that?"

"He thinks I'm holding Ken back from his work. What if when he sees me, he hates me and sends me off to some island?!"

"Whoa, Misa, lay off the movies for a while. He's not a mafia boss or anything. Relax a bit."

"I can't. I couldn't sleep thinking about this. And now I have to have it on my mind for the rest of the week. It's going to drive me crazy."

"Oh, here comes Sano. People have been asking him questions since he walked through the doors. I think you should talk to him," Katie said. She turned and went ahead to class.

"Wait, Katie!"

"Hey, Misa." Sano had approached me.

"H-hey, Sano. How's your ankle?"

"It's fine. I told my mother about it, and she made me go see a doctor and said I shouldn't run for a while."

"Really?"

"Yeah, I'll be fine though. It seems people have found out about you coming to my house and getting the wrong idea though." he said.

"Yeah, I'm sorry. I've gotten you mixed up in something that's not your fault."

"Well, it is my house you were going to. I should have some fault to it."

"I should probably stop coming for the time being. Until this all dies down," I told him.

"That's probably for the best. I don't want to cause any trouble for you or Ken. But the kids would really be sad if you suddenly stopped coming all together. Why not come over today so you can say bye to them?"

"Oh, really? That's not a problem. They're fun to be around," I said, putting aside their hyper and excessive need to play.

As we talked, I noticed two girls walking past and whispering to each other while looking at us. I shouldn't talk to him too much at school while this is still a big issue. We ended it like that and went separately into class.

The bell rang as I walked into the room. That gave no time for anyone to say anything to me. I can feel the daggers in the back of my head from Jennifer. Without even looking, I can see her perfectly arched eye browns and glittery purple eyeshadow scrunched together waiting for her chance to say something.

I didn't give her that chance because every time I saw her, I turned the other way. It was like that all day. I don't know what she's planning, but she didn't go out of her way to say anything to me. My suspicion meter was going all over the place. How could she cause a scene like that yesterday then suddenly act as if I don't exist?

Like I promised, I headed to Sano's house after school. I know it's for the kids, but I'm still surprised he wanted me to come by even with everything going on. When I got to his place, sure enough, I was attacked like an owner that went on vacation and left the dog alone for a few days. I told the little ones I wasn't coming around for a while and they all got extremely sad.

"Misa, are you really not coming back?" Mia asked.

"Yeah, are you not coming back ever again?" Cindy frowned.

"I'll come back to visit. Something just came up, so I won't be able to come every day anymore."

"Did you steal something? Or did you rob a bank?" Brian asked me. "I saw that in a movie." Their ideas were more than a seven-year-old should think.

"No, nothing like that. Don't worry, everything is fine I promise. And I promise I'll come back," I said. I played a game of tag with them, and then went to find Sano.

"I've never seen them take a liking to someone so much," he said when I found him in the kitchen.

"They're nice kids. It's good they have a nice home and a good older brother that takes care of them so well. Few people would take this kind of responsibility so easily themselves."

"It's not so hard once you get used to it. When they first came and were younger, it was a bit hard for them to adjust. As time passed, they opened up more and it became a lot easier. The only issue at any point was having enough money to cover food, clothing, and everything else. But with the money we get from my father, I've managed to make it work."

"Well, even so, I still hate to leave you to do so much by yourself."

"I was able to do it all before you came. I still can, so don't worry so much," he told me.

"It's not that I'm worried, just concerned a little." I said. Sano looked away like he wanted to say something but couldn't.

"I've been wondering," He started, "We've had a class together before, but we hardly talked. You didn't know much about me, so why did you want to come hang out with me?" His question took me by surprise. Was this supposed to be my chance to confess? This would be my last time spending this kind of time with him for a while.

"Well, you seemed like you were a nice guy, and you're even good at sports. Then when you helped me in the rain that day and told me about your situation, it just made me want to help you."

"Is that so?" He asked.

"Y-yeah. You don't seem like you're the type to do wrong, so I wasn't worried about you being a bad guy or anything. I mean, hanging out with someone new is the way you learn about a person to be able to make a friend. And by now, you could probably call us friends, right?"

"Yeah, I consider you a friend, a good one that looks out for others," he said with a smile. I looked away a bit embarrassed.

I wanted to go ahead and tell him that I liked him. To finally get it out. There we stood face to face with no interruptions. The kids played happily in the yard while it was only us in the kitchen. I parted my lips in hopes it would finally just come out. I've come this far, and the moment couldn't be better. But this sudden feeling I got made me swallow those words. I couldn't say anything.

"I don't want to cause you more trouble keeping you here," Sano started again. "You should probably get going before it gets too late."

"Yeah, don't want to cause anymore misunderstandings. Guess I'll see you in class tomorrow," I said going to grab my things. I don't know what this feeling was, but it caused me to freeze and miss my chance.

"Oh, and Misa," he called out to me again, "I enjoyed having you around. Thanks for the company."

"Oh, no problem." I felt my face grow warm hearing him.

He said it with a lot of sincerity. It's almost like I wouldn't be coming back again. There wasn't anything else I could say, so I took my leave. And just like that, my Sano adventures were done. Or at least until this storm blows over. It feels like I just closed a chapter of my book and about to start a new one. And the remaining character is Ken. I felt a bit sad that my time with Sano was done, but why didn't it hurt more like I thought it would?

16

"Come on, Misa, we have to get going. You look great no matter how you dress," Ken was yelling at me to hurry up. The week flew by so quickly I never got the chance to prepare myself for this meeting with the head of this game. It was nine in the morning. A beautiful clear Saturday. And I was going to spend it talking to a very important businessman.

"You can think that, but what if your father doesn't think so? I have to make sure I look presentable." I told him.

"Misa, we're just going to my house, there's no reason to go overboard." I heard a horn honk outside the house.

"Our ride is here, so we should get going, I don't want to keep him waiting."

"Okay, okay, I'm coming." I rushed down the stairs, still fixing my shirt. I had to dig in the back of my closet to find my black-and-white dress shirt to go with my leggings. I felt more comfortable in this, so hopefully it would make talking easier.

"Oh, Mimi, you look so nice. I could just lock you up for myself," Ken said watching me.

"Um, thanks, but no thanks. Let's just go before I freak out. And stop calling me Mimi!"

"Alright, next stop, my house!" Ken was the only one excited to be going. I grabbed my bag and some confidence to follow him out the door. "Make yourself comfy. It's going to be a long ride." He opened the car door for me. First, the nice black matte car, now I'm getting into a dark blue car with a jaguar on the front. I think I've already touched more than I can afford for one lifetime.

"Oh, my sweet sugar! Who is this fine young thing getting into this car, Kenny-kens?"

I was taken aback when someone spoke from the driver's seat. It was a young man pushing his side bang aside and lifting his sunglasses looking at me.

"Jay, this is Misa, and Misa, this is Jayson. I guess he's what you'd call my guard," Ken said introducing us.

"Guard? Oh Kenny-ken, that sounds so formal, just think of me as his older brother, with the better-looking genes that is," Jayson said with a little laugh. "Why haven't you told me you've been with such a gem like this? Have you been keeping her all to yourself and having fun without me?"

"Yeah, it's just been me and Mimi," Ken answered.

"Didn't I *just* tell you to stop calling me that?" I hissed.

"Oh Kenny-kens, I know you can do better than that. How about... MI-SA-KY. It has such a nice ring to it," Jayson suggested. First Ken and his Mimi. Now this Jayson guy is trying to change my name completely.

"Your father has been waiting for the both of you." Jayson spoke again.

"I'm sure he has," Ken said, "But will the *others* be, you know?" He emphasized the *others* when he said that.

"Oh, don't worry about them. They won't be back until tomorrow evening, and good thing too. I don't know why, but they have been so fussy lately. What have you been doing to those poor things?"

"I haven't done anything. You should know how they get about things going wrong." I was so lost on what or who they were talking about.

"And with them gone, Papa Masy should melt down like butter to you, Misaky," Jayson said.

"Oh, um, good?" I didn't know how to respond to that.

"Oh, she's just so adorable!" Jayson said like I was a child. Ten minutes into this new world, I can already kind of see where Ken gets his behavior from.

It was true that Ken came a long way to my house. I was in that car for what felt like hours. The open road seemed like it went on forever until the open road turned into a green grassland that led to a large building off on its own in the middle of almost nowhere.

"We're here!" Jayson said like we made it to Disney World.

"Masidone Manor! Come on, Misaky, let me give you a tour."

"That has to wait, Jay. She must talk with my father first."

"Oh, all right then. But she won't be leaving without one. I'll let the big guy know you're here." Jayson walked away first, up to the house that should have its own zip code.

"Uh, Ken, can I ask you a rather odd question?" Ken looked at me with an expression that says he knows what I'm going to say.

"If it's about Jayson, I'll have to explain him later. For now, just focus on making this a short and sweet visit."

"I'll try," I answered. Looking at the outside of this large grey stoned house made me wonder if I could. It looks to have about two floors and stretched wide. Small fountains surrounded the area around it while a big one was placed in the center of the lawn. Statues and other lawn ornaments were out on the neat and manicured lawn. A small glossy black fence sitting on grey bricks lined the walk and driveway. It was still morning, so the clear morning sky was making the place stand out more than it already is. You'd think this place was a tourist attraction.

We walked up to the front doors where a big, scripted *M* covered them. And without either of us touching them, they opened, showing us a small group of maids, or at least what I thought were maids. The traditional black-and-white dresses weren't on, but they were all still dressed in the same black suits. If I didn't know any better, I thought I was going into some secret agent meeting.

"Welcome back, Mr. Masidone," they all said. I was a bit startled by it. It was like I entered a movie scene. There were like six maids all happy and ready to serve us.

"I think my father is trying to impress you," Ken whispered to me. But that was already done. This is just over the top.

"Welcome, Miss Macky," one of the maid slash secret agents to my left singled me out. "If you could just follow me this way, please."

She directed me to come with her. I looked to Ken who gave me a nod of approval. I went ahead and left Ken to go with her. She led me through a hall that angled back. The click of her heels hit the polished marble floor tile hard, making an echo sound throughout the entire hallway. It was quiet in here. And with it being so big, everything else seemed louder. I just hope she couldn't hear my increasing heartbeat.

I tried taking my focus off of where I was being taken and looked at all the pictures and paintings that hung everywhere. The stone stands with large flowerpots on them. The bathroom on the left that, in passing, looked to be triple the size of mine. When we reached the end of the hallway, it led to the only average thing I've seen since being there, a door. A regular door stood before me. No writing, fancy letters, name plates on it or anything. It made me feel nervous like I was about to be put in the dungeon.

"President Masidone will be with you momentarily," the lady said.

"Um, thanks." I didn't know if I was supposed to give her a tip or not, but she just nodded and went back down the hallway.

Now it was just me and the regular door that I still wasn't sure if it was a dungeon or not. Ken's father is going to appear from somewhere. My meeting him was going to happen sooner or later since he's staying at my house. But the way Ken was going made it seem like I should be very weary of him, and I should make it seem like I'm not the distraction he thinks I am. I wouldn't even know what to do or say to appear as a non-distraction.

"Well, if it isn't the infamous Misa Macky."

The sudden voice took me by surprise. I looked and saw the regular door was opened, revealing a man that favored Ken a little too much in a dark grey suit.

"So, you're the one that has captivated my son. How are you today, Miss Macky?" He asked.

"I-I'm good, sir." Although he isn't as intimidating as I was imagining, I still wasn't trying to let my guard down.

"Ah come on, no need to be so stiff. I'm not going to hurt you. Do I look like I bite?" he asked pointing to himself.

"N-no, sir."

"Then drop the sir. I feel old. Don't need to be older than I already am. But please, come in." He held the door open.

"Yes, sir. No! I mean…" I was still nervous and searching for words.

He started laughing. "I see why my son has taken a liking to you." He walked in and I followed. He went and sat at his desk and motioned for me to sit at the chair in front of it. The room was huge. His desk was in front of a large picture of one of the company locations in between two windows that gave a gorgeous view of the wide-open land of the side of the house.

The rest of the room was filled with filing cabinets, a table that was on the other side of the room, pictures, and I'm sure a trap door somewhere. I took my focus back to him. He didn't seem like a bad guy at all. He really looks like Ken if he were a bit older with shorter hair. He seemed laidback and talked with a friendly and casual voice.

"Well, let's get right to it shall we." He wasting no time getting down to business, "You seem like you mean well, Miss Macky. However, I've found new knowledge about you."

I felt a squeeze in my chest. "New knowledge?"

"Just a few things. However, those few things were enough for me to need to have this meeting arranged. Now, it is to my understanding that Ken has taken quite an interest in you. He went through a lot of trouble to show that simply by convincing me to let him stay at your residence." He said. I could only imagine what Ken did to get him to agree.

"It is also to my understanding you haven't been reciprocating this infatuation. I know you all are still young and in high school. Still free to act and do what most teenagers enjoy doing. But Ken isn't like most teenagers. He has a very important future awaiting him. As soon as he finishes all of his schooling, and proper training, he will be in an office much like this one, if not this one. And what good would it do to successfully run a business if he doesn't have a nice, good companion by his side?" He asked. I hope it was a rhetorical question because I didn't answer. "Now, you know of Jenny, yes?"

"Yes." I *unfortunately* answered.

"Well, as you may or may not know, Jenny was originally the one that was thought to be the perfect person that fits the good companion bill. Those two have known each other for quite some time now, and she does anything for Ken. But the thought of her becoming his significant other isn't something Ken is willing to cooperate with and won't let this wonderful young lady be anything more than just his friend." I'm not sure if he should call her wonderful, but this isn't the time to bring that up.

"That brings me to my next question. There was one day Ken was going through something with your parents' name on it. It was then he mentioned them having a daughter his age. And before he even met you, he felt that something better could come from you than with Jenny. Do you both have a past together that he isn't telling me about?" I was shocked. Is that how this all came to be?

"Um, not exactly. Well, we met once a few years ago."

"I see. So that's the reasoning. I guess it runs in the family when it comes to love at first sight." He said with a chuckle. I've been listening to him the whole time, but as he continues to talk, my mind keeps wandering elsewhere, like it's telling me something about him.

"Miss Macky?"

"Y-yes! Um, Mr. Masidone."

"Still so timid," he told me, "I'm sure you're wondering what I want with you, and where is he going with this, right?"

Again, I hope that was a rhetorical question.

"Well, I've had one of my servants look into you for a few days." He told me. Does spying also run in the family? I knew that wasn't the end of it! "I was just trying to gather my own information since Ken didn't want to share. And I did find something very interesting."

"W-what was that?" I asked. I felt a cold sweat coming on the side of my face. Obviously, he knows about Sano and wants to send me to the dungeon for wasting Ken's time and his with some other guy not a part of this. I better brace myself in case the floor moves.

"Well, it seems that you have also been getting close with my other son." The floor didn't give away, but I felt my heart drop to my stomach.

"Y-your other son?"

"Yes, my other son, Sano."

17

"Y-your son Sano? As in Sano Sanders?" I asked in disbelief.

"Yes, that is who I'm referring to. Your response tells me you didn't know?"

"No, no I didn't." I thought he reminded me of someone else, but not like this.

"So, neither of them told you?"

"No, they didn't."

"Well now, I wonder what their reason for that is," he thought out loud. I wanted to know too.

"Well, continuing on, I'm very interested to know, what does Sano do?"

"What does he do?"

"Yes, what does he do? Does he play sports? Does he have a job, anything like that?"

"Well, he runs track. And he stays home to watch after his brothers and sisters."

"Ah yes, those foster kids. How many were there? One, two?"

"Three." I told him.

"Three? I see. That's why he requests so much money." He thought again out loud. So, this is Sano's source of income?

"I take it he doesn't go out much?"

"Um, not really."

"I see. He's still so aloof," he said.

"Um, Mr. Masidone, if I may ask, why does Sano live by himself?" I didn't think I'd actually ask. My mind is so blown, the question came out on it's on. Mr. Masidone had a look of confusion.

"Himself? Doesn't Sasha, his mother I mean, live with him?"

"She's been in the hospital for over a month."

"Oh really? That's a new bit of information. You're telling me he's been taking care of the house and children on his own?"

"Yes." I answered. He became quiet while slightly shaking his head.

"Well now. This is certainly news to me," he said. Just like Sano, he kept a composed expression, but it was no secret he was taken by surprise. "Sano," he went on, "he's been through a lot, I can admit that. We all used to live together. Me, him, Ken, Jayson of course…" He paused for a moment, "And Kelly." he added.

But who was Kelly?

"Everything was fine up until some years ago when Sano figured out the truth."

"T-the truth?" I repeated.

"Yes, the truth about who the Kelly woman was I mentioned. Kelly, who was my wife at that time, has only one son, which is Ken. After finding that out, Sano wanted to know who his mother was. Once he found out who she was, he packed his things and moved out. Sano has never forgiven me for never telling him. It wasn't until about two years ago that he started to talk to me again. We made a deal that I'd assist him and his household with any monetary needs if he kept in touch. But that didn't really last, however, I still give him support." He explained. I didn't know any of this.

"But Miss Macky, what I'm trying to say is that I want to be on good terms with my son, but he refuses to talk to me. The only one he kept in touch with after the move was Ken, but then I heard he stopped shortly after as well. But you Miss Macky," He pointed at me and said, "You can help me in this matter."

"How would I be able to do that?" I asked.

"Ken and Sano did everything together, but at times, he would close himself off to everyone, even Ken, and kind of just kept to himself. So, the thought of him letting someone in his personal space much less inside his home, a person's safe space, is mind-boggling indeed. And that happened with you. He let you in his space. If you could just stay with him and be an inside support, then maybe he'll begin to open up more." Mr. Masidone wants me to stay with Sano. He's asking me to be with Sano… and not Ken.

"But, Mr. Masidone, wouldn't that put Ken in an awkward position?" I'm so overwhelmed by everything, but him telling me to give my attention to Sano, where does that leave Ken? He was quiet for a second looking at his desk. I didn't think it was possible for me to feel even more uneasy without blacking out. But the new look in Mr. Masidone's eyes as he looked to me sent a dagger straight to my chest.

"Miss Macky, what do you call your relationship with Ken?"

"My relationship?"

"Yes, your relationship. For example, if the two of you were walking down a busy street together, how would you want people to interpret you?" he elaborated. I had thought this same question once and still don't have an answer for it.

"Um, I-I'm not sure."

"From what I've been told, you don't see Ken the way he sees you. But from what I put together, you want Sano to see you the way Ken does. Am I wrong?"

I looked down at my hands that were in my lap. I didn't want to answer that question, but I think he still found his answer.

"Miss Macky, I run a business here. That being said, I don't really have the extra time to have one little teenage girl try and stop my business from moving. Ken may not be doing the real business now, but he has to keep a well, steady, and progressive life until then. This is but a small kink that needs to be fixed before it gets knotted into a bigger problem. Do you understand what I'm driving at? For Ken to be able to focus on what he needs to do and keep moving forward, you must make a decision. Before I have to make it for you." His cool laidback tone was gone and was replaced with a more serious and almost threatening speech.

"That's all I wanted to say." He reached for his desk phone and pushed a button. "Looking for Jayson. Are you there, Jayson?"

"Yes Papa Masy, what can I do for you?" I heard Jayson say through the intercom.

"Bring me my medicine and show this lovely young lady around this beautiful estate, would you?"

"Roger that! Be there in a hottie." He let go of the phone after that.

"Oh, that Jayson. I don't think there's ever a time when he's not energetic. No matter the situation, he's always been there. Alright, Miss Macky. It was a pleasure meeting you. You are dismissed."

I didn't know what else to say, so I stood and awkwardly walked out into the hallway in a daze, which is why Jayson startled me when he showed up holding a small tray.

"Oh, Misaky, I'll be right with you. I just have to hand this off. Are you all right? You look like you just saw a ghost."

"I-I'm okay." I obviously lied.

"You sure? Did Papa Masy do something to scare you? I'll have to talk to him about that. Scaring our little Misaky like that. Just wait, we'll get that cute smile right back on that cute little face of yours." Jayson smiled and walked into the room that looked regular from the outside but held the dangerous beast inside.

It was silent in the hall. This silence was heavy enough to finally bring me back to reality. A reality I didn't know until now. Ken and Sano are brothers. Not stepbrother. But brother, brothers! And that guy is their father? Sano and Ken don't look anything alike or act the same or at least not that I noticed. It never dawned on me to think so. Sano always told me his father was overseas. This guy seems pretty close to me. I think this is the same country we're in. Why did he lie? What would be the reason for him to do that?

Those two are in the same class, but they never talked to each other. You'd never think they actually knew each other, let alone were brothers! Ken has never mentioned this. I remember he told me he taught his brother how to drive. Is Sano the brother he meant? Did he actually know this is what his father wanted to talk to me about?

I feel like I don't know anything anymore. I want some answers, and I want some now. I'm not about to sit around waiting for that Jayson person. I want to go find Ken. I only have one route from here, so hopefully it won't be hard to find him. I probably shouldn't roam around myself, but this is urgent.

I kept straight down the long hallway back to where I came, but I think I went too far. I'm faced with ever more doors and rooms. I guess I could be heading in the right direction. He could probably be in one of these rooms. But all the doors I'm passing are closed. I can't just open them. I continued walking and passed so many pots, plants, pictures of people that must be in the family.

A maid went by dusting a large vase not caring for me now. How could Ken go from living here to a place like mine? His dad's office was almost the size of my house! I finally reached the end of this hallway and saw a door cracked opened. I walked up to it to see if I heard any voices. There weren't any I could hear coming from the room, so I got closer. I peeked in and saw an unexpected scene.

The walls were painted bright purple and pink and flowers all on them. Fuzzy sparkling carpet covered the floor. Everything was colorful and flashy. There were two beds with matching pink and purple comforters and pillows, two dressers, and closets, almost like two rooms in one. I wondered who could enjoy living here. I peeked in closer, and the door moved.

I looked at the door like I was caught but instead I saw something else. There was a name plate. And the names were the things that frightened me the most— Jenny and Jennifer. The name plate had Jenny and Jennifer's name on it. There's only two people in the world that were related with the same name. And for some reason, I feel this is their room. Why are they living here? Why are they giving the impression that they're girly? Those two are witches!

"Are you having fun snooping around?" The sudden sound of someone's voice nearly made me jump out of my skin. I turned and saw Ken, which meant I was busted. "Are you surprised?" He asked me.

"Surprised? I was just looking for the bathroom and uh, whoops, guess this isn't it." It wasn't what I wanted to say, but hopefully it'll buy me time to remember what I did what to say.

"You left Jayson, and he got worried, so he asked me to help look for you," Ken said.

"Sorry, I left without him. I went to go look for you actually."

"For me? Oh, you couldn't go long without seeing me? Don't I feel so special," he said putting his hand to his chest.

"Um, no that isn't the reason exactly."

"Darn, I was hoping that was the reason."

"Do they really live here?" I asked, remembering what was going on.

"Does their living here make you jealous?"

"No, it just seems kind of strange that they're living here, when you're not." I said. He didn't say anything right away.

"Well, I can't really explain that" he answered.

"Why not?"

"Actually, I don't really know the answer myself," he replied. I didn't buy that, but I asked something else instead.

"Okay then, can you explain why you never told me you and Sano were brothers?" He stayed silent then. "Well?" I pestered.

"I didn't know until recently that you two were hanging out."

"Are you sure about that?" I asked. I know for sure that was a lie.

"What?"

"You, you all, there's something wrong with your family. You've been watching me, your father has been watching me, what should make me think you aren't still doing it? How do I know you weren't watching from the beginning? Do you get some kind of joy out of me hanging out with your brother and you're the one that has all this talk of marriage? Or do you just want to make his life more difficult than what you all have already made it?"

"Hold on, what did my father tell you?"

"What difference does that make? Is what he told me going to change how you answer anything? You trying to avoid the truth?" I couldn't control the confusion and anger I felt.

"Misa, it's not like that." Ken tried telling me.

"There you two are!" A ray of sunlight came in on our storm. "You've found Misaky. I thought I lost this sweet bowl of sugar." Jayson was too bright for the atmosphere he just entered, but either he didn't notice, or he's good at avoiding confrontation.

"Sorry I left without you. I wandered without thinking," I said.

"Oh, it's not your fault, you were just curious about the house. Come on, let me take you around properly. Kenny-kens, you can tag along too. You're not doing anything, right?"

"No, no I'm not." Ken was able to act normal about it too, but I can tell what I said wasn't just being overlooked by him.

"Alright. Let's start from the beginning." Jayson took us back to where we came in. "I say we should've painted here a different color like a light blue, or maybe something like a marble. But Papa Masy insisted on this less than appealing shade of brown."

The color was a little dark. It gave the room an older style feel to it. But with the layout of this house, it was anything but old. It was almost like a maze. There were four different halls leading out of this area. I've already seen the back two. To the left leads to Mr. Masidone's chamber. To the right it seemed to have rooms. One of which belonged to Jenny and Jennifer. In the middle of these halls where we stood were the split staircases that curved going up. From here, I could just see the railings of the balcony view.

Jayson continued the tour of the house, going to the living room down the other left hallway. As he mentioned how they had done renovations recently and added the new eighty-inch smart TV above the fireplace, I drifted more into my own thoughts. Why did Ken lie and keep this all a secret? We've only been around each other for a couple months and he's already keeping secrets and not telling me things I should know. Sano is at fault too. He told me his father was overseas and never said anything when he would mention Ken, which he did a lot.

"Misaky, watch out for the wall!" Jayson's words didn't register until it was too late, and I was stumbling back to the ground.

"Misaky? Are you okay?" he asked helping me up.

"Y-yeah, I'm fine," I'm not even sure when we got outside.

"You hit your head kind of hard, would you like an ice pack or anything?"

"Thanks, but I'll be fine."

"You know, you seem a little unfocused."

"I do? I was just thinking how big and really spacious this house is." Now doesn't seem like the time to say what's really on my mind.

"Well, it is a big house. I don't know why Papa Masy got this place so big and only a few people live in it. Even the help as you saw have their own separate housing. But I guess that's Papa Masy for you. Always going above and beyond to show how far he's made it." You could hear the second-hand pride in his tone and the glow in his eye. We continued going through the house until we finally got to a location where my nose agreed with.

"Alright, I don't know about you all, but after all that walking, I'm a bit famished and I must keep my figure up to date. And what luck, I've come to the last stop of the tour, and the most loved area of the house, the kitchen!"

We entered the kitchen through the doors in the dining room. It was almost like we stepped into a whole different house. The kitchen was huge and looked as if it was dipped in silver. Chrome counter tops and cabinets with a light and dark grey back splash that matched the glossy grey floor tile. The island in the center was shaped like an open box that had a second sink on it and a couple black stools at the far end. Being in this place felt almost unreal. To think I'm seeing what it's like to live in luxury with my own eyes and not on the internet or TV.

"How are you holding up, Misaky?" Jayson asked me, leaning on the island counter.

"I'm fine. This house is amazing. I wish I had a house like this," I said, minus the thousands of sculptures and paintings of everything in the world. I have to remind myself to check to see if I've ever seen this place on TV somewhere.

"I'm so happy you like it here. Now my next question for you. How good are you in the kitchen?"

"Um, I'm decent."

"If by decent you mean you have enough skill to poison people then decent is the perfect word." I looked over and almost forgot Ken was with us. He was so quiet.

"Who asked you?"

"Well, if it's skill you're looking for then look no further! I, the best Jayson in this kitchen, can be of great service to you. Come on, Misaky, help me make us all some lunch. Kenny-Kens, you go wait in the other room. You've spent lots of time with her, now it's our time to bond." Jayson waved his hand shooing him out.

"Alright. Just don't get too close to her. She wouldn't be able to keep up."

"Oh, don't worry. No one can keep up with this." I was afraid to ask what I should be *keeping up* with. So, I just watched Ken disappear back into the dining room.

"Alright, Misaky, what are you in the mood for?" He asked me.

"I'm not sure. Anything is fine."

"Come now, I'm sure it's something your taste buds are just dancing for. Pasta, fish, chicken, we have it all."

"Um, I don't know. I guess I haven't had fish lately."

"Mmm, I love me some fish! I just knew we had some things in common!" He said sounding a little too excited about it.

"Could you go grab the fish from the freezer? I'll get the pans and stuff. We'll have what they call fish and chips. I'll grab the potatoes too." He walked over to a cabinet above the stove to grab a pan.

I went to the freezer in search for what could pass for a fish. I've never actually seen my mom cook fish, and nothing in here looks like the things I see swimming in the water. I should've just said I wanted a sandwich. That would make things a lot easier to do.

"Misaky, did you find the fish?" Jayson asked after about five minutes of me looking.

"Um, yeah, I think I found it." I wasn't sure what it was I was holding, but I hope it's right.

"Here, I think you're looking for this?" He came up behind me and grabbed the package above the one I had.

"If Kenny-kens were in here, he'd start going crazy. He gets serious about his food."

"Yeah, I know. He did flip on me before," I said remembering his rant about wholehearted Kool-Aid.

"You know, I wasn't going to say anything, but you two didn't talk at all during the little tour just now. And before, when I found you both, you seemed like you guys were having a serious talk. Did something happen? You two look like the cutest little couple, it's a shame for something to be wrong."

"If by cute couple, you mean Ken giving me nothing but confusion, troubles, and headaches, then call it what you'd like." I don't know why I blurted it all out like that to him. He stopped what he was doing and looked at me with disbelief.

"All that with Kenny-kens? He's just about the sweetest bowl of pudding. What could he have done to you?" He asked. I wasn't sure if I should tell him, but the vibe I get from him is way different from his dad.

He seemed a lot easier to talk to, and I needed to get everything off my mind.

"It's just that, he comes out of nowhere and claims I am his fiancé, and I didn't even know him. No one ever stopped to think if I could've already been with anyone or liked anyone. And I did, and with this small world we live in, it so happened to be his *half-brother*." I said it like it was untrue, which it still felt like that. But the loud gasp and surprised expression he showed meant that it had been true.

"Are you talking about our lovely little Sano? He goes to your school?"

"Yeah."

"Oh, my sweet sugar, I thought they moved away. So that's what Kenny-kens wasn't telling me." He was in shock. Ken was even keeping Sano a secret from the people he knew. "Oh, Misaky, you poor thing. But don't put the blame on Kenny-kens. Maybe he didn't know."

"Even when he knows everything else and keeps watch of me through surveillance? And then there's Sano too. He could've told me." I wasn't sure who I was more upset with, but both of them played a part in this.

"Misaky, you have every right to be upset, but as a big brother to those sweet little boys, I can guarantee they had a good reason for not telling you. Now, I'm not too sure about my lovely little Sano, but as for Kenny-kens, I know he likes you. When he comes home, he's always telling me about you. I felt I knew a little of you just from hearing him talk about you." I glanced the door Ken left out of. I didn't know he was going home and talking about me with someone.

"However," Jayson continued, "he can move a little too fast. Especially when it comes to something he wants. I was surprised when I heard that he wanted to go stay with you when those other little kittens were already here for him." I assume he must be talking about Jenny and Jennifer. But using *kittens* to describe them is a stretch.

"You must understand that Kenny-kens can be a free spirit at times. Things aren't always easy for him around here, so he tries to stay positive and act in a way that keeps those troubled feelings away. With that being said, I know he keeps a lot of things in. Not always for selfish reasons, but more so to try and protect others too. Also, he tries to make sure that he isn't going to do something to ruin his father's business or reputation. I've lived here long enough to understand this much."

He did his best to get me to see why Ken can be… Ken. Everyone has their share of secrets. I understand that. With Ken being from this kind of background, it's almost expected to hold things in. But something like this? Maybe if I can get him to explain himself, I could understand why.

"I would like for you two to talk about things," Jayson said, "but first, we have to make this nice little lunch. I don't know how much longer it'll be until I need to take you back, but I would not be able to face that handsome man in the mirror if I let you two go like this." Jayson smiled and went back to get what he needed for us to make lunch.

Unlike with Mr. Masidone, I don't feel the need to keep my guard up with him. He seems to care about Ken a lot. If he's going to have us talk, he must really feel Ken had good reason to lie and act like he didn't know anything. I just hope he did.

18

"And here we are! A meal fit for a king, prince, and princess," Jayson announced as he and I went to the dining room. Ken had been sitting there on his phone when he saw us coming out with our plates on trays.

"It looks and smells good, Jay. I almost got concerned for a second when I thought I smelled something burning a little bit ago," Ken said.

"Oh that. There was just a small miscommunication of directions," Jayson answered, but I really thought he said turn *up* the fire, not turn *off* the fire.

"Here you go, Kenny-kens. And Misaky, you sit right here." He went around the table pulling out the seat across from Ken. "And I'll take my plate to my room."

"You're not eating with us?" Ken asked.

"I would have loved too, but Misaky told me about the situation going on with you two, and I want you both to take this time to talk about it. I'd even bring my lovely little Sano in too if I could. I just hate seeing such cute faces looking so sad and distressed. You know I'm an advocate for saying what's on your mind. This is how good communication is built. So, if you need me, just give me a page." Jayson took his stuff and left the room, leaving just me and Ken there alone to talk.

The dining room, surprisingly, wasn't as big as I thought. We sat at this glass wood table I was almost afraid to touch in fear of breaking it. A large marble glass vase sat in the middle with flowers. I noticed the clock on the far end of the wall was shaped like an almost clear snowflake. I could actually hear the seconds ticking away as the room stayed quiet. Neither of us has said a word since Jayson walked out. I didn't know what to say anymore. Just a little while ago, I wanted to yell at him. Now, sitting here, watching him calmly eat as if there isn't anything to talk about, nothing I wanted to say is registering.

"Once again, Jay outdid himself. This is delicious," Ken said taking another bite.

"Actually, I made that one," I said. I was able to tell since mine came out a bit darker and a little thinner than Jayson's did.

"You mean you made this? Seriously?"

"Gee, thanks for the compliment." I sarcastically replied.

"I didn't mean it like that. It's just that it's good enough to be considered Jay's work. And knowing your past w—"

"You mean the past you dug up through hidden spies while still keeping your profile low?" I cut him off.

He sighed, "Misa…"

"Oh, or is it that you actually thought you got to know all about me in the little time we've been together?"

"It doesn't take a million occasions to understand that a person isn't skilled at cooking after they've tasted it and seen them try more than once. I was just taken by surprise when you said you made it. I'm sorry if that offended you," Ken said taking a sip of his drink. He wasn't yelling, but it felt like he was. I was taken aback.

"Well, he did take me through it step by step, so it wasn't so difficult that way," I said. It was the only thing I could say in response.

"He's a great teacher. You can learn a lot from him."

"Could he teach me about why guys are liars and so secretive?" I asked.

"Yes, he could." He answered as if that's the response I was looking for. "I guess that wasn't the answer you wanted to hear," he said reading my mind. He wiped his hands with his napkin and made a big sigh. "Look, it's not that I didn't want to tell you, it's just that I couldn't."

"What do you mean you couldn't tell me?" I asked. The way he's acting, he really doesn't seem like he wants to talk about it.

"Well, Sano and I, we were close growing up. But then something happened between us that weakened our bond. He must have been taking that harder than I thought since he hasn't contacted me or even breathes in my direction at school."

"What happened between you two?"

"It's not that easy to explain. And I rather not go into detail."

"Well, even so, should you just leave him like that? He has a lot on his plate and all you're doing is sitting in this wasted money about to inherit a worldwide company. That doesn't sound fair. If he's your brother, why couldn't Sano have the inheritance?"

"He's the one that left us!" He snapped. I had never heard Ken raise his voice like that. I didn't move as I watched him try to pull himself together. "In the middle of the night, he packed his things and walked away. My father tried to go after him, but he didn't want to come back here. And who could blame him? I wasn't exactly proud of what they did either when I found out. We were both confused and felt like we'd been betrayed. And about the inheritance, he couldn't take over the company anyway."

"Why not?"

"At the time my father found out that Sano's mother was pregnant, he was already with someone else. His mother found out and didn't want her son to be raised by him. She wanted to keep him, but he fought for the rights and won. But after the years passed, and we were told the truth, he ended up leaving." He explained.

"How do you know all this?"

"I made Jayson tell me a while ago. He didn't want to, but he did in the end."

"That still doesn't explain why he can't get the inheritance."

"Sano's mother wanted him to have her last name so he wouldn't seem to have any ties with us, so at that point he was already out of the game. She wasn't going to have him do it with or without custody. Then I came along. With me being born, there was no reason to keep fighting that particular battle." His voice was a bit bitter. Like he felt at fault. I stayed silent. I felt a pain in my stomach listening to him. I almost wished I didn't ask. To think all this happened and Sano had to go through so much. Their father is really something else.

"Do you understand now?" Ken asked, "I... I did know that he was who you were with after school, but that was only because when I first came to your house, I heard you say to your mother you liked a guy named Sano. When I got to school and saw him in class, I just put two and two together. I couldn't say anything. I hadn't seen him in years and didn't feel I had a right to." I didn't think he could say anything else to surprise me. This whole time he knew that I had liked Sano. And he never said anything about it? "With you two hanging out, I didn't want to say anything. I thought it'd be fine, and no harm would come from it."

"So, what about me then? Do you think it's fine and okay for me to hang out with him and then come back home to you? I don't know who you think I am, but I'm not the type to go around like that."

"I didn't say you were. But you told me that you're just helping him out, right? If you guys are just friends, I didn't see anything wrong with you having more than one guy friend."

"But, what... what if we become more than just friends?" He knows I like him. So why is he all right with me being around him?

"I'd just have to step my game up before that happens. Is it a problem going for someone who is still available?" He certainly has the attitude of businessman. He doesn't give up until the deal is completely off the table.

"Wouldn't that mess up your already broken bond further?"

"If it did get to this point, in the end, one of us would be out of luck anyway, right? I know Sano would want you to choose who you'd want, as would I, but neither of us would know until you say who it is you chose to be with."

So, in the end, it all really does come back to it being about me and my choice. From the way he's talking, it sounds like he's been thinking about this more than I thought. Does he really like me that much? I know we've been around each other for a while now, but I still don't know.

"That's all there is to it. Do you still think I'm hiding anything?" Ken asked.

"I do. There's always something not said, But I do have a better idea about everything."

"Misa, I told you what you wanted to know about. What else do you think I'm not telling you?"

"Just because you answered a couple of questions doesn't mean you're out of the doghouse yet. I still don't know much about you. For all I know, you could be hiding your real name.

"My real name is Kenneth Jacob Masidone Jr."

"Kenneth?" I said as a question. "That's the first I've heard of that."

"It's because I don't like going by my full name," he said.

"Why not?"

"Because it reminds me of someone I'm not." He almost whispered it. I guess he's referring to his father since he's a junior. I just looked down not wanting to press that matter more.

"Hey, since you've already talked to my father, why don't we go and finish talking elsewhere?" Ken said after looking at the clock.

"What's wrong with talking here?"

"It's probably too late already, but it would be better to take this elsewhere. The walls have eyes here.

"What?"

"Hey, Jayson, you read me?" He pulled out a little walkie from his pocket not listening to me.

"Yes, Kenny-kens? Have you and Misaky finally settled your differences?"

"Um, yeah, we're ready to leave now."

"Oh pooh, really? I guess Misaky and I will have to play some more another time. Just give me a sec then, I'll be over in a hottie." Ken put the walkie back in his pocket after Jayson spoke.

"As you heard, Jayson will be here soon. I'm going to the restroom. Did you need to go?"

"No, I'll be fine." I told him. I watched Ken leave down a hallway. It feels like his whole attitude changed again. What did he mean by the walls have eyes? Is there someone watching us or something? I wouldn't be surprised.

"She's here!" I heard someone through the hall that led back to the main entrance. Then I heard the doors opening.

"Welcome home Mrs. Baker!" The maids greeted someone. Who else were they trying to impress?

"I'll take your bags for you," one of them said.

"Thank you, ladies. Julie, could you prepare me a meal? Anything is fine. I've already had a long morning. I'll take it in the dining room." The person who came in was a woman and she was coming in here. I wasn't sure if I should leave or not. By the sound of heels clicking this way, I could say I was already out of thinking time.

"Oh my, such a long day. Oh?" She stopped as soon as she saw me.

"And who might you be?" She asked.

"M-Misa Macky." A full name introduction felt needed as a tall and slim woman with a silk red shirt and straight legged dress pants came in. Her black hair was in a neat ponytail. Her red and black strapped high heels clicked more as she walked over toward the table next to me.

"Oh right, right. You are the girl little Kenneth likes." She smiled even though she didn't sound excited.

"Um, y-yeah."

"I see. I've heard about you." She kept a good eye on me.

"My name is Jocelyn Baker. You can call me Mrs. Baker. I'm with Kenneth, the older one of course." She introduced herself. She's with Mr. Masidone? I thought he said Ken's mother's name was Kelly.

"I've been looking after little Kenneth for three years now. He's like a son to me. So, you should understand that I've wanted to meet the one little Kenneth's been with."

Well, you aren't the only one.

"I'm a bit surprised you're here. I've asked him to bring you here many times, but he refused to."

"His father wanted to talk with me." I told her.

"He wanted to talk to you. What's he up to?" she asked herself out loud. "Well anyway, I can see you both were chatting over lunch?" She asked looking at our plates of food.

"Um, no. Ken and I were here. Jayson suggested that we have lunch, so we made some," I said. And just as I mentioned his name, he came into the room.

"Misaky, you here? Oh, Mama Baker, I didn't know you were home!" Jayson said all smiles.

"Yes, yes. I'm here. And didn't I tell you no nicknames for me Jayson?"

"Aw, but you're missing out on all the fun with them."

"I just heard that you and this young lady were cooking together. It looks good. I think I'll have some." She said, ignoring what he said.

"I'd be happy to make it for you, but first I have to take this sweet little thing and Kenny- kens back. Come on, Misaky, let's go," Jayson said. He seems fond of this lady. She talks and walks with confidence. This is the woman beside Mr. Masidone.

"Misa dear, since your visit here is over for the day, I'd like to bring you here one more time next weekend if it isn't too much of a hassle. Would that be a problem? I'd like some time with you as well." She asked me.

"Um, no it isn't." I sort of answered. Obviously, I couldn't say no. Something about her aura makes it hard to even try. What does she want with me?

"Come on, Misaky, Kenny-kens is already waiting," Jayson said again. He took me back to the main entrance. We walked outside before we stopped. Ken wasn't there.

"Misaky, how long were you two talking?" Jayson asked me.

"Um, not very long, why?" I asked.

Jayson's bright smile dimmed. "Well, I think it's best to tell you now before it's too late." He sounded more serious than he's been so far. "I'll be very blunt about it... Misaky, stay away from her. That woman is not to be trusted."

"Huh?" That was a bit too blunt for me.

"Kenny-kens and I aren't exactly found of her. He tried so hard to prevent them from getting married, but that didn't stop them. Now you can do what you like, but I advise you, don't be alone with her and do not go with her next weekend." Jayson told me. He talked to her like they were best friends. Now he's telling me not to go near her.

"B-but she didn't seem that bad of a person."

"Who doesn't seem that bad of a person?" I turned and saw Ken walking out the house.

"Oh, Kenny-kens, you're here." Jayson said.

"Who are you guys talking about?"

"Can't we have a conversation without you butting in?" I said to Ken.

"Now, now you two. We were just talking about Mama Baker."

"What? She's here already? She didn't try talking with you, did she?" Ken asked me.

"Yeah, what's the problem?" I watched as Ken and Jayson exchanged a look.

"I thought she wasn't supposed to be here until later?"

"She wasn't. One of her meetings must have gotten cancelled or something. I didn't stay long enough to ask." Jayson told him.

"Hey, what exactly is wrong with her? She wants to meet with me, but the way you two are going on makes me worried." I was already getting a nervous sweat, and nothing has happened yet.

"She said she wants to meet with you?" Ken asked.

"Yeah." I answered. Ken looked at Jayson again, who just shook his head agreeing.

"Well, isn't that nice. Let's just go," Ken had a new look of frustration. I don't know what's going on in this house, but I'm starting to wonder if going in the dungeon would have been better.

The long drive home away from the palace of the Masidone mansion, which holds the most mysterious family of untold secrets, was long and bittersweet.

"Thanks for today, Jay," Ken said as we pulled up to my house.

"No problem. Just give me a ring if you need anything. See yah, Misaky! You can also count on me for whatever you may need."

"Alright, thanks for today, and the cooking lesson. It helped me a lot." I told him. Everything else aside, that was the better part of today.

"Oh, anytime. Kenny-kens, you better continue to look after her."

"Don't worry I'll keep a good eye on her," he assured him. And somehow, I don't doubt that. I walked into my house almost forgetting how small it is after leaving the mansion. My regular, unscripted doors. No maids, and average decoration.

"Even though my house is bigger, I actually would rather live like this," Ken said reading my thoughts.

"Why would you trade all of that for this?"

"It's like you said. It's just a waste of money. Instead of investing all his money on all that stuff, he could use it on something worthwhile," he said. I guess at times, even he can be humble despite what he has. "I know you're wondering who that woman is, so I'll tell you. She's my father's wife that I strongly disapprove of." He suddenly stated.

"What exactly made you so against her?"

"Just know that she's one you don't need to get to know."

"There you go again avoiding the question."

"I'm telling you that she isn't the one to be friends with."

"That's not a real answer to my question." I told him. I heard him sigh again.

"Alright," he said. "It's hard to explain, but I'll try anyway. I'll tell you all about her. What I know at least. I'll tell you anything you'd like whether it's her or me. Now that you've met my father and that woman, it's probably for the best anyway."

"Really?"

"Yeah, really," he said looking at me. He gave in so easily, I'm almost afraid to ask anything now. "So, come on. This could take a while.

Give me your best shot," he demanded and went to sit on the couch.

"O-okay then, let's start with you. Who is Kenneth Jacob Masidone Jr.?" I sat down on the couch next to him.

I don't want much really. Since he told me about him and Sano already, I feel like I already know more than I wanted to know. His background is much more complicated than I imagined. I don't know if I care about his family. Maybe I can take this chance to know more about him.

19

The closer I think I get to a solution to this unusual game I've been thrown in, the further I seem to get from it. I wake up every morning remembering everything that's happened since Ken got here. Starting from him moving in, being able to finally get to know Sano, and being threatened inside the single best house I'll ever step in.

When I realize it's no longer the beginning of the semester and see that this is all real, I wonder just how a normal teenage girl trying to pass her classes really managed to get caught up with two rich high school boys. After all the truths were told at the Masidone mansion, I finally managed to understand Ken, and why he did and acted the way he did. Who knew all it would take was a little home visit. Too bad that home visit came with a price. A price I'm still not ready to pay.

"Katie, I'm freaking out!" I ran to find her when I saw her at school.

"Why? What's wrong?"

"Don't you know? Today is Thursday!"

Katie looked at me like I was insane. "Yeah, and tomorrow is Friday because yesterday was Wednesday, it's just how things work in the real world."

"No, I mean there's just another day and a half before I go see a person that I was specifically told I shouldn't meet! What if I do or say something I shouldn't?"

"Didn't Ken tell you how to deal her or something?"

"He just told me to be myself. What if being myself is wrong?"

"If you made it through a visit with the father, then you should make it through a visit with the wife."

"But he doesn't really like me either, so why would the wife like me at all?"

"They're two different people. Just relax. It'll be fine."

"I don't know. Maybe." I looked up and saw someone walking our way.

"Oh crap! It's Sano! Come this way!" I grabbed Katie and hid in the nearest bathroom.

"Misa, you've been avoiding him all week. When are you going to talk to him?"

"I'll talk with him, just not yet. I'm still not sure how to approach him."

"How about going up to him and saying, 'Hey, Sano, how's life without Ken'?"

"I can't do that! That's moving in way too quick."

"Well, ducking behind lockers and bathrooms and running home after school every day sure isn't going to cut it," she said. I've been trying so hard not to run into him.

"Well, he's already enduring so much. I don't want to bring him down any more than he probably is.

"You're so caring. But that caring behavior is going to be your downfall."

"Okay then. How should I do it? Should I ask him directly, or call, maybe send a letter?"

"How about we start with not running away every time you even imagine him around? Asking over the phone isn't a good way to do it. You should probably just ask at school, just not when many people are around."

"I don't know if I can do that," I said.

"Why not? You've been talking with him just fine before."

"I know, but this time is different."

"Not really. You're just trying to find out the truth is all. It's not like you've been sent on an assassination mission or something." Katie always makes it seem like it's nothing.

I wish I could see it that way. Right now, it's more than just something simple. He lied to me and never once said anything about Ken after pretending he didn't know anything when asking about him. Ken and I have talked about this for a long time, but he won't say anything for him. He said he couldn't tell me if he wanted because he doesn't really know what's going on with him right now anyway.

The school day was so long, but it's almost over now. And I was still avoiding Sano. If I ever plan to sort this out, I'll have to stop hiding. I still don't know how to approach him. Our last conversation was the good-bye at his house, and he was being just a little strange then. Did he know that I was going to find out everything?

"Hey, player." Another person I've been trying to avoid came up to me.

"What do you want, Jennifer?"

"Oh, not much. Just saw you here. Are you waiting for the betrayer?" She asked.

"What?"

"Yeah, I heard the story. I know all about Sano now."

"And who told you?"

"Papa Masy did." Hearing that only makes it certain that she did indeed live at Ken's house, and that Jayson is the only one that can get away with calling him that.

"Well, if you heard the whole story, you'd know it wasn't as if he wanted to go just because."

"Oh, I heard the whole story. And I know Papa Masy had good reason for holding the truth. It's that Sano who couldn't understand that and left them in despair. That's some guy you picked up." She rolled her eyes.

"Who could understand and accept that the woman they grew up with wasn't their mother so easily?"

"So that is the reason you've been avoiding me." My blood flow stopped as I turned and saw Sano standing there.

"Sano! W-when did you get here?"

"Well, if it isn't the man of the hour," Jennifer said with a look of disgust. "I have no more to say to either of you." I watched as she flung her head around and left, finally leaving me alone with Sano. But this isn't how I wanted it to be.

"So, I guess you know now," He started after an awkward silence. "And I guess you're upset that I didn't tell you."

"Well, it was surprising." I told him.

"Yeah. I'm sorry. I guess I thought it was better this way."

"Why would you think it would have been better to lie about who your father was and who Ken was to you?"

"Well, it's a little hard to explain. And right now, isn't the best time to talk about it." He said, looking past me.

"Hey, Misa, you read- Oh hey, Sano." Katie was walking up to us and stopped realizing I was talking to Sano.

"Hey, Katie. I should probably go. We'll talk later," Sano said before walking off.

"Sorry, Misa. I didn't know that was Sano you were talking to," Katie said apologetic. "Did you guys talk things out?"

"Not completely. And if it weren't for Jennifer, we wouldn't have been talking in the first place. I'm so glad you came when you did."

"What did Jennifer have to do with this?" She asked.

"She was blabbing about everything just when Sano was coming around."

"So, she knows who he actually is?

"Yeah, she does, and now she'll be even more annoying to have around because she's taking Ken's father's side."

"Speaking of Ken, how are the two of you doing? In class today, you hardly even looked in his direction. Are you still upset with him?

"Oh, that. It's nothing."

"That doesn't sound like nothing," she said reading through me.

"Everything is fine. I was just trying to focus in class today.

"You? Trying to stay focused in class? On your own will?" she said with disbelief.

"Yeah, is that a problem?"

"For a regular person, no, but for you, I'm a bit skeptical."

"Well accept it because that's what I was doing."

"You know, Misa, if you're trying to hide something, you should at least learn from those two on how to do a better job at it," Katie said. That hit a little harder than it should have.

I made a mad dash for home once the coast was clear for leaving the school grounds. It feels so good to be home. But I couldn't continue to run from him. Especially now that he knows, us talking will happen soon than later.

"Mimi, you home?" Hearing Ken's voice coming from the kitchen made me forget what I was thinking.

"Hey, Mimi, how's about we go out somewhere?" He asked.

"Go out? Like, in public? I'd rather not."

"Aw come on. Are you still mad about this morning? I said I was sorry. How was I to know you were still taking a shower?"

"I had the water running! It's not exactly silent either."

"Not at the time I came in. Besides, you were covered, *mostly*," he said, lingering on that last word.

"You're such a pervert!"

"You say such harsh words." He said acting hurt.

Things between me and Ken managed to go back to how it was. After that side of him on Saturday, I got to know a little of his background. But at no point did I get to understand how he became such a perv.

"That's beside the point right now. What are you doing home so early?"

"Early? This is roughly the time I always arrive. Were you expecting me to be out?" He asked.

"Well, you have come in later before and take random trips back home."

"That has happened before, but after all that has started to develop, I managed to limit my many unexpected summoning to the weekends."

"So, you won't be like, going home or anywhere?" I haven't forgotten what's coming for me this weekend. I was trying to find a subtle way to bring it up.

"Is this about this weekend?" He figured me out. "Misa, if you're that worried about meeting Jocelyn, you don't have to."

"No, I already said I would." I can't tell her I don't want to and have her wondering about me and why I couldn't make it after saying yes.

"She might not even take long with you. She's been quite busy lately. She may even be leaving soon. But I doubt she'd go before her meeting with you Saturday," he said. I guess I couldn't get out of it from inconvenience.

"How long has she and your father been together?"

"Jayson told me she's been around since he was with my mother. But he never knew how long, so he's not certain."

"And you both don't get along with her?"

"Well, as I said last time, since the time I first met her, she's been trying to play the mother role, but there have been times she wasn't 'motherly' when my father wasn't around. I really believe she's up to something, but I don't know what it is yet." He said. There's actually something he doesn't know. I mean who wouldn't want to be with a successful businessman. But if she's been around for this long, she's either not that bad, or really good at whatever it is she's doing.

"But anyway, she may not even ask you anything. She probably just wants to get to know you. However, I do advise you don't tell her too much," he added.

"Why do you say that?"

"One thing she has is a good memory, and she'll remember any little detail given to her." Now I have to be really cautious about what I say. "But hey, on a brighter note, it's still nice out. How's about that outing?" He asked again. He must want to change the subject.

"My answer is still no!"

"Aw come on. I said sorry already. Do you want to punish me to make it even? Come, punish me however you want." He braced himself as if waiting to be hit.

"The punishment is me not going," I said walking off.

"That's it? No spanking? No physical abuse?"

"No, you freaking perv!" I was about to head upstairs when I heard his phone start ringing. He looked at it before answering.

"Misa, if you don't mind, I'm taking this outside." He answered it as he walked out. It must be a call from his dad or someone. Thinking about it now, Sano and Ken really are related. They act the same way with everything. They both have their own responsibilities that they take on without much complaint, and they're both good at everything they do. I just wonder what it was that made them break apart.

"She's here now?" I heard Ken's voice get loud after standing outside for about ten minutes. I peeked out the window to see what was going on. He was talking to someone standing out there with him. It looks like Jayson.

"Oh, Misaky!" Jayson waved to me after spotting me in the window. Ken turned and saw me there then opened the door. "Oh, it's been forever since I last saw you!" He said as if he didn't just see me five days ago. "It's good to see you again. But unfortunately, I've brought you some good news and a tiny bit of bad." Jayson put his fingers close together showing the *bit*. But a drive all the way here for a *bit* of news seems like a stretch.

"Okay then. Let's start with the good news?" I said.

"Well, the good news is that you don't have to take time out of your precious weekend to see Mama Baker." he said.

"Really? That is good news. But what's the bad news?"

"Well, the bad news is that she's here today." he said throwing his head in the direction of his car. My eyes widened as I looked to the street and saw someone sitting in the back seat of his car.

"She's here to see me today?"

20

"I'm sorry, Misaky. But she has to leave, and she refuses to go before seeing you first. But it won't be for long, just a short ride." Jayson looked at Ken. "And it'll be just those two."

"So, I can't go?" Ken asked.

"She wants it to be just the two of them so they can have their 'girl talk' together." He air quoted girl talk. "But luckily, I managed to let her have me drive, so I won't let anything happen." He tried assuring me. I feel like I'm about to go into a job interview I didn't prep for. "I can give you about five minutes, I promise I'll try to make this as painless as possible." He held up his pinky finger as if to pinky promise. "I'll be waiting in the car for you." Jayson gave a look to Ken and turned to head toward his car.

"Misa, I know how you like to overthink things, so just relax and don't think much of it." Ken tried giving me a pep talk.

"Easy for you to say, you know how to handle her. Jayson had even said to stay away from her."

"Okay, so we probably exaggerated when you first met her. She isn't that bad."

"Yeah, you say that now."

"I know things have been a little overwhelming for you the past week, but you have nothing to worry about. And Jayson will be with you. He already said he'd step in if things get bad." Ken's trying his hardest to put my mind at ease. It's strange, but I guess I should just listen to him and hope this'll be all right.

It's time again I got back into this high-class lifestyle. I took a big inhale as I started my solo walk to the car. I went around to the back seat on the driver's side since Mrs. Baker was on the other side.

"Well good afternoon, Misa." She said to me as soon as I got in. She was all smiles wearing a black dress that had a low ruffled cut and stopped just at her crossed knees. She looks as if she's going to a business party. I hope this stays a drive since I have on a simple white shirt and jeans not thinking I was going anywhere special until the weekend.

"Alright, Mama Baker, we're ready to go," Jayson said to us.

"Jayson, would you take us to the villa?" She asked.

"The villa is our destination? It's so far away. We don't want to keep Misaky out too long."

"It's not as far as the house. I already checked traffic, and it shouldn't slow us down. I have something to do there, so it's the perfect distance for our little get to know each other session." She looked at me when she finished talking. I tried looking away without being obvious.

"Alrighty then, Mama Baker." Jayson pulled off.

"Haven't we discussed that name issue?"

"Sorry, it's just so catchy!"

"I'm sure you believe it is," she said with a hint of irritants in her voice. We started our journey to this villa place. Jayson had music playing low, so it helped with the awkward silence.

"Well now, Miss Macky, I'm sure you're wondering why I suddenly came today." She asked me.

"Well, it was unexpected."

"I know, so please excuse the surprise visit. Turns out, I'm unavailable this weekend, so I didn't think you'd mind my dropping by today."

"Oh, no, I didn't have much work or anything today."

"I see. You have the opposite of my schedule. But speaking of your work, how is school for you? Do you have friends? Are you in any activities?" The interrogation began.

"I guess I'm okay in school, but my best friend and Ken sometimes help me."

"So, you only have one friend then?"

"I have some others, but I only have one close one. We've known each other since we were in the first grade."

"That's an impressive friendship. Does Little Kenneth know about this friend."

"Yeah, we all have the same first period class together."

"That's nice for you all to be together so much. You know, I used to have a good friend back when I was in high school, but then something happened, and we stopped being friends after that."

"What happened?" I asked curiously.

"Well, to make a long story short, it turned out that my friend had been dating my boyfriend while I was still with him." She said it short and sweet without much emotion for something like that to have happened.

"That did set me back dating wise for a couple of years. It wasn't until I met Kenneth that I was able to date comfortably again. But of course, we didn't date right away. He was with someone else at the time." He must be a popular guy.

"Have you had any relationships, Misa?" She asked next.

"Me? N-no I haven't."

"Really? You're a pretty little thing. I would have expected for you to have been in at least two or three relationships by now."

"I mean, I've had people I've liked, but never more than that."

"Ah, I see. What about these boys you've liked?" she got curious.

"Misaky, it's getting a bit chilly in here, do you mind if I turn down the AC?" Jayson asked.

"No, I don't mind."

"What about you, Mama Baker?"

"I don't mind either, Jayson. I am starting to feel a bit of a chill as well actually."

"Alright then, taking it down a peg." He adjusted the temperature in the car. "It feels better already. We'll be having warmer bodies in a minute. We'll also be at the villa shortly as well," he informed us.

"Thanks for the update, Jayson. Now where was I?" She seemed a little bothered as she remembered where our conversation left off.

"Oh right, about the boy you favored. Tell me about him. Is he still around? Do you still like him?" I wasn't sure if it was a good idea to mention anything about Sano. She probably knows who he is.

"Um, no." I tried lying.

"No, he isn't around or no you don't like him?" She and Mr. Masidone may have talked about me since I've been there. If Jennifer knows about Sano now, lying about him isn't the best thing to do.

"I may still like him, but since Ken came around, I guess things haven't felt quite the same."

"What do you mean by that?"

"Well," I started, but I don't know exactly how to finish it without saying too much. "It's just that Ken is around with this marriage thing, so I thought I'd see what he was about."

"I see. So, you're just seeing what he has to offer before you make a move."

"Uh, when you put it that way... I mean, Ken is a nice guy, he just can be a little confusing sometimes."

"Confusing? Lately, I haven't been able to spend much time with him, so I can't say for certain what his behavior could be like these days. Tell me, why do you say he's confusing?"

"I just don't always understand his motives."

"His motives? I see. He is a growing boy in his teens, and he's also living with another girl whose parents are rarely at home, so I would understand that he may be, in other words, tempted?" she asked. Unlike Mr. Masidone, I couldn't treat it like a rhetorical question. She was waiting for an answer.

"Uh, I guess you could say that." I'm not sure what I'm saying anymore. This conversation is headed down a dangerous road.

"Of course, I was against a sixteen-year-old boy living together with a teenage girl. I don't understand why Kenneth agreed to such a thing." She said. I guess it wouldn't help my case if I told her I didn't necessarily agree to it either.

"But so far, things haven't turned out for the worse as I thought they would." She continued on. I looked past her and out the window wondering if I could figure out where I was so if I needed to make a quick escape, I could. But I couldn't make out the area as we were up driving by the lake. "Now, you are aware of Jenny, right? Little Kenneth's first choice?" She asked.

"Yes, I know who she is."

"How do you feel knowing someone else has a high interest in little Kenneth?"

"Um, I'm not sure."

"You're not sure? You don't mind that someone else is also trying to get his attention?" Her tone changed.

"W-well it's not that. It's just um, it's Ken's choice so it's up to him who he wants to choose I guess." I told her. Why do I feel so much déjà vu?

"Interesting. You know, it sounds to me like you're not all that serious about Little Kenneth," her entire tone and expression turned serious. "Misa dear, I'm sure you heard this from his father when you talked with him last week, but Little Kenneth can't go around playing little games. He needs to know that he will be well on his feet when the time comes. And to have a good and healthy life, he should have a good loving partner that will help him and not bring him heartache and stress while managing a big company. You do understand that, yes?" She looked at me with stern eyes.

"Yes, I do."

"So, what will you do? Are you going to get serious about Kenneth, or go with some other boy?" She asked so bluntly. She was staring at me, waiting for my answer. I was searching for one, and honestly, in that moment, I felt whatever I said could've been wrong.

"Alright! We are approaching our destination!" Jayson broke the tension thankfully. The house we were pulling up to was almost as big as their mansion. The driveway was longer as it wrapped around in front by the lake. The house looks like it has a fresh coating of white and the large clear windows make up most of the walls on both floors. There was an outdoor pool by the far side in the backyard surrounded by the extended deck. I'm almost positive I've seen this place on TV somewhere.

"Ah, this is my stop then." Mrs. Baker looked out to the house as she gathered her things.

"So, you don't intend to talk more with Misa here?" Jayson asked.

"Even though our time was short, I do understand Misa can't be out too late. But I also have a meeting here soon. I'll let her be today. Misa dear," She turned back to me, "I'll be looking forward to speaking with you again to finish where we like off all right? I expect by then you'll have a more concrete answer." Mrs. Baker and Mr. Masidone must be around each other a lot as they've both given me the same look, waiting to hear the same thing from me.

"Um, okay." I answered her. She seemed satisfied with that simple reply as she uncrossed her legs and stepped out of the car.

"I'll see you later Jayson," she said to him.

"See you later Mama Baker! Don't work yourself too hard!"

Jayson waved to her and drove off after she entered through the gates.

"Misaky, I drove as fast as I felt wasn't too illegal and took all the short cuts I could find." Jayson started after he got back to the highway. "But she still managed to say a bit too much. I was getting a bit worried if she kept going."

He could say that again...

"I can't help but think she was just a little off today. She still got under my skin toward the end there."

"I wasn't sure what to say for some of the things she asked me." I admitted to him.

"Yeah, she had no right to ask you about personal relations like that so soon. But I also think you shouldn't have mentioned liking someone else. I don't know if Papa Masy told her the whole story on our lovely little Sano, so it's probably best not to mention him."

"I wasn't sure either."

"It's good you didn't mention any names. I know she's already in favor of Jenny, so giving her more fuel wouldn't do anyone any good."

"I figured as much." Just listening to the way she said Jenny's name was enough to know she liked her more than me.

"Well, regardless of it all, she's going to be tied up for a while, so, you can rest easy." He tried to assure me.

Mrs. Baker was just Ken's stepmom. She acts like she could be his real mom. Which means I have to watch her like his real mom. I may be free of her for now, but I must be ready for the next time I see them. They're both waiting for an answer from me, so I know we'll see each other again.

21

"Alright! Home again. Not too late, not too early. The perfect time to go clubbing!" he laughed at himself as he pulled up in front of my house. Once again, my house feels so small compared to just looking at that other house of theirs. I wouldn't mind seeing the villa again. Just not with Mrs. Baker around.

"Thanks for the ride, Jayson."

"Oh please, call me Jay. And no problem. I assume Kenny-kens is waiting for you."

"Yeah, he probably is," I said as I looked at my small house that holds the richest mysterious teenage boy.

"That reminds me," he started again, "there was one thing she said that I did kind of agree on."

"What was that?"

"When she asked you about Kenny-kens and how you felt. I think you two should spend a little more time together. I could tell that you didn't have an answer to that, so you should see more about him so you can have an answer. I know you both are still young, but you're old enough to know who you do and don't like."

"Yeah, you're right. I guess I should. I mean, he isn't all that bad. He even came clean about the everything... but he won't admit to being a pervert." That last part slipped out, but Jayson laughed anyway.

"Oh, Misaky, I should apologize for that one. I guess I taught him about one too many things. He was a growing boy, and his mother wasn't around as much since Mama Baker was there, so he couldn't go to anyone with certain questions."

"I guess that's understandable. But why do you always call her that when she doesn't like it?"

"Trust me, Misaky, if you lived with her as long as I have, seeing her get all bent out of shape because of a name is very amusing." He said with a grin. The more I talk with Jayson, the more I wonder if he's really Ken's father. "Well, Misaky, I should let you go. I'm sure you have homework or something that you need to do. Tell Kenny-kens to give me a ring."

"Will do."

"Alright then. See you on the fine side!" He waved to me as he pulled off.

I was finally back home. Looking at the time, we weren't out that late. It still felt like the longest trip I've had to endure. But after being with Jayson and Mrs. Baker, I somewhat got to understand where Ken is coming from. It seems like Jayson was a big part in his life. The way they talk to each other makes it seem like he really is his big brother.

Speaking of Ken, it seemed awful quiet for someone to be here. Did he leave and go somewhere? I went into the kitchen, and it smelled like he made something before he left. I might have made something good last weekend with Jayson, but I don't think I'm good enough to be left alone yet. Maybe I could make something simple like a sandwich. It's no fish and chips, but I can do this on my own.

Ken and I haven't really been spending a whole lot of time together. I've been around Sano more with the frequent house visits. It was only just recently Ken, and I tried hanging out together, and he's been here for months it seems. He kind of knows about me. But even though he gave me the opportunity to ask what I wanted to know about him, I wasn't really sure what it was I wanted to ask, so I couldn't ask him anything. I think it would be easier to just do a little more with him than to just keep asking questions.

"You sure have a strange way of making sandwiches."

My heart did a complete flip at the sound of Ken's voice suddenly close behind me. "K-Ken! When'd you get here?"

"Just got in. But what's this you got going on here?" He was looking at the plate that had the bread slices and meat on, still in the package sleeve.

"Oh! How did this happen?" I've made sandwiches plenty of times, but always managed to take the meat slices out of its packaging first.

"My guess is that brain of yours was focusing on something else. Am I right?" He asked. He knew that he was right, so why ask?

"Where were you?" I asked him instead.

"Well, mom, I was out talking with someone, but that took longer than expected. However, you're back sooner than I expected. How was it?"

"It was okay. It wasn't as bad as I thought."

"That's good. Where'd you all go?"

"The villa."

"The villa? You made it there and back so soon? It's over by the lake at least an hour away. Why did you go there?"

"Well, with Jayson's driving, it wasn't that long, and she needed to go there for a meeting or something."

"A meeting? That doesn't sound right."

"What do you mean by that?" I asked.

"No, well, I mean, she doesn't normally make appointments there."

"Is she not supposed to?"

"Meetings were always done at the office. But I'm sure she got that approved by my father before doing it."

"I see. How is your father?" I suddenly wondered. Ken raised an eyebrow at my question. "I mean, when I saw him last week, he asked Jayson to bring him his medicine, so I wondered if there was something wrong," I explained.

"I see. Well, he has been a little under the weather these days. I assume his work isn't helping him."

"Is he going to be alright?"

"My dad won't let a little illness get in his way. He went to the doctor the other day and said nothing serious was going on. Why the sudden curiosity of my father?" He asked.

"Well, both your father and Mrs. Baker keep saying how you have an important life ahead of you, so you need a good wife to support you. I was wondering if this job is so important and so stressful, would I really be able to help you?"

"Are you concerned about me, Mimi?" He looked at me and smiled.

"It is a very intense line of business at times, but my father had complications long before it."

"How do you know so much?"

"I overheard him talking about it before. And I did try to ask him about it once before, and he didn't tell me." Even something as important as health is kept secret. They have to be spies or something.

"But I think what Mimi is worried about is whether she's actually able to handle and fit into all of it. Remember, you aren't actually the one who's getting this position. I am. So, the only thing you have to worry about in that area, is working on accepting me first, and then you can worry about things like not trying to poison me," he said looking at the still assembled sandwich with the wrappings. He continued giving me that smile of his like he's super confident about everything.

"Now that this is sorted, how about we make something that you can get your teeth through?"

He started helping me fix the mess. But for some reason, I feel that he's got something he's not telling me again. Now that I think about it, he did say he was meeting with someone. Who was that someone? I should bring it up, but I didn't want to start any trouble again, so I left it at that for today since this day just seems never ending.

The rest of the night went smoother, and morning came before I knew it. I got up on time and made it to class early. I was looking for Katie who actually hasn't shown up yet, and she's never late for class. I kept looking at the door and the next person to walk in was Sano. I can't hide from him now. I should probably ask him about what he wanted to say today after school when I know he'll be alone.

But his face looks slightly distressed. Something must have happened.

"Hey, Misa." I turned and saw Katie.

"Katie. I didn't see you walk in. It's weird that I'm on time, and you aren't. And you look horrible. You all right?" Her hair was thrown in a little ponytail, and she wore her glasses, which she hardly ever wears to school. Contacts are her preference.

"That's exactly what I need to hear right now. I was feeling sick last night and overslept."

"Are you alright now?"

"Yeah, I slept like a brick. I actually feel great. I just didn't have time to look it. But you also look a little anxious. Something happen?"

"Not just something. It's a big something."

"Something like?"

"She came yesterday."

"She? As in that lady? Why yesterday? I thought she wanted to see you tomorrow."

"I thought so too. But she's like super busy so she came yesterday."

"Oh. So, what did she say?" Right as I went to reply, the bell rang, and everyone went to their seats.

"I'll tell you later." Now that the room is quieting down, I wouldn't want anyone like Jennifer to hear. She came strolling in with her hair in loose curls bouncing around just as she walked to her seat. She side-eyed me as she passed. But she stayed in her place and just sat down. Her sudden quiet behavior made the time and day go by unexpectedly smoothly. I kept bracing myself for an attack, but nothing. It was already the end of the day, and I found Katie at her locker and told her about yesterday.

"On the plus side, she wasn't what you thought she was and was going to do away with you."

"Yeah, but it still wasn't a pleasant evening. It was so uncomfortable. And I'm pretty sure her view of me got worse."

"She's probably going to make it more uncomfortable now that she knows you got other options you're looking at."

"Yeah, I know, I spoke too much."

"And since Jenny and Jennifer are living in their house, they have the upper hand on staying on everyone's good side which is why they're on her side."

"I just want to know why they're living in his house anyway," I said.

"We don't know the minds of rich people. Her parents must really want to get into Ken's family like yours do. And if that's the case, you need to step your game up."

"What do you mean step my game up?"

"Well, if you want Ken, then you have to compete with some top-notch people." She reminded me.

"Who said I wanted Ken? I- I still haven't decided."

"You need to do something. If he was willing to let you go to his house, then maybe Sano likes you too."

"But he lied to me."

"And so did Ken but you forgave him. It's hard to find good guys these days," she shook her head.

"What are you talking about? I haven't seen you and Eden fight even once since the two of you have been together."

"Yeah, but we still have some minor disagreements on things."

"That's nothing like choosing between these two mystery guys." I told her.

"Okay, well then, I have another idea. Why don't you choose neither of them?"

"What?"

"If it's such a problem for you, then why don't you ditch those two and find someone else?" She suggested. I know that that is a possibility, even more so now that I've met Ken's parents and they don't agree with me, but could I just let them go? That thought never crossed my mind. "Hey, I think I see Sano up ahead," Katie gave a head motion behind me. "Now's your chance to go ask him if you two can talk."

"Yeah, but I think he's talking to someone," I said looking in the distance. I was trying to see who it was, and I gasped slightly as I saw it was Ken.

"I thought you said those two don't talk anymore." She said seeing the same thing I was.

"I thought that too. Or at least that's what he told me. What could they be talking about?"

"Want to go and see?" she asked, walking forward.

"Wait no! I can't do that. They're like... together. It would be too weird!" I held her back.

"Well, what then Misa?"

"I don't know. I mean if they don't talk, what's there to talk about?" I asked.

"Oh, I don't know. Old times, back in the day... you." Katie pointed to me.

"Me?"

"Yeah, I mean now that the cat's out the bag, they're probably talking about it." Katie thought.

I looked to her, then looked back down the hallway with kids shuffling around wanting to go home. Except for Ken and Sano standing and talking calmly. My heart started skipping beats. What was Sano telling Ken? Or what was Ken telling Sano? Or what is being said period! The suspense was killing me!

22

"If you're going to just stand here and eavesdrop, you might want to get closer to be able to hear," Katie suggested since I haven't budged from the lockers where we stood just looking at them.

"I can't, Katie. What if they see me?"

"That's why it's called sneaking."

"Yeah, and I'm obviously not good at that!" I admitted.

"Yeah, you have been getting caught."

"Gee thanks. That really helps," I said. But then I suddenly felt an unwanted presence.

"—sa!" I heard something that sounded like my name in the distance.

"What was that?" Katie asked.

"Sounds like…" We both turned behind us to see what it was.

"Misa!"

"John!" We both whispered.

"If he keeps shouting like that, they'll definitely know we're here," Katie said, so we walked back to him.

"Misa! Mi—" I ran up to him and covered his mouth.

"Keep quiet!" I said.

I heard him gasp, "You must be reconsidering me with this kind of physical contact. Oh Mi—" I cut him off again holding my hand to his face this time.

"Will you keep your voice down? I don't want them to hear." We looked back behind us.

"Who don't you want to hear?" He asked.

"Misa, I think they're looking this way," Katie said.

"Let's go!" We started walking away leaving John behind. He hasn't been anything but trouble these days, it's best to keep him at a distance for now.

"Misa, you can be so childish sometimes," Katie said following behind me. "If you were just going to run away if they saw you, then there was no point in staying."

"I know, but John was being so loud, I panicked. Now I really won't know what they were talking about."

"You can just ask them." She said like it was the most obvious thing to do.

"If I was going to do that then there was no need to wait over there."

"Well, unless you can read minds, then your only way of knowing is if you ask."

"Hey, Katie. Misa." We looked and saw Eden coming toward us.

"Hey." She waved to him getting that light bounce in her step she gets every time she sees him.

"Are we still going tonight?" He asked her.

"Of course we are."

"Where are you two going?" I asked.

"We're going to that new restaurant that opened last week," Katie answered.

"Oh, sounds fun."

"Yeah, I heard the food there is really good, so we thought we'd give it a go."

"Yeah, so I'll pick you up at seven?" He asked her.

"Sounds good Eden," she said. I wonder will I ever look at someone the way she looks at Eden. The sparkle in her eye shows she's really into him. The only look I have in my eyes is confusion.

"Oh, right. Before I forget," He looked to me, "Misa, can you give this to Ken?" He handed me a folder.

"Sure, what is it?"

"It's the layout of our science project. He, Sano, and I are in the same group."

I gasped, "You're all in that AP class?"

"Yeah, and that project is really important so would you be able to get that to him ASAP?"

"Yeah, no problem."

"Alright thanks, see you guys," he said, walking away. I looked down to the folder, then looked to Katie.

"I didn't even know they knew each other, let alone all had a class together," I said.

"I didn't either. He never told me, and I always tell him about you and Ken." Katie looked betrayed.

"Oh, well I'm glad my situation is a nice conversation starter for you both."

"I don't tell him the private stuff, just basic. But at least that's one thing they could be talking about."

"I guess, but why are they all in a group together?"

"I don't know, but I have to get going. I'll ask him that later. Why don't you find Ken, give him the papers, and ask him your questions?"

"You always want me to do something."

"I'm not going to do it for you. This is your real-life drama. You have to complete your own storyline. See yah." She said walking away.

"You're doing that confusing thing again," I said to her. But she kept going.

Walking back home on my own, I couldn't help but be curious about what kind of project they were doing and took a peek inside the folder. It looks like they're building some kind of rocket. I knew Ken had advanced classes, but it looks like they're using some pretty complex formulas. It must be more than just a simple rocket for this to done in an AP class. But if Ken, Eden, and Sano are doing this, it'll be done with ease. That brings me back to the real question. Why are they in a group together?

"Misa, you're home." My mom surprised me as I walked in the door, and she was coming from her room.

"Mom? What are you doing here?"

"What, I can't be in the house I'm paying for?" She said.

"No, you can, it's just you never are."

"I know, but I just got a few days off."

"Aren't you still working for all that vacation time you took?"

"Are you trying to get rid of me? They just hired more people in this branch, so they're giving some of us some extra wiggle room for taking a few extra days. Your father will be here next week actually. I wanted to make it where we had the same days, but we couldn't get the days changed. So, you have me now, and your father is coming Monday." This is probably the longest my parents will be around in a long time.

I went upstairs and passed Ken's room and thought to just put the folder there.

"Oh, Ken, you're back too." I heard my mother's voice just as I was about to enter his room. I can't remember the last time those two talked alone.

"How is everything going?" She asked him.

"It's going well. I'm enjoying my stay here more so than I do at home," he replied.

"It's good to know you're enjoying yourself. Has Misa been giving you any trouble?" There she goes asking unnecessary questions.

"No more trouble than I'd expect. She's been a delight to be around." What does he mean 'than he'd expect'?

"I'm glad you're both getting along well. I was so worried that things weren't going to be working out."

"Everything is going fine here thankfully. How have you been doing? I haven't seen you around here lately." He turned the conversation around.

"That's sweet of you to ask. I'm doing just fine, thank you. I guess your dad's been hiring some people out here, so he gave me and Misa's father a couple days off. But he won't be here until next week."

"Really? He must be working on something big this quarter. But I'm sure you must be tired from all the working you've been doing, so I hope you rest up on your time off."

"Thanks for your concern, but I'm one of the rare few who loves working, so I'm not as tired as you may think. But maybe I should take it easy."

"You should. I'd hate for you to put a strain on yourself and ruin your beauty with worry." I can practically see the phony smile on his face. Is he trying to hit on my mother or something?

"If only Mark was here. He could take some notes from you. Such a sweet boy you are."

"What can I say, it is true. I have no reason to lie." He said. I must put a stop to this! I ran downstairs as fast as I could.

"Misa, you've come back down," Mom said. "I knew he was a sweet boy, but you didn't tell me what a charmer he is."

Lies, it's all lies he's feeding you! He's a pervert in disguise!

"Have you been telling her false things about me, Mimi?" Ken asked.

"I told you not to call me that, and here." I was upset and just handed him the folder.

"Oh, it's the project outline, great. How did you get this?"

"Eden gave it to me to give to you. Said you needed it ASAP."

"Yeah, it's going to take some time and careful planning, so we have to memorize everything about it. Mrs. Macky, you don't mind if my group comes over to work on our project next week, do you?"

"Oh, not at all, you're always welcome to invite your friend's over." She told him. So, this means they're coming here?! As in Sano will be in my house? At the same time as Ken? This just isn't right.

"Thank you. Oh, and unfortunately, I won't get to enjoy your company while you're here because I will be leaving for home for the weekend in a few hours. That will give you two ladies some quality mother-daughter time that I'm sure is well overdue," he said.

"That does sound like a nice idea, Misa, why don't we go somewhere together tomorrow?"

"Sure, why not?" I was still trying to come to terms with them being here in my house. Now is not the time for mother-daughter events.

"That's great for the two of you. I guess I should go gather my things and get ready." He left and went upstairs just like that. Something about the way he left made me wonder.

I didn't know he was going home this weekend. That means if I want to talk to him, I should do it now before it's too late. I won't know anything unless I ask. I'm just so curious about everything now. They couldn't have been discussing the project that long after school if they could've done that in the classroom.

"Since you're standing in my doorway, I guess I should ask you now since I didn't downstairs, but you don't mind us working here, do you?" Ken asked me. I somehow found myself standing in Ken's doorway.

"How many of you are there?"

"Just three of us— Eden, Sano, and I."

"I didn't know you all had the same class together."

"Yeah. Turns out I wasn't the only one who learns things quickly. But it's still going to take time and preparations to make. Probably will take at most a few days," he said as if that wasn't a short amount of time to complete something with those formulas.

"I guess it's not a problem. But just curious to know, why is it going to be done here?" I asked.

"Eden's house is small, and we need a bit of space. Sano doesn't want the children to be around our materials."

"But he's the only one taking care of them, where will they go?"

"He said something about taking them to a relative's house. You worried?" It wasn't until he asked that I realized I said that out loud.

"W-well I just wondered."

"He's a smart guy. He wouldn't abandon them and leave them home by themselves."

"Yeah, I know. He wouldn't let anything happen to those kids," I said. I paused for a moment before I continued. "So, you and he are like, friends now?"

"Hmm, I wonder about that. Right now, we're just working on this project that's worth almost fifty percent of our final grade." That's sounds intense.

"If you still aren't on good terms with each other, why are you in a group together?"

"Everyone had to be in groups of three, except for the one of four, and we were the only ones left. This project didn't allow us to work individually."

"Did you want to work by yourself?"

"I usually prefer to since whenever I'm put in a group, I do all the work anyway, but I know that wouldn't be the case with us three." I know Sano would never put all the work on one person.

"What's got you all curious?" He asked.

"What do you mean?"

"You only ask me a series of questions when something's up." I felt a bit of cold sweat down my face. He's seen through me.

"N-nothing is up. I was just wondering what was going on before you turned my house into your after-school hangout spot."

"You don't like people in your house?" He asked.

"It's not that. I'm just not used to many people being here."

"It'll only be us three and we'll try to finish as quickly as we can." I guess he answered my question, but something still isn't sitting right with me.

"Do you still have something to ask? You have that cute, worried look," he said.

"Humph! Only creeps find other peoples' misery cute."

"You are always calling me a pervert, so what can I say? Your expressions are so cute! Oh, see now you're showing that cute angry face," he said as I was slowly getting annoyed. "Is this your way of trying to get me to stay with you this weekend? I can stay here, and we can cuddle all day."

"Um, no. And thanks to you, I already have plans this weekend with my mom."

"Ah, that's right. I'm sure that'll be fun."

"Yeah, not really," I said.

"You should be happy you can spend some time with your mother," Ken said with almost a bit of envy in his voice. It made me realize his first statement wasn't sarcasm. I forgot he doesn't get to spend a whole lot of time with his mother since he has a stepmom.

"It'll be better than doing nothing by myself all weekend. What are you going to be doing?" I asked to get off the subject.

"Well, that depends on if my father has work he'd like me to do. If not, then I have something else I need to finish doing that I left there." He does so much, yet he's always smiling. What keeps him so upbeat? "You know, it's refreshing to hear you asking about me when there's not a catch to it."

"You're always doing something. I was simply curious to know what." Although I did originally come here wanting to ask about Sano, now we're here talking about him.

"Mimi's been thinking about me? That's so cute. I hope I'm going through your mind all the time."

In a way, he kind of is since I'm trying to figure out what to do with him. But I could never tell him that. Just being here talking to him really isn't all that bad. Maybe it's because he lives a life I could never fully understand.

And Sano and I aren't exactly the same, but we're more alike than he is to Ken since he doesn't live in their mansion anymore. Ken has been trying to make things work between us and I haven't been doing anything. Thinking about what Katie said earlier about letting them go, imagining how things would be without them now really wouldn't be the same. I haven't talked to Sano yet to even build back up our relationship we were getting. Maybe I should just work with one at a time. But which would be easier to start with?

"Hey is this bag of M&M's open or not?" Ken started waving his hand in front of my face.

"What? Hey! Don't use that old name."

"I called your name like three times just now and you weren't responding. You should work on that spacing out thing. I just got a text from Jay. He said he's coming earlier than planned, so he'll be here soon to get me. Guess that'll give you even more time to be thinking about me," he said holding that same smile. "I'll take my things and go wait downstairs."

"Okay then." I watched as he picked up his book bag and another small bag he usually takes back home with him, and walked towards me.

"You alright there, Mimi?" He looked at me confused and I looked at him in the same way. In this position reminds me of how Katie was looking at Eden and I saw sparkles in her eyes. I wonder how I would know it's in mine?

He was waiting for me to respond to him. I looked down trying to understand this sudden impulse I was beginning to feel. I don't know why, but since he's leaving, I feel the need to say something to him now.

"Um, I'm fine, but uh, n-next weekend, how about we go somewhere?" I spat the question out so fast I don't even know what I'm saying. I looked back to Ken, and he looked even more confused, and I just looked away.

"Are... are you asking me on a date?" He couldn't believe it, and neither could I.

"I didn't say date. It's two people going out into public at the same time, which happen to know each other, and going to the same place."

"Sounds like a date to me, and I'm going to think it that way! Of course, I would love to! You just made me so happy, Mimi, I could kiss you."

"Hey, let's not go that far." I took a few steps back, not sure what to expect.

"You've made me really want to stay, but Jay's already on his way so I have to go. Wait for me Monday!" He said with the biggest smile I've ever seen him with. I'm not sure if this is really what I was sorting out in my mind, but I can't take it back now. He's like a puppy when it gets a treat. I can't take it away from him. Although, part of me thinks letting the puppy have one treat isn't so bad.

23

"So, Misa, how was your weekend with your mother?" The usual check-in with Katie happened when we got to class.

"How do you think it was?"

"I don't know, I thought you and your mother were close."

"Yeah, when I was younger. Now it's awkward. She kept asking me how things are going with Ken and then telling me about her job and the company."

"Well, how is it?" She asked.

"I don't know. I wasn't paying attention. I was spacing out."

"You've been spacing out more than normal. What's all going through that head of yours?"

"I'm not even sure anymore. I still can't believe I even asked Ken to do something this weekend."

"You did?" Her face was a lot more surprised than I thought.

"I didn't tell you that?"

"Uh, no you didn't."

"Oh, well, yeah, that somehow happened."

"You really must be out of it. Or you finally came to your senses about how you feel."

"Well, I don't think it's that exactly. I don't know what made me ask it, I just did."

"It's a start I guess since you aren't trying to get out of it. Have you talked to him since?"

"No, he hasn't come back yet."

"Oh, you can talk to him now. He just walked in," Katie said gesturing to the door.

Ken came in looking as well dressed and laid out as perfectly as he always does, but more so since he's coming straight from home. I'm pretty sure he owns every type of button up there is. Today's color was navy blue with some splashes of a silver designs. His hair was styled up like it usually is, but it's gotten a little longer, so he ran his hand through it letting it fall to the side.

"Hey, Mimi. I've returned," he said coming to me, "Did you miss me?" He leaned on my desk as he grinned.

"You were gone for like, two days," I reminded him.

"I know. So long right? And just after you finally asked me out." He said sounding guilty for leaving.

"I told you that's not how I meant it."

"Aw, don't deny your true feelings. You were thinking about me, weren't you?"

"Nope, she was probably thinking about other people." Surprisingly, I wasn't ready to hear Jennifer showing up. "Ken, I don't see why you still put up with her after knowing her true wicked nature." I think she's finally breaking her silence and coming back to attack.

"I see no wickedness here. Plus, a wicked person wouldn't ask me on a date," Ken bragged.

"She did? Is that why you rejected Jenny on her date offer? Don't you think you'd have better time with her than *her*?" She said, eyeing me. I noticed Katie, who didn't budge from her spot, getting agitated. I shook my head, telling her not to do anything because I knew she would.

"I think I'll stick to my date with Mimi here. She's way more fun," Ken said.

"You know Jenny isn't going to like this."

"Sorry, I can't control her emotions," he said without a hint of remorse.

"Ken, what's gotten into you? You've changed," she said.

"I think I'm starting to like Ken more and more." Katie whispered to me.

"That's only because you don't like Jennifer either," I said.

"I approve of your relationship." She gave me a thumbs-up.

After that, Jennifer flung her hair and sat at her desk and stayed quiet like she was on time out. I looked to Katie who had a look of satisfaction, and I looked to Ken who had the same look, but his look wasn't because of the look of defeat from Jennifer.

She kept her distance from me all day. But that was mostly because she's talking to a lot of people. I didn't know she became so popular already. I wonder do they know the evils behind all her make up. She smiles and laughs with them, but they must not have heard the part where she specifically came to this school to destroy my relationship with Ken just so her sister can have him.

"Misa!" It was a good thing I had already passed Jennifer and her crew in the hall. I don't know what it is about John that likes to show up at the wrong time, but that always seems to be the case. "Misa, Misa!"

"John, do you really have to shout my name every time you see me?"

"I can't help it. I get so excited when I see you. Plus, I have something to tell you!" He said.

"What is it?"

"Remember how the other day you were trying to see what Ken and Sano were talking about? Well, after you left me there, I stayed around to see what was so special, and I heard some of what was being said, and I'm sure you'd like to know what it is. Do you want to know?" He asked me. That was what I wanted to ask Ken about, but instead asked about an outing, so I still don't really know what went on that day.

"Sure, what were they talking about?"

"Mmm, well, here's the thing. It sounded like something that was kind of serious but, I won't say unless you agree to go out with me."

"Don't you think you're asking a bit much about something that doesn't concern you anyway?"

"You may be right as always, and probably knowing the condition of Sano's mother isn't that important anyway," he said turning around.

"Her condition? What about her condition?" I asked spinning him back.

"Oh, so you are interested in knowing?"

"Yes! I want to know. What's happening? Is she getting better?"

"I'll tell you if you agree to our terms." John was getting a little full of himself. He must be following Ken when I'm not around with that behavior.

"Okay, by go out, do you mean go out somewhere that's not school?" I asked hoping that'd be it.

"Yes! I mean unless you really want to go out with me and be my girlfriend."

"Um, no." I don't know why I keep finding myself in these critical no-way out situations. "I'll agree to the first part of that. So, tell me what's up!" I demanded.

"You mean you'll really do it? All right, finally! I get to go on a date with Misa! Someone pinch me I must be dreaming!"

"I'll gladly do that if you don't hurry up and tell me what he said." I haven't been able to be around Sano lately and he said he was going to see her more, so he must know more of her condition.

John told me all that he heard. I sold myself for information I didn't want to hear. I felt almost sick walking home. His mother's condition is taking a turn for the worst. And they may not be able to help her. She's already been in the hospital for so long. What will happen if she doesn't make it? He can't be left to raise the kids on his own. And why was he talking about it with Ken? This must have just happened, so why the rush to tell him? John left before he heard what Ken had to say, so I don't know what he could have said to that. Or rather, what can you say to that?

"Ah, Mimi, you're here!"

"Hey, Misa." When I got home, Ken and Eden greeted me in the

living room.

"Oh, hi." I had forgotten that his group was coming this week to work on the project.

"Eden and I were just about to sketch out the model of the rocket until we realized we didn't have any color pencils and markers. You wouldn't happen to have any, would you, Mimi?" This guy has all kinds of money but doesn't have any color pencils?

"Yeah, I do."

"Oh, you're a lifesaver!" Ken said.

"Thanks, Misa." Eden added.

"Yeah, you're welcome. I'll be right back with them." It's not every day I could watch guys sit around coloring.

It's been a while since I used them myself. They were all the way at the back of my closet. I probably don't need to waste my time finding all of them since it's only Ken and Eden. I wonder what happened to Sano.

"Oh, excuse me Misa."

"Sano!" I bumped into him as I was leaving out of my room and nearly dropped everything.

"I hope you don't mind that I used your bathroom." He said pointing behind him.

"Oh, not at all. Uh, here, they said they needed color pencils and stuff." I handed them to him.

"Ah, thanks." He said. There was a short pause. This is extremely awkward. Instead of being in his house, Sano is in my house this time. And I just heard about his mother. I highly doubt now is the proper time to bring that up. So, I had to think of something else to say.

"Will this project be hard?" I simply asked him.

"Not really. The teacher showed us an example model, so we know how to make it. And since I don't do track anymore, all three of us will be able to work on it to make this go faster."

"So, you're done with track for good? Is your ankle not healing well?"

"No, that's not a problem anymore. It's just that some things came up, so I thought it would be better to sit out for now." He has to mean his mother. He's stopping what he's been enjoying for years because of this. That sick feeling was starting to come back.

"I'm sure it's probably better that way."

"Yeah, and um, look. I know I haven't explained to you why I did what I did yet, but I want to because I don't want you to get the wrong idea. But I think it'd be better to wait until we finish the project. So maybe this weekend we can talk somewhere," he suggested.

"Sure, we can do that."

"Alright cool. I should probably be going back downstairs now." He was getting ready to leave when we heard someone coming up the stairs and coming up fast.

"There you are, Cocoa! It feels like it's been forever! Come here and give your old man a hug!" I was suddenly grabbed in the world's tightest bear hug by my dad.

"Ugh, Dad, you're here. Welcome back." I could hardly breathe from the tightness.

"That's right! I'll be here for the next three days. It's been so long. My have you grown!" He looked like he was getting teary eyed.

"Dad, please…" He was embarrassing me.

"Now I've met the two gentlemen downstairs, but you're another face," Dad said taking his attention straight to Sano.

"Um, this is Sano. Sano this is my dad."

"Nice to meet you, sir," Sano said extending his hand. My dad took the offer.

"Likewise, and my, what a firm grip you've got. Cocoa, you never told me you've become so popular with the fellas. And here I thought you enjoyed our father daughter time at the circus and carnivals."

"Dad, seriously!" I saw Sano grinning a little.

"Oh, all right. I'll stop, but you'll have to promise to spare a little of your time with your old man… unless you think you're too cool for me now." He looked away a bit too dramatically. I seriously can't believe him!

"Yeah sure, sure I will, just stop talking."

He laughed. "Are you feeling embarrassed? They haven't heard the story of when you cried when the clown gave you a balloon."

"Oh my gosh, Dad, that was like, ten years ago!" I heard Sano actually laugh this time. I need to find a place to hide.

"I think I'll head back downstairs now," Sano said.

"Oh, okay." I could barely look at him as he walked away.

"Nice meeting you again, son," Dad said as he was going down.

"Same here."

It's been a while since my dad has been this embarrassing. He's always trying to be 'cool,' but that 'cool' dad usually makes me want to go jump off a cliff somewhere.

"This is really something Cocoa." My Dad said as he looked down the stairs. Ken, Eden, and Sano were at the table trying to figure out where to start on drawing the rocket. They all may be smart, but arts and crafts might be an area they don't overachieve in.

"I don't know how I let your mother talk me into this." He said more as a thought than something meant to me. He continued to look down to the three guys sitting in our living room.

"Dad, please don't do anything." I begged.

"You know, your mother said the same thing to me. Except she wasn't as nice about it." He said. I knew mom probably threatened him or something.

"Since you just got in today, how about we catch up tomorrow when I get out of school?" I offered to take his mind off what he was looking at.

"You mean just the two of us? No other boys?"

"Yes, just us two."

"Alright, that sounds like a plan. I'll head to my room, and I'll be keeping an eye on our guests." He said going back downstairs.

My dad is protective. No matter who it is, he doesn't like it when I'm around people he doesn't know. And he really doesn't like it when it comes to me being around guys. He was nice to Sano just now, but I could tell he didn't like any of this.

If I didn't tell him that I'd do something with him, who knows what he would've done. This is also the fourth arrangement I've made with someone. I never thought I'd be dealing with so many guys at one time! How am I going to do this? I peeked down the stairs again and watched the three of them continue to work. I also saw my dad walk back over to them.

"Looks like a fine project you're working on. I'll be just over there in that room. If you all need help or anything, Mr. Macky is here to assist." He patted his chest as if to make sure they knew he was 'Mr. Macky.'

"We'll be sure to keep that in mind. Thank you, Mr. Macky." Ken didn't hesitate to reply.

My Dad was about five foot nine or ten, so he was a couple inches under Sano and Ken. And he was kind of small for someone who finds working out a chore. So, looking at him with them, from this angle, was kind of funny. But the subtle warning he just gave them wasn't. Watching them color would've been fun and all, but I think it would be best for me to lay low for today. That would be for the best for everyone. Plus, this'll give me time to figure out how I plan to go meet up with Ken, Sano, John, and my dad all in one week.

24

Ken must have gotten the idea that smooth talking my dad like he did my mother wasn't the best option because he went to his room as well when they finished up for the day. It was a good thing my dad could sleep in until noon on his days off, so we were able to get ready for school without his disturbance and left peacefully. I had to split up with Ken in order to go talk to Katie about my master plan I had so much time to figure out.

"Alright so I figured something out. Ken's been going home over the weekend, so I'll go out with him Friday. Then, Saturday, I see what Sano has to say, and then I'll humor John on Sunday. That way, nobody knows and would have to run into each other. How does that sound?"

"Well, Ms. Macky, playing the love game can be difficult, especially with all three bachelors coming for your heart and you can only pick one. And dealing with these three contestants, especially, is a very unusual set up."

"Katie! This isn't some kind of love game!"

"Really? Bachelor one, who comes with the proposal of marriage. Bachelor two, who is determined to get you to see the good in him. And bachelor three, who is hopelessly in love, seems to make it so. So, what will our lovely maiden do?" Katie did her best to sound like some host of a show passing me an imaginary mic.

"I told you how I was going to do it, but it seems you're having too much fun hosting a show that's not happening."

"I have always thought it fun to be the host of a game show, and this just seems like the perfect opportunity. But what you said seems fine to me. Our little Misa is finally growing up. It feels just like yesterday that she was crying about that silly little nickname the kids gave us back in elementary school. And now you're growing up and going out with all these boys. You're getting that much closer to being a woman." She held up her fingers together.

"Hey, I never cried because they called us that."

"Yeah, you did. You used to get so embarrassed when people would call you M&M's and call me Skittles."

"Why did they call us that again?"

"Remember that day I had Skittles and offered you some and one kid was like 'M&Ms and Skittles don't go together.' And then another kid was like 'they don't go together either but they're still friends' or everyone thought it was so funny it kind of stuck around after that since a lot of them never understood why we were friends. So, they called me Skittles whenever I was around you. I swear kids had way too much free time on their hands."

There was always a reason for me to be the center of attention no matter how much I try to avoid it. But no matter what people said about me, Katie never left my side. She really is a good friend.

"But after a while that got really annoying, so I had to put an end to it." She said. She put a stop to her name, but my name stayed a little longer.

"Even with that attitude, you still managed to get a boyfriend."

"Yep! Eden loves the way I am."

Eden is kind of quiet and probably doesn't have any kind of anger problems. But Katie isn't so quiet and has a very short fuse, yet they've been going together for almost three years. I guess even though they have almost completely opposite personalities, that still didn't stop them from getting together. Love really has no boundaries.

"Suddenly, I'm not so prepared for this weekend anymore." I said.

"Oh? Not ready for your hot dates? Well, think of it this way. At least your father has met Sano and Ken, so meeting the dad scenario is over."

"Oh, that reminds me I'm supposed to spend time with him after school today. I hope he won't do much. I'm so tired from all this thinking."

"Your dad can be pretty laidback. And it's a weekday, so he can't ask for much," she said. But somehow, I don't agree with that.

I met up with my dad after school. Ken was home with his group being scientist, and here I am in his car, pulling up to the park.

"Come on, Cocoa, let's get on the seesaw!" It was a beautiful spring afternoon. After school hours meant kids were also out here enjoying themselves on the swings and playing tag around the slide house. We were over by the teeter-totter, kids no older than eight just got off of. We just arrived and he's already going overboard.

"Dad, don't you think you're just a little too old to be playing at the playground?"

"Too old? I feel just as young as I did when I was your age."

"And how many years ago was that?"

"Come on. Get on the other end," he was ignoring my protest, so I had no choice but to get on.

"Put some energy into that push Cocoa!" I got on, but I didn't particularly put much of the 'teeter' in the 'totter.'

"It can only go so high. And please don't call me that in public."

"Why not? You're the one that chose that name."

"I didn't choose that name. It was just my first word." I reminded him.

"And I'll never forget that moment. I gave you a sip that one time before you could even walk. Your mother was so mad at me for giving you chocolate so young, but after that first taste, you became hooked. And then the one time when your mother was all 'no hot cocoa for you' you started crying your eyes out and shouting 'cocoa, cocoa' and she was so proud of you, she gave you some." I could see my dad getting teary eyed again as he went down memory lane, telling me this story for the billionth time. "It feels as if that was yesterday. But now you're growing up into this fine, young woman right before Daddy's eyes."

"Dad, please don't start crying," I pleaded.

"You're just growing up so fast. And now you're at that age where I can't really stop you from dating because Daddy knows he wants to throw all those bad boys out since none of them are good enough for my little girl."

"Dad, I won't be your little girl forever."

"I know. You just have to give me time," he said, calming his emotions down. "So, who are those young men exactly?" He asked.

"They're just there to work on a project. Only one was the one staying there."

"That was the one you were talking to in the hallway yesterday?"

"No, that wasn't him. The one staying there is Ken."

"That's right, that's him. He was the first to introduce himself. It seems like he has his head on his shoulders right. But the one you were talking to…"

"You mean Sano?" I asked trying to finish his sentence.

"Yeah, that's his name. If that wasn't him, then why were you two getting all chummy in the hallway?"

"It wasn't like that. We were just talking."

"Talking separately from the others?"

"It wasn't supposed to be like that. He was coming from the bathroom, and I was leaving out of my room."

"I see. So, you're into this Sano kid then?"

"W-what makes you think that?" I was surprised he got to that so quickly.

"Hmm, I don't know. I guess it's a parent thing. Am I right?"

"W-well um, p-possibly." I always found it hard to lie to my dad.

"I was right! My Cocoa is leaving me!" His dramatic outbreak made people look at us.

"Dad, we're not like, dating or anything."

"But you like him. You might as well tell me you're getting married tomorrow."

"You're overreacting. If that were the case, then Ken wouldn't be here."

"Hmm, that he wouldn't. He is the one that wants the marriage. Why does it have to be my little girl? It's not like we're rich like them. And we don't have much to offer." He wondered. I'd be digging Ken's grave if I told him, it all started because he had been spying on me after we met once. "Of all the people there, it just doesn't add up. Anyway, why haven't you kicked that guy to the road if you're interested in that other one?"

"It's not that I'm not. I mean um, I don't know. I um… can, can we talk about something else?" I desperately wanted to change the subject. It feels weird talking about this with my dad.

"Cocoa, your mother has already warned me about interfering with this… numerous of times," he took a pause. I can see my mom threatening him now, "So I'm not going to tell you what you should and shouldn't do. However, if things get out of hand, then I will be there to put a stop to it. I will say this: I've been working for his parents for well over a year now, and sometimes when I'm there, I get this bad vibe."

"What do you mean a bad vibe?"

"Well, it's just that some of the things I hear around there just don't add up. I've been trying to figure out the rumors, but haven't been able to get anywhere without seeming suspicious myself. Of course, any business has its dirty laundry. All I'm trying to say is, make sure this guy is who he says he is."

"Sure thing, Dad," I said humoring him. I already know it's something different about them. But just how different was the question.

"That a girl. I guess this thing isn't meant for people my age," he said slowly pealing himself off the teeter-totter.

"Why don't I treat you to some ice cream from the store." It's been a while since I've spent so much time with my dad. Even though it was hard to explain it all, I still always found talking with my dad easier.

After ice cream, more stories of the good ole days, and fifteen minutes of me convincing him not to take us to the circus that was apparently in town, he took me back home.

"Mimi, you're home! Did you enjoy your time out?" Ken was still in the living room, but Eden and Sano were gone.

"Sure, it was fun."

"Glad you enjoyed your time out. Where is your dad?"

"He went out. He said he'd be back in a couple hours."

"Ah, I see." If I'm not mistaken, I saw a bit of relief in his eye.

"You finished working on the project?" I asked, wondering if I could breathe my own sigh of relief making sure Sano wasn't in the bathroom again.

"For today, yes. The other two had something to do, so we stopped early. It looks like it'll be a bit more work to do than we originally thought, so this may go into next week. The teacher gave us three weeks to finish, so we still have plenty of time left to turn it in. We're not going to meet Friday to work on it," His face lit up after he said Friday, "That reminds me. Leave that day open because that's the day I'd like us to go out. Can you do that?"

"Um, yeah that works," I said giving myself a mental pat on the back for already having this planned.

"Good. Now just to find a place to go. So many possibilities." Ken was really thinking about this.

"Aren't you going to go back home for the weekend?" I asked.

"Oh, right. I have made that an obligation recently. Darn, guess that idea is out." He said, scratching his head.

"W-what idea?"

"Well, there are still plenty of other things to do." He continued thinking out loud.

"What exactly do you have in mind?"

"It's a secret." He turned to me and said.

"I'm the one that came up with the idea, and you won't even tell me what you're plotting?"

"Hmm, that is true. It was your idea. What did you have in mind then?" He suddenly asked.

"Me? I don't know." I never thought about it. I was too busy trying to figure out when but not the where.

"I know there's somewhere you want to go, or something you want to do." He asked. I thought about it, and really couldn't come up with anything fun to do.

"Uh, well, you probably wouldn't want to, but skating maybe?"

"Skating? Oh, I know of this great ice-skating rink not too far from here."

"Wait, I didn't say ice skating. I don't know how to." I told him. I barely know how to regularly skate.

"Oh, I can teach you. It's simple."

"Easy for you to say, you know how."

"Actually, I don't." He said.

"You don't? You can't do something? Then why are you trying to go somewhere where you can't even do the main event?"

"Jayson told me about this place once and it seemed fun to go to. And I'm a quick learner anyway. I learned how to ride a bike the same day I got it."

"Really? How old were you?"

"Let's see. I want to say four, maybe even three. My dad ordered me a tricycle, but they sent a regular little bike by accident. They tried putting it away for when I was older, but I found it and tried riding it anyway. I fell a few times but after the third fall, I realized I wasn't doing something right. At this time, we were visiting relatives, and I noticed other kids riding bikes outside and saw the trick was to not lean so much to one side, and it worked out just fine after that." I think I'm reaching a point where I'm not even surprised by the things he can do.

"So, it's ice skating then, right?" He asked again. He might be able to learn fast, I on the other hand take a bit more time to get something. He knows that, but he's still willing to give it a try.

"Sure. Why not?" I gave in.

"Alright! Ice skating with Mimi is going to be so fun!"

"Why do you insist on calling me that?"

"Because it's cute." was his reply.

"I don't see what's so cute about it. Just sounds like a bad name to call someone."

"Okay then, would you rather I call you Cocoa then?"

"No! How do you know that name?"

"When your dad came in yesterday, he asked where Cocoa was, then corrected himself and said Misa. I also heard him say it again when he saw you yesterday. So, I'm thinking it's a name for you?"

"Yeah, it is. It's something he's been calling me since I was little, so I've gotten used to it."

"You've got such a good family bond. The last time I spent time with my mother was on my birthday, and the time spent with my dad is normally doing some kind of work or seeing him in passing," he said. Thinking about it, a lot of his stories involved Jayson and hardly his parents at all. It must be hard for him.

"Alright fine. You can call me the stupid name," I said.

"Really?" He asked surprised.

"Yeah, but just don't get carried away."

"Oh, Mimi, you just keep making me so happy!" If I didn't know any better, I swear I saw a tail wagging.

"Yeah, yeah, I'm going upstairs."

"Upstairs? But you've just given me so much energy, let's do something now!"

"No. I've already done something today. I'm done." I said. I was never much of the party- all-day-and-night person.

"Aw, you're no fun." Ken looked at me and pouted as I went upstairs. I don't know what it was about seeing him like that, but something made me laugh slightly.

Never in my life did I expect that I'd have a run-in with someone like him. Ken Masidone. Wealthy heir to the family business that turns into an energized puppy whenever I do anything, and pouty when I say no. One day, I'll understand this guy, but it isn't today.

My dad's mini vacation ended before I knew it. He was gathering his things to head out. "Alright, Cocoa, I have to start first thing in the morning. I should be going now so I won't have to wake up at two in the morning to make it on time." He made it to the door before he turned back to me, "If you need anything, I'm only a phone call away," he said. Even though with the distance, he wouldn't make it in time, but somehow, he'd find a way. "You better watch after her, you hear me?" My dad went to Ken.

"Roger that Mr. Macky. I'll make sure nothing happens."

"Good." My dad leaned down to me. "I don't care whose family he's from, you better tell me if he tries anything funny," he whispered to me.

"Will do, Dad."

"Alright then! I hate to go so soon, but I'll be back before you know it. You kids stay safe and behave yourselves."

"See yah, Dad."

"Have a safe trip back." Ken and I watched my dad leave before he turned back to what he was doing. Eden and Sano were still here over by the table holding the pieces that needed to be put together.

"Hey, Mimi, we're going to take the parts out in the back to spray paint. Can you be so kind as to go up to my room and get the cans of paint for me please?" Ken asked as he returned to his work.

"Fine."

"Thanks. We'll be outside."

Can't this guy understand that I'm trying to stay away from them? I know I said he could use the nickname, but he doesn't have to so casually around other people. It's good he never said it when my dad was around. I went upstairs to get the paint. He didn't really specify where it was. I didn't really want to have to search his room, but I had no choice.

Just as I was about to look around his bed, I heard something vibrate. It was coming from his desk drawer. I went to see what it was and saw his phone. He normally keeps it with him, but he has it in his drawer on vibrate. I don't want to go through his things, but that didn't stop me from taking a look at who was calling him at this time. The number wasn't saved in his phone. His phone was so much bigger than mine. I don't think I'll ever do that upgrade...

"Hello?"

"Oh no!" My finger slipped and answered the call.

"Hello, are you there?" The voice called out again.

"H-hello?" I said on a whim.

"Hold on, who is this?" The voice sounds familiar. "Who is picking up my Kenny's phone?!" It was Jenny!

"H-he's not around right now—"

"Wait a minute. Is this that girl that he's temporarily living with? Why are you answering his phone? Did he tell you, you could?" She asked.

"Uh, n-no, it was an acc—"

"Oh, so you just picked up his phone because you think you can? The nerve of you! What gives you the right to answer his phone? Give Kenny the phone now!" She was yelling so loud I wondered if he could hear her.

"Ken is busy. He'll have to talk to you at another time."

"Don't you tell me when I can and can't talk to him! Now I said give him the phone!"

"Sorry, he's doing work, but I'll let him know you called. Bye." I hurried and ended the call.

My nerves started going all over the place. I answered Jenny's call and hung up on her. I wouldn't be surprised if she suddenly appeared here. I quickly put the phone back and closed the drawer. That was when I noticed the bag of spray paint cans next to the desk. I hurried up and grabbed them so I could leave and not get myself in more trouble.

"There you are. Did you get lost?" Ken asked when I got back downstairs.

"Here, next time do your own errands." I shoved the bag to him.

"Did something just happen?"

Yeah, your crazy fiancé called, is what I wanted to say, but I can't very well tell him that. "I'm going back in," I said instead and turned away.

"You don't want to help out?" He asked.

"I'd rather not."

"Alright, party pooper." The last thing I need is to hang around them, risking one of them saying something about this weekend.

The inside of the house was quiet as I went back upstairs. I went passed his room again. I could hear a rumble coming from his dresser. She must be calling back. She's really mad that I answered his phone. I don't want to deal with her more than I have to, so I went on to my room ignoring it.

"Are you sure I'm putting this on the right part?"

"Yeah, the wing will go there so only spray half of it." I could hear them talking outside from my back window.

I went over to have a look. I've never seen Ken or Sano look so focused and serious, and all they're doing is painting and putting a few things together. This further proves those two are related. They both take after their father and his dedication to his work. It feels so weird now. It started with a crush on one of them. Now I'm living with the other. The two guys that were brought into my life. When I asked for cupid to shoot his arrow, I was hoping he knew what he was doing when he went around shooting people.

25

"So, are you ready for your awesome weekend, Misa?" I shut my locker and looked at my very sarcastic best friend.

"No."

"Well, you should be. You're the one who arranged it."

"I know, Katie, but can't I reconsider?"

"It's a little too late for that now. Your lover boy was singing all day. You can't let him down now." I'm not sure if she's talking about Ken or John because I saw them both doing that.

"I just want to get this over with. Of all things, Ken wants to do something neither of us knows how to do."

"Eden and I went ice skating before. It's not that hard."

"Katie, this is me we're talking about. I can't even inline skate.

How do you expect me to move and balance on a slick surface?"

"Oh, yeah. You're right. You should probably take a helmet and padding. It can get slippery out there."

"Thanks for the warning. I'll try not to fall," I said, giving sarcasm back to her.

"But if you do fall, you'll have your prince come in at just the right moment to save you from total embarrassment. Then you'll look into each other's eyes and have this romantic moment where it's just you and him and everyone else disappears and—"

"Katie!" I had to bring her back to reality. "Take some of that emotion and write a book because none of that is happening here."

"You have to be open minded."

"Why would I hope for all of that to happen?"

"Because all it takes is one fell swoop and boom! You'll be walking down the aisle before you know it."

"Your love filled brain is taking over. Why don't you take some of that to Eden or someone."

"Don't worry. You'll experience it sooner than later," she said. I wonder about that though. I've been out with Ken before, but somehow this time feels different.

I went straight home to get ready for day one of my long weekend. I wasn't sure what to wear, but I was running out of time.

"Mimi, you ready? Jay's outside waiting!" Ken shouted up to me. He told Jayson where we were going, and he insisted that he take us there.

"I'm coming." I was finally ready and headed downstairs. I kept it simple this time and put on my long, grey shirt and black leggings. I'm also bringing a jacket since I heard it's cold in there.

"Are you ready to have some fun?" He asked.

"Aren't you a little too excited about this?"

"How could I not be? We're just about done with this project like two weeks early, and now I'm going to go on a date that was offered by you. I have a bit to be excited about." He explained. There goes that tail wagging again. "So, you're ready, right?"

"Yeah."

"Alright then. Onward to skating!" We headed out and got in the car. Jayson took off for the rink. I don't know what Ken meant when he said it wasn't far from my house because it took forty-five minutes to get here.

"Okay now," Jayson started, "You kids have fun. Kenny-kens, don't you let her fall and hurt herself."

"I'll make sure that doesn't happen."

"And Misaky, you go out there and show them the skills I know you have."

"I'll try," I tried making my answer sound as confident as Ken's was, but I don't think it was.

"Oh, this reminds me of my first skate date. We had so much fun. But since you have me, Jayson, the best chaperone in the car, I can't let you two stay out like we did. Papa Masy would not approve. But you two will still have fun," he said. We got out the car and I looked to the big stone building that stood in front of us.

"See you later Jay." Ken said as he pulled off. And now it begins.

We walked in and the temperature instantly dropped twenty degrees. The rink was huge, but still filled with people shuffling on and off the ice, getting skates, and sitting on the side stands.

"Misa, you wait over here. I'll go get us some skates,"

I went over to a seat that was close to the rink and watched Ken go over to the shoe stand. Then I noticed a girl on the ice with a long ponytail and a black and white leotard dress, jumping around like she's in the Olympics. She moved so gracefully through the air and landed so smoothly. She's probably been an ice skater for years. I noticed three other people around the edge of the rink holding on for balance just hoping they don't fall. That's probably what I'll be doing. Neither of us knows how to ice skate, so it's best we keep away from Miss Spins a lot in the center.

"Alright, back with some blades of fun," Ken said handing me a pair. "The shoe sizes here run a bit bigger, so I got you a smaller size." The fact that he knows my shoe size doesn't surprise me.

"Are you sure we should do this? Wouldn't we get in the way or something?" I said referring to ponytail girl.

"Ah, don't worry about that. We're here to have fun just like them. Let's lace up and go." He started putting on his skates. The blade was so thin, yet the shoe was so heavy. I hope I'll be able to stand on theses. "Do you need some help?" Ken offered.

"No, I got this." I managed to get the shoes on and went to stand up slowly. All went well until I tried taking a step and lost all control of my legs and fell.

"We haven't even gotten to the ice and you're already falling."

He helped me get up. I haven't even worn them for five minutes and I've already embarrassed myself. "Just pick your feet up as you step. The floors are rubber, so you won't slip and fall." I did what he said, and it was easier to walk.

When we made it to the entrance of the rink, I took in the sight of the large white floor with the markings from skaters that have moved so many times over it. It all looked even bigger now that I was so close to it.

"Alright, I'll go first so we both don't fall in." Ken went straight in without any hesitation. He let himself get balanced and he was gliding along the ice. "This isn't so bad. Feels like regular skating," he said moving his leg and gaining a little speed. He still wasn't going too fast, but he looked like he got the hang of it already.

That meant my turn was next. I know myself and I know I'll slip like I stepped on a banana peel, so I was depending on the wall for balance like I saw the others doing.

"Whoa!" I slowly stepped on and slid but caught myself. I looked over and saw Ken skating in circles like he's been doing this his whole life. I tried taking another step without falling. It was a success! Now another step...

"Would you like some help?" He came over and asked.

"No, I can do this on my own," I said. I won't be having him help me twice in ten minutes. I continued taking steps. I was getting better at every go. He wasn't the only one who could learn fast.

"Look at that. You're doing great." He said watching me.

"Yeah, you're not the only one who can do it," I was feeling good about myself.

"I agree, you're doing well. You haven't made it far, but it's a start."

"What?" I turned and saw where I started still near reaching distance. I swear I was further than this.

"Just keep going. It'll get easier as you go." He sounded like a coach encouraging his student.

I kept on going taking baby steps trying to get the hang of it better. The weight of the shoe made picking my feet up harder, and keeping my legs together isn't as easy as it looks. Ken was still doing his own thing, but he stayed near keeping an eye on me. He got the hang of things so easily, and I'm still here inching along. He won't have any fun if I'm glued to the wall like this the whole time. If I go for it like he did, maybe I'll get it too.

"Balance," I repeated to myself. I let go and was still standing, which was the important thing. The next issue was moving. I don't think I had thought that far yet. But before I was able to think that far, I felt a breeze on my face as I was grabbed into motion. "H-hey, Ken! You can't suddenly grab a person like that," I said.

"I figured you were trying to move on your own, but you weren't going to get anywhere standing in place. So, I decided to help get you going." He was skating while he had his grip on me.

"I-I can manage by myself," I said. My legs still hadn't moved. With Ken holding on to me so closely, I didn't want to risk taking us both down.

"We'd be here all night if I let you do it. Come on, I'll help guide you. Just move one foot at a time," he said as he slowed down so I could try to join in. I tried picking my foot up and skated as he did. One leg at a time, we were moving further and further along the ice.

"Yeah, just like that. You're doing fine." He told me. But I was really only able to do it because he was holding on to me, keeping me up.

"How did you get this so easily?" I asked.

"Well, it's not so different from blading. Just center your weight and don't spread your legs too far." He said as he started going a bit faster. So, I had to go a bit faster, and I was still standing.

"This is actually starting to get kind of fun. I haven't been skating or anything in a long time," I said. I felt this sort of free feeling as we were gliding across the floor with the light breeze against my face. We swayed back and forth keeping a nice steady pace.

"See, it wasn't a bad idea to come here. Let's try going even faster."

"I don't think I'm ready for that yet." I said.

"Come on, I got you. We don't want to look like the slowest ones here." Ken kicked up the speed more. In order for me not to fall behind, I had to do the same. I don't know how, but I was still keeping up. We passed by the ones still hanging on for support. I thought that would be me the whole time, but here I am ice skating.

I, the girl who can't even rollerblade, was actually ice skating!

I was out here actually doing this. I looked over at the person beside me. Ken was helping me a lot. He hasn't let go once since grabbing on to me. I should thank him. I'm pretty sure I would've fallen a long time ago if he had let go.

After becoming more aware of Ken's presence, I started to feel more anxious. He's holding on to my side as I skate alongside him while he guided me. It almost felt like a real date with the guy helping his girlfriend because she was having trouble. It gave me the feeling that he's done something like this before. Has he gone skating with another girl, possibly with a girlfriend? Maybe he's done this with Jenny or Jennifer or maybe someone else?

"It's kind of hard to turn when you're keeping straight," Ken said.

"What? Oh, sorry." We were coming up to the turn, so we had to shift over. I tried turning my body as Ken did to make the turn. The sudden thought took my focus away.

"Your speed went down a bit. Is something wrong?" He asked reading me.

"Um, no, it's nothing."

"You sure?"

"Yeah." I didn't want to suddenly ask him if he's been out on dates with other girls before and make things awkward. Something like that shouldn't bother me anyway.

"How sure are you?"

"I'm quite sure."

"Positive?" He kept asking.

"Yes, I'm fine!" I was getting annoyed.

"You're lying!" He said to me. And that's when I saw the world around me spinning. Ken pulled me fast toward him as he moved us in a circle.

"Ken! Don't just go spinning people. I nearly fell!" My feet were moving all over the place from the shock of the spin. I had to get my footing back.

"You're not being honest with me. If there's anything I've gotten to know is that facial expression you get when you're in thought. So, tell me what's up or we're going to try our own fancy tricks that's better than that person who is doing all the twirls over there." He looked over to the girl that was still in her own world gracefully jumping through the air and landing perfecting back in motion.

"Wait! That's not fair. You can't make me tell you what I'm thinking! Especially at a time like this." I was able to control my feet, but I don't think I could take another move like that again.

"I bet we can do a seven-twenty too." Ken didn't pay attention to what I said.

"No! I just got the hang of this, and that's only because you're holding me. I still haven't done anything on my own." I had to remind him.

"Ah, so you want to be great on your own. Be my guest," he said. Then he did the worst thing a person could possibly do. He let go.

As soon as his weight lifted off me and he disappeared from my side, I began losing all my balance. I tried my best to get my position back. I was slowing down, but not fast enough as I was headed straight for a wall. I hadn't figured out turning on my own yet, so I could only go straight. I was just gliding along to my doom, so I closed my eyes hoping it'd make things better. I still crashed. However, the wall was unexpectedly soft. That is, until I opened my eyes and saw what I ran into wasn't the wall.

"I'm sure you could've found a better way to stop than this." Ken said looking down at me as I was caught in his arms.

"Ken! Are you crazy? What if I really fell!"

"You looked a little tense, so I wanted to change things up. Wasn't that exciting?" He asked.

"Not at all! I can't trust you anymore. I'm getting off the ice." Although it was fun, I couldn't handle another rush like that. I found the nearest seats and took the skates off. The way they were rubbing against my skin made a sore. My falling when I first put them on didn't help. He knew I wasn't going to make it, that's why he put himself in front of me to save me from total wipeout. I hadn't realized how strong a build he had until now. Then again, I was never thrown into his arm before.

"Aw, you're done skating?" Ken finally showed up holding cups.

"My legs are killing me."

"I think some nice yoga classes can help that."

"And be forever stuck as a pretzel? No thanks."

"Well, if that's how you feel. Here." He handed me one of the cups he was holding. "I bet a nice cup of cocoa will help warm your pain."

"Thanks. I haven't had this stuff in a while."

"Really? I was under the assumption you loved it."

"I did, but then I stopped drinking it hoping my dad stopped with that ridiculous name. But that clearly hasn't worked."

"I think it's a cute name."

"You think everything is cute."

"That's because you're always doing something cute. The nicknames, the way you do things, your cute expressions, which remind me of the one you had out there. Are you going to tell me what was bothering you?" He asked again.

"I told you already it was nothing. I was… I was just wondering if you ever had like a girlfriend before."

"Oh? What brought that on all of a sudden?" I could see he wasn't expecting that question.

"I don't know. You are like, seventeen and a guy who also happens to be rich at that."

"Well, I don't really go around bragging about my status in society. I like to try and live regularly." He answered, taking a sip of his drink. But he lives anything but a regular life, so that was kind of hard to believe.

"But, to answer your question, yes, I have had girlfriends." I almost choked on my drink when he answered. He not only had a girlfriend, but he said it as a plural! He's had more than one?

"I've only had three." He continued answering my unsaid question. "Two of which were my father's choosing. But they were only in it for the money. The other one was someone I knew from my old school. But she didn't last long either." I don't know what I was expecting to hear, but it certainly wasn't that. "What? Isn't that what you wanted to know?"

"Y-yeah it was. Just that, I mean, the way you went on about me and everything…" I didn't know how to finish that sentence, but he got where I was going with it.

"Ah, that. Well, the time in which all that happened was after I had them stop gathering information."

AKA: stalking me.

"During that point, a lot of things were going on. But then that twist of fate brought your parents to our company. I didn't notice right away, but when I did, that's when I was able to ask about you." He explained. So, he's had girlfriends before coming to me? How long was he with each of them? Did he also act like this to them? For some reason, these questions flooded my mind.

"I can sense Mimi's mind turning. Before you think too much, none of them were serious or anything. It kind of just sprung upon me. They didn't even last more than a few months," he clarified. It's normal for people to have been in relationships, so why is it so surprising to me? "Would you like to know more about them?"

"No, that's not necessary. That's your business." Talking about ex-girlfriends wasn't something I wanted to hear him talk about.

"I don't want you to think I'm hiding something, and I don't want Mimi to think too much and get jealous."

"Shut up! Who's jealous? I'm just surprised someone was able to be with a pervert like you!"

"On the contrary, you're still with this pervert, so score one for me!"

"Who's with who?"

"Such rejection hurts," he said clutching his chest, "And here I thought we had a nice time together."

"I did have fun. But that doesn't mean we're together now. It'll take a little more than ice skating to win me over."

"So, what will it take?" He asked.

"I... I don't know." I couldn't answer because I didn't even know the answer.

I've never been with anyone before, so I'm not sure. If I could just figure that out, then this would be a whole lot easier to understand. We've been out together, he's great in just about everything he does. He seems to only have an interest in me, we've even kissed, and he's currently living with me. What does it take to win me over?

I looked at him, and he looked as if he wanted to say something else, but he didn't. I still couldn't bring myself to answer that question, so I had to change the subject.

"So, when is Jayson supposed to pick us up?"

"Ah, don't tell me you're ready to go now."

"Well, I'm not going back on the ice. And it's..." I reached in my jacket pocket for my phone, but I didn't feel it.

"I think my phone is gone."

"Really? Did you drop it somewhere?" He said looking on the ground.

"I don't know. It must have fallen out. Oh! Maybe when you suddenly spun me, it probably fell out on the ice."

"I'll go check." He got up and headed back to the rink. I only had a one-track trail, so I went to check around the outside by the other seats I sat at.

I hope no one picked it up. How did I not notice until now? Stupid Ken and his conversation. At least now I know he's had previous girlfriends. They must have ended badly since he didn't seem all that thrilled about them.

"Oh, my goodness! Are you okay!?" I was looking under the seats by our shoes when I heard a panicked voice.

"Oh no, it looks like somebody got hurt out there!" Another person next to me said. I looked up to see what the commotion was.

I don't think I've ever felt an ocean wave of fear, shock, and panic take over me as fast as it did after noticing someone lying on the ice.

"Ken!" It was him on the ground. I don't think I ever moved faster than I did just now to get over to him. I almost slipped a few times after getting back on to the rink without my skates, but I had to keep going. "Hey, Ken, are you alright?" I asked, crouching next to him.

"Well, the good news is your phone was out here. The bad news is the ice cleaners are going to have to work a bit over today." He said as I looked down and saw blood coming out of his lower thigh.

"You're bleeding! Wh-what happened?!" The red stain was growing on his pants, and I wasn't sure what to do.

"Hey! Are you with him?" I looked up and saw ponytail girl coming toward me.

"I'm so sorry! They told me not to practice while other people were around, but I had an event tomorrow and I just didn't see him. My blade- I was spinning, and it hit his leg. I'm so sorry I didn't mean to. I was just about to call an ambulance," the girl was shaking and speaking a mile a minute trying to explain. I was having a hard time understanding as my nerves were also all over the place.

"No, I'm not hurt that badly," Ken said to her.

"Are you crazy? You're bleeding everywhere. We got to get you to a hospital."

"No, Misa, just call Jay. We have a doctor."

"O-okay." My fingers were shaking, but I managed to dial him and told him what happened.

"H-he's on his way," I said.

"I'm so sorry. I'll go get someone to help you." She turned to go get help. I looked up and saw a crowd of people looking at the horrible scene. Looking at Ken on the ice with a pool of blood around his right leg.

"No need," Ken said. "You just keep practicing. You're good by the way." He gave her a thumbs up.

"Uh, th-thanks." She said. But she was still too far in shock to take the compliment well. This sudden turn of events has us all in shock.

"Misa, can you lend me your shoulder?" He asked me.

"Sure." He slowly lifted himself up on his other leg. I was trying to help him up, but I was afraid I'd hurt him more. "Are you sure you should be moving? That looks really painful."

"Oh, I'm all right. Actually, this isn't what I'm worried about at the moment. What I'm worried about now is-" Ken was interrupted by the sudden sound of a loud thud of the main doors bursting open and people scrambling to move to the side.

"Kenny-kens!" We heard Jayson when he spotted us in the middle of the ice rink.

"Jay's reaction." Ken finished his sentence as we both saw him headed this way. Fast.

Jayson came running over to us. He didn't hesitate at all getting here. He barely stopped to understand the situation. He simply grabbed Ken and got him in the car as quickly as he could for us to go to a doctor. Once we were all in and Ken had a rag over his leg Jayson had in his car, he drove like mad to the hospital. No one really spoke other than Ken telling him to slow down a bit every now and then, but Jayson didn't listen. He just kept driving. He already called ahead to have their doctor waiting for him. They immediately took him in to check out the damage once we finally arrived at the hospital. After getting him signed in and everything, we were in the waiting room. After what felt like forever, I looked over to Jayson, who looked to have finally exhaled. The waiting began.

26

My head was cloudy as I was sitting in the waiting room letting my hand mindlessly play with a magazine I wasn't really looking at when the doctor came out. "Nothing life threatening to worry about," he said to Jayson so he could change the expression he's had since getting us. "We did some X-Rays, and it does show the blade did reach far enough to fracture his femur. That wasn't a small cut, so he got a few stitches. He'll need to stay off his leg for some time to heal, but he's doing fine now." I was relieved when he said there was nothing seriously wrong. "He's bandaged up and laying in his room, you can go in and see him." He added.

"Oh, thank you so, so much for all your help," Jayson said.

"We had no trouble at all with Mr. Masidone. Very good kid."

"Come on, Misaky, I'm sure you want to see him." Jayson gestured for me to go. I still haven't said anything since getting here. If he hadn't gone back to the rink to look for my phone, we wouldn't be here. It's that thought that's sitting heavy in my throat, making it harder to speak. "Oh Kenny-kens. How are you? Are you doing all right?" Jayson went in like a concerned parent over to his bedside. Ken was sitting up and had his covers over his lower half. His badly stained pants were sitting on the chair with his other stuff.

"Yeah, I didn't think it was that bad, she must have had some freshly sharpened blades to go along with that powerful spin." Ken said.

"My heart almost stopped beating when I got the call from Misaky. I didn't know what to do." Jayson had that worried look again. Ken must not get hurt often from how he reacted. He nearly drove into the building and mowed through everyone getting to Ken. Then he almost left me when I went to get his shoes and stuff.

"You know Papa Masy isn't going to be happy." Jayson went on.

"Yeah, don't remind me."

"And Misaky, you poor thing. Seeing all that blood must have frightened you. You even got it on your pretty outfit," Jayson said looking at the bottom of my shirt stained from when I went by him on the ice. I tried washing it off in the bathroom while we were waiting, but it had already set in.

"And your phone got cracked," Ken added for kicks. But it wasn't the time for jokes.

"Forget about my phone. It's because of that stupid thing this happened." I finally spoke with more anger than I thought.

"Well, it started because I surprised you with that spin, so it's my fault. I should've been more careful. I saw that girl coming around, but I didn't think she was that close to me."

"Oh, come now. Don't put the blame on yourselves. You are both beginners, so you didn't know anything or what could possibly happen," Jayson tried to comfort us, "And that poor thing who did it. She looked like she was about to have a breakdown. I can't even be mad at her. It was all just a really, really bad accident. The important thing here is that Kenny-kens is all right, and just needs some resting time before he's like new again." Jayson got his composure back trying to calm us. "Speaking of resting, it's getting a bit late, and we have a long drive to get you home. Misaky, are you sure you'll be okay going home tonight?" Jayson asked me.

"Um, well actually, could you take me to my friend's house?" I asked. Katie wouldn't mind me coming over late. Right now, the last thing I want to be is alone at home just thinking about this.

"Alright then. I'll feel a million times better knowing you're not by yourself."

"Guess I'll have to wait to have Mimi become my personal nurse and help me out." Even after being hit, stitched, and given a couple shots, he's still able to joke. I guess if he's being this strong about it, I can breathe a little easier. This heavy feeling in my chest is still there.

Jayson took me to Katie's house, and they returned home. I told her what happened and used some of my emergency clothes I have in her room to change out of my probably-unable- to-wear-again clothes. It feels like old times when I lived here. Her parents welcomed me in without hesitation. I had to explain that I wasn't the one that was hurt after they almost had a heart attack looking at my clothes. Once I was able to talk about it, I was finally able to calm down and fall asleep.

"If I didn't wake up in your room, I really would've thought everything was a dream." I told Katie after getting up.

"Well, you did go from a wonderful evening to a horrible misfortune all at the same time. Who knew ice skating could be such a dangerous sport."

"Yeah, and it was to Ken. I didn't think things like that could happen to him. I just hope he's all right. It really looked bad."

"Aw, is Misa worried?"

"Well, he got hurt looking for my stuff." I reminded her.

"Ken looks like a strong guy. I'm sure he'll be all right. But what are you going to do about Sano? Don't you meet with him today?" She asked.

"Oh! I almost forgot about him. What time is it?" I looked for my now cracked phone to see the time.

"What time were you supposed to meet?"

"He said around like 2pm."

"You do realize it's 1:15pm, right?" Katie said looking at her phone.

"Did I really sleep that late? Why didn't you wake me?"

"It was way after midnight when you went to sleep. I didn't want to bother you after the night you had. At least that'll make for a good conversation if you need one." She thought.

"Should I really tell him?"

"Well, it is his brother. And he told Ken about his mother too."

"Yeah, but wouldn't that bring up how I know and how it happened? I still don't feel right telling him we were out yesterday and the two of us are meeting today."

"I guess that could bring up questions."

"So, what should I say?"

"I say you should get ready and worry about that later," she said reminding me of the time.

My body felt heavy getting up with the weight of yesterday still on me. By the time I finished getting dressed, I had about ten minutes to get to our meeting place before I would be considered late. I set out on a power walk. If I could beat all the lights, I could probably get there a few minutes behind. I'm starting to get a bit anxious about what he wants to say. I know it's going to be about why he lied and was keeping the truth about him and Ken from me. It could be something else since he's going through the trouble of needing to meet alone. I was just across the street from my destination when I had a run in with someone who was approaching the corner from a different direction.

"Oh, I'm sorry. S-Sano?" The person I bumped into was him.

"Oh, sorry, Misa, were you on your way to meet me?"

"Yeah, I was. I was in a hurry because I thought you were already there."

"I was running a bit behind schedule too. I had to drop the kids off at our aunt's house."

"I see. How are the kids?" I asked.

"They're doing great. Every now and then they ask when you'll be over again." he said.

"Well, we are going to the park. You could have brought them along." I said as we crossed the street heading to a kid's play land.

This one isn't the one my dad took us too. This park was much bigger with a walking path for people to jog or bike around. The field was open and had a spot for people to bring small barbecue pits to cook out, which one family was doing. There was surprisingly a small number of people and kids there for a sunny Saturday afternoon. We walked around to an area away from the others to a table under the tree.

"You know how energized they can be. I didn't want to have to worry about them. But I did promise to take them tomorrow since I've been leaving them so much."

"Oh, because of the project?"

"Yeah, that, and I've been going to the hospital more." He said a little low.

That's right. His mother isn't doing so well. I looked around past the family barbecuing, and past another father and daughter playing frisbee farther down and seeing them all so happy while he has to make frequent visits to the hospital to even see his mother.

"Is your mother going to be okay?" I asked on a whim.

"It was a bit rough a few days ago, but she's holding up for now." I could see the worry in his eyes.

"That's good she's doing better. It must be hard for you doing everything. The project, other schoolwork, taking care of the kids, going to the hospital, when do you have time to rest?"

"I find the time. It's not the worst thing in the world to be doing. There are worse things to be going through," he said with a light smile like what he's doing isn't much at all.

"Well, let's not take too long so you can get back and try to relax some," I said. I don't want him to overwork himself more than he already is.

"I guess I should get started then," he said with a little exhale, "It's not much to say really. Ken, our father, and I haven't been seeing eye to eye since we had a huge incident happen about five years ago with the family." He must be talking about the hidden mother thing.

"As you had figured out, they tried to hide who my real mother was, and I had a hard time forgiving them for that. I ended up leaving the house and moved in with my real mom. I only kept in contact with Ken for a little while after I left, but then we had a little falling out and I stopped contact with him as well. I actually hadn't seen any of them since I left. When Ken came to our school, that was the first time I saw him in about five years. I was shocked, never expecting to see him there, but then after I figured out the reason, it didn't surprise me that he would be doing this." He took a little pause.

"It's just that, when you started coming around me, I didn't want to tell you we were related because I didn't want you to think I was like them in any way." He didn't want me to think he had any ties to their family. Even if he kept asking about him, he couldn't tell me the real reason why thinking I would change the way I see him.

"But aren't things going better for you two? I mean, I saw you both talking in the hallway before."

"Oh that, we were passing each other, and we just started talking. I decided to tell him about what's going on. I was a bit surprised when he seemed concerned about my mother. That did kind of change my opinion about him, but it's still a lot of things to resolve, and this is something I haven't been able to let go of so easily."

"I understand what you mean. I'm sorry you had to go through so much by yourself. I didn't think they were all that bad, but with your stories, it makes me wonder."

"Did Ken tell you something?" he asked.

"Um yeah, when I first found out about you guys, I asked him about it, and he told me some of what you said."

"Really? I didn't think he bothered to remember it all."

"He did. He sounded upset as we talked about it. Actually, he was really upset about it."

"I see," he said softly. Another silence came through as some falling leaves fell onto the table. Sano and Ken are brothers. They were close brothers at that. It wasn't Ken that hid the truth, so his problem isn't really with him.

"From how I see it, I feel it's more of a problem with your father than with Ken. I-I mean, I probably shouldn't say that..."

"It's okay. You're right actually. He's the one that started the whole thing, and then everything started spiraling. I'm sure Ken probably knows that's where the real heart of the matter lies, but it's not much we can do about it."

"Yeah. Ken's always doing something because of his dad. I wonder how he's going to hold up now that he's injured."

"He's injured?" He asked. That last part slipped out. I didn't intend to bring it up so soon. If at all.

"Y-yeah, he got injured yesterday. He'll have to use crutches for a while."

"Oh really? What happened?"

"Um…" I stalled. Should I tell him it happened during a date?

"I-it happened during…" I trailed off searching for the right words.

"So, you injure my Kenny and then go out on a date with someone else!?" Sano and I both turned to see Jenny. They must have a tracking device on me. How did she find us?!

"Jenny, don't waste your time with them." Jennifer walked up behind her. They were both here!

"How could you!?" Jenny was holding a drink as she came and stood next to me, "Do you know what you put me through after hearing about Kenny and how hard it was to see him in that state!? So very hurt and just so helpless?"

"He said it didn't hurt that much, you're exaggerating," I said not really looking directly at her.

"Exaggerating? Who are you to tell me that I'm exaggerating? My Kenny is strong, but I know he is hurting a lot right now. And why? Because of you!"

"I-I didn't cause him to get hurt. It was somebody that ran into him that caused him to get hurt."

"But it was because he was out with you that it happened.

Something like this has never happened before he started hanging around you!" She was close to crushing the cup in her hand, but instead, she suddenly removed the lid and splashed it on me.

"Whoa! Hey!" I yelled out. To have suddenly been hit with what smelled like green tea took me aback. My face was soaking along with my hair and shirt. I think she's finally crossed the line.

"Hey," Sano got up, "I don't know the whole story here, but I think you're getting the wrong idea and taking it a bit too far. I asked Misa to meet me, so this isn't her fault. And whatever happened to Ken still doesn't give you the right to do this."

"And who are you again?" She asked him, looking him up and down.

"That's the no-good brother," Jennifer whispered to her.

"Oh. So, this is him," Jenny shook her head still staring him down.

"I hope you feel proud of yourself for what you've done to that wonderful family."

"Hey, this is between you and me, so don't bring Sano into this." I was standing too at that point trying to wipe my face the best I could with no towel or anything.

"He shouldn't have said anything then."

"He only said that because you're being crazy out here where there are other people and kids," I said noticing the barbecuing family looking over at our argument.

"Oh, boo-hoo. It's just a few kids, they're not important," Jenny said fanning them away like they were flies.

"I think you should apologize to Misa, and leave," Sano told her.

"Apologize? For what? I have nothing to apologize for."

"Uh, how about pouring your drink on me?" I pointed to myself.

"Oh that, sorry. For a second, I mistook you for the trash."

"What?"

"Look, I don't even know exactly who you are, but I'm not going to sit here and let you disrespect Misa like this." Sano stood next to me. I've never seen him look so upset.

"Oh my, Kenny-kens was right after all." We all stopped and looked over at Jayson who was slowly making his was over. Maybe there is tracker on me. How did he find us?

"Girls, you two should be ashamed of yourselves. What are you doing all the way out here? I didn't want to believe Kenny-kens when he said to watch out for you both. He even tried to leave himself. It's a good thing I called your driver to see what you two were up to today. What have you done to my Misaky?" He asked looking at me, still wet and the smell is somehow getting stronger. Then he looked and noticed Sano next to me and his expression changed again. "Oh, my sweet sugar. Is that my lovely little Sano? It's been so long since I've last seen you! How are you doing?" He went toward Sano like a mother who hadn't seen their child since leaving for the military.

"I'm doing fine." Sano tried sounding believable, but he wasn't exactly in a reunion mood.

"That's so good to hear. But that smell, Misaky, what happened to you?"

"She was suddenly hit with a drink." Sano told him and looked to Jenny who still had the empty cup in her hand.

"Oh no. Jenny you didn't, did you?" She looked away and didn't answer.

"I think it's just about that time for you girls to head home. Sano dear, could you take Misaky home, so she won't get sick?" Jayson asked.

"Yeah, I was going to." He answered.

"I'll apologize on behalf of these girls and how they've behaved toward you. I'll be keeping a close eye on them. I cannot believe you went searching this city for her. Now I want the both of you to apologize." He demanded.

"I didn't do anything." Jennifer protested.

"Exactly, you should've stopped her. So, the both of you, come on now." Jayson was waiting.

"I'm sorry," they both halfheartedly said at the same time. But they can forget getting an 'apology accepted.'

"Alright, now let's go the both of you. I'll see you later, Misaky." I've only met him a few times, but Jayson really is a helpful guy to have around.

"Bye, Jay." I said. They left, and now that the mood was destroyed, so did we.

I'm two for two on ending the day badly. Seeing Sano get so upset was a new side of him I hadn't seen before.

"Are you okay, Misa?" He asked me after what seemed like the longest and most awkward silence since we left.

"Yeah, I'm fine. It's been a while since I've smelled green tea." I tried joking. I wanted to hide from the shame actually. I didn't want him to see such a thing like that.

"If I had a better understanding of everything, I could've helped more. But that other girl is from our class, right?"

"Yeah, she's pretty much there to watch Ken at school. The other one was her sister, and also Ken's other fiancé."

"I see. Guess there's not much you can do with a person like that. If she can even find you out in public so easily, you should probably keep watch of her." he told me. I'm already ahead of him on that one. "But um, to get back to what we were talking about, I hope what I've told you gives you a better idea of everything and that you'll be able to forgive me for not telling you before."

"It does. And don't worry, I will." I told him. I understand what he went through was rough and he did that to protect himself and hope I'd still want to talk with him since I knew Ken. Now that I think about it, it's kind of like Ken too. He didn't say anything to make it seem like he didn't know Sano so Sano could keep his life the way he had it.

He didn't say much else after that as we walked back. It was almost like he was thinking whether to say something else or not. But I didn't press anything about that. We got to my house, and he stopped.

"I don't know if this is asking too much, but are your parents usually gone most of the time?" Sano suddenly asked me.

"Yeah, they are. They stay closer to the job and come back when they get enough time off. I don't always stay by myself. I stayed with Katie for a while, but since Ken came here, I moved back."

"When my mom first got to the hospital, it was kind of weird not having her at home, but with the kids there, it keeps things from being lonely. I guess it's good that you at least have Ken around." He said. He had been thinking of my living situation. It does seem unusual, but seeing as I am the only child, being on my own hasn't really been that bad. "I guess I'll see you around then." Sano parted ways with me after we said goodbye and I went inside.

I went straight for the shower to get the smell of that horrible green tea out of my hair. After everything that happened, Sano didn't really seem like himself. But at least he was honest and told me the truth. I'm glad he wanted to clear the air. I wonder how he feels about Ken now. The real source of the issue is their father. I think he may have a misunderstanding about him.

I'm starting to understand them both more now that I know what happened between them. You really don't know a person until you hear their story. I would never have thought for either of them to have that in their past just by looking at them. The scary part is, the more I hang around the both of them though, the more my original thoughts keep changing. And that's the part that isn't processing well.

27

Sleep is really a wonderful thing. It's so easy to do when you want to forget about something that happened. Especially if that thing is wanting to forget how a jealous fiancé came and ruined a nice Saturday afternoon. I tried letting go of the encounter that happened earlier after changing and settling back in, but my rest was interrupted by a knock at the front door. I wasn't expecting anyone, and day had already turned to night. I looked to see who it was, and it was slightly shocking to see who was standing there.

"Ken?"

"At your service," he said all smiles while resting on his crutches.

"W-what are you doing here?"

"Well, I mean I partially live here. Just needed a little help with the door." He said.

"Yeah, but you went home for the weekend, and you're injured." I reminded him as he shifted in stance.

"I decided to come back early. It was awful just sitting in that house."

"Don't you listen to him, Misaky." Jayson said appearing behind him with his bag, "After I told him what happened, he nearly hurt himself again trying to get here. I tried to tell him to just wait it out, but he kept insisting like a broken record."

"I'm sure Mimi doesn't mind me coming back." Ken nudged me.

"Well..." I didn't expect to see him again so soon after he left the hospital yesterday.

"It's okay Misaky, if you have other weekend plans, just say the word. I'll take him right back." Jayson said. He came all the way back here after hearing about what happened earlier. Just to see how I was doing.

"Um, no, no I don't mind him coming back today."

"Perfect! See, all is well. Everything is fine and dandy." Ken hobbled into the house.

"Alrighty then. I'll see you next week. If you need me for anything, you know I'm just a shake away. See you guys then. Oh, Misaky, are you okay now?" Jayson turned back, remembering the incident.

"Yeah, I've gotten cleaned up so I'm fine."

"That's good. You kids behave yourselves. Kenny-kens, don't worry her too much."

"I'll try not to." Ken waved to Jayson as he left. The door slammed shut. For whatever reason, that slam reminded me about one last date I forgot about. John and our meet up tomorrow.

How am I going to go with Ken here not able to walk much? I'll have to tell him that I can't make it. Now that Ken's here, I have no choice but to stay with him. Although the real question is, will he accept my canceling?

"Misa," Ken called out to me, "I want to apologize for Jenny. She went overboard today. I told her not to try coming out here looking for you like she did when we were out the first time. She's just been more on edge since you answered my phone the other day." I knew that wasn't the end of that.

"Oh! Um, sorry about that. I didn't mean to. Something was vibrating, and I was curious to know what it was, and I accidentally answered it."

"Oh, you were curious about who I talk with? Was it jealousy that sparked that interest?" He looked to me with that sly smile.

"N-no! I just didn't know what it was. Then when I looked and saw an unknown number, my finger accidentally answered."

"I thought I blocked her number. She must have gotten another number change."

"Why did you block her?"

"Lately, she's been a bit much to handle. I don't know what's gotten into her. She would call over thirty times a day. I've tried talking with her, but she just blows up at everything. And since you're her competition, she's not planning on backing down." He said. Guess I'll have to be on my guard 24/7. "She also has Jennifer as her partner in crime, so it's kind of hard to maintain both of them."

"So, if you don't like them, why do they stay at your house?"

"Well, I've known them for a while. It's not that I don't like them entirely. It's just that I never liked her romantically, but I guess Jenny did, and when this whole thing of finding someone for me came up, she just flipped. And since she's close to my father, he has a strong approval of her, so he doesn't mind her being around."

"I see why getting rid of her would be hard." I said with a hint of annoyance.

"Well, she's gone now and it's just the two of us. Let's do something!" Ken must have noticed that annoyance and tried changing the subject.

"Have you forgotten that you're hurt? You can't do anything."

"Oh, right. So, are you going to assist me in doing simple everyday tasks?" he asked.

"Your arms are perfectly fine. You can do simple task on your own."

"But I can't move to do it. You'll have to bring me everything. You'll have to help me to my room, to school, and everywhere else. So much time together." He sang. You would think nothing is wrong with him by the way he's acting.

"Only because the doctor said for you not to move much. You shouldn't even be going to school so soon. You're supposed to be staying put."

"You don't have to worry about me so much. If I rest and relax now, I should be able to handle it."

He's so calm about it. He could have easily been paralyzed but he's acting as if he were just a little scratched. I should do all I can to help him since he's like this because of me. As I look to see the brace on his leg, the image of him on the ice with blood everywhere makes this sort of guilt swell up in me. John should be able to understand that I have to watch after him.

The horrible weekend ended, and the week started. The warning bell sounded, but thanks to a certain guy that needs like an extra hour to get around, I was in class early.

"Hey, Misa, how's life with cripple over there?" Katie asked as Ken was adjusting himself in his seat, trying to find a place to put his crutches.

"He's so needy. I never realized a person needed to move so much." I told her. He tried his best to get me to help him in the shower, but I drew the line there.

"I feel your pain. Eden sprained his ankle once. But that isn't anything like an injury to the femur. That'll take longer to heal."

"So, you really don't know my pain then."

"Misa!" My chat with Katie was interrupted by John when he showed up in my class.

"John? What are you doing here?" I asked him. The hurt expression on his face showed it was obviously about my canceling.

"Misa, you gave me hope, and you took it away. I know I don't have a chance, but don't give me a mile if I can't even have an inch!" He was serious. That's a first for him.

"Look, I'm sorry I had to cancel, but I needed to help Ken since he's injured." I calmly and quietly said as he's already attracted the attention of almost everyone.

"I know and that's completely understandable. Coming to someone's rescue like you always do. But I still feel cheated, and I want compensation." He walked closer to my desk.

"W-what do you mean by that?" I felt a cold sweat unsure of what he was going to do. John was upset. John is unpredictable. And most importantly, John was heartbroken.

"I understand now I don't stand a chance since he's hurt, and you'll be spending your time with him. So, I think, as a good replacement for our date, this should do." He stopped talking and put all his focus on me.

John was a lot of things, and crazy was one of them. I never thought he'd have a breaking point after going on for so long. But here it was as he brought our faces closer together, closing that personal space I did my best to keep. And before I knew it, John was kissing me.

28

John was kissing me. Me! I was frozen. My eyes wide unsure what to do. Katie went to pull him back from me.

"John, what do you think you're doing to her? Have you finally lost all of your mind?"

"W-wow, I actually did it," he said in disbelief.

"Yeah, you did. You finally lost your mind and went insane." Katie said, getting upset when I think I was finally coming to.

"Misa, I'll cherish this forever! And maybe with this, you'll be able to feel-" with my hand going across his face, he wasn't able to finish his sentence.

"What's wrong with you? Are you that crazy that you can't control yourself?" I glanced at the classroom, and everyone was looking. They all saw!

"Alright, let's get this week going," The final bell rang, and Mr. Hallens came strolling in.

"What are you doing here Banks? This isn't your period. Get to class!" he told John.

"Y-yes, Mr. Hallens." John rushed out of the class still holding his face. I don't think I've blinked yet. I just sat forward in my seat and didn't dare to look in any direction. If there's anything good about this whole this is that Jennifer hasn't shown up yet. Everything would be over if she had seen that.

"You cancelled on him?" Katie whispered to me, "Why would you do that? To John, of all people?!"

"I had no choice. Ken came back early."

"Why did he come back early?" I didn't tell her what happened Saturday. If I did, she would've been the reason why Jennifer hadn't shown up yet.

"I'll tell you later," I told her. She looked at me with a face that says she'll be waiting.

Class got started, and for once, I paid full attention to distract myself from what just happened. Ken and I had already arranged for me to help him with his things to his second period class. He was allowed to leave a little early to beat the crowd. I was not ready to face him yet. But class was ending along with my preparation time.

"You are taking his things?" Katie asked.

"Yeah."

"His mood seems different, but I can't tell if he's mad or not. He has a good poker face. But that was quite the scene earlier. If you hadn't slapped him, I would have. In fact, I think I should still."

"It's okay, I'll handle this myself."

"You sure? Cause I'll do it. Just give me the word and one good hit, he won't know left from right, up from down, east from west, acute from obtuse, squ—"

"Katie! I got this. I'll talk to you later." Knowing Katie could do away with John didn't stop my accelerating heartbeat as I stood to go face Ken.

It was five minutes before the bell, and I walked over to his seat. I can't exactly tell from his expression, but I'm sure he's upset.

"Are you all packed?" I asked.

"Yep. Just need to put these books in my locker before I go to my next class."

"Alright." I couldn't sense any anger in his tone. But I did start hearing whispers around me.

"So, what was that about with John if she's still with him?"

"Maybe she's with both of them." I tried not to notice the two girls in the row next to him, but Ken didn't ignore it.

"Hey, if you're trying to whisper, you need to talk just a little lower." He whispered back to them. "Let's go Mimi." He started hopping out the door, and I just followed behind him. We headed to his locker in silence.

"I just need this one book for now. I shouldn't have my assistant holding too much."

"Your assistant?" I asked.

"Yep, my *personal* assistant."

"You do know we only have this one class, so I won't be carrying your things after this."

"Aw, couldn't you leave your other classes early?"

"I don't think it works that way. You'll have to have someone in your other classes to help."

"Well, that's no fun." He was acting all sad about it. I'm still waiting for him to ask about that situation with John. I remember he was looking the whole time, so I know he saw it. And he heard those girls talking too. Does it not bother him?

This is the same guy that got super jealous when I was going to Sano's house. I thought for sure he, of all people, would be upset about it.

"My class is upstairs, so we'll have to take the elevator." Taking the elevator alone with him. Maybe I should say something in case I'm reading him wrong. "Something wrong, Mimi?" Ken looked at me asking if something was wrong when I should be asking him that.

"Uh, no, I mean, well, about what happened earlier..." I was trying to find the right words, but then I heard a clicking sound in the hallway.

"Hey! Can you hold the elevator?" I held the open button as I heard someone coming.

"Thanks. I didn't have anyone to help me today." A girl who was also on crutches got on with us. With her here, I won't be able to finish what I was going to say.

"I just got my classes changed and I'm not used to this side of the school yet. I only need it for the elevator, do you know where the art hallway is from here?" The girl asked after we got upstairs.

"Oh um, it's right around the corner here," I said, pointing left.

"Oh, really? Thanks."

"Did you need any help?" I offered. She looked like a freshman, and I remember my lost days going through the halls of this large school.

"No, that's okay, I got it. Plus, you seem to already have your hands full. Thanks for the offer though." She said as she headed to her class. The girl had most of her left leg wrapped up and a boot on her foot. She must have been in a bad accident.

"Isn't Mimi so nice? Always wanting to help and come to people's rescue. "Ken said.

"She just seemed a little lost. And don't call me that at school."

"Fine, fine." The bell had already rung, and everyone was moving around to their next class. I guess I'll have to tell him later as I followed him to his.

"My class is here." We stopped at a room in the science and chemistry hall.

"Oh my, Ken, what have you done to yourself?" His teacher asked as soon as we walked in the room.

"Nothing. Just got hit by a shoe." He simply stated as he headed to his seat.

"A what?"

"It's a long story." Ken must be on good terms with his teacher to be able to say it like that. "My seat's here." He told me. "Thanks for the help." He was in the front row. That should make leaving and entering easier for him. He can just ask whoever sits next to him to help him to his next class.

"Is that the girl everyone talks about?"

"She isn't that special." I heard more whispers coming from behind me.

"He rejected me for her?"

"Wow."

"I'll find you after school to help you then." I said. I hurried out of there after that. Those girls that were talking must all like him. They all will probably volunteer to help him. I guess I never paid that much attention to him during school to notice he had so many admirers.

"Hey, Misa." I rounded the corner to see Sano coming this way. We have to stop meeting like this.

"Oh, Sano. You headed to class?"

"Yeah, I am. You just dropped Ken off?"

"Yeah, I did. Your class around here?"

"We have the same class. This is the class we're doing the project in." He pointed to the room I just walked out of.

"Oh, I see. You all going to finish it today?"

"Probably. It's not much left to do. Even though he's not going to be able to move much, we'll still be able to get it done."

"I'm sure you all can do it." I replied.

"Thanks for the encouragement."

"No problem." This conversation feels forced. He seems kind of distant.

"I guess I should be going." I said, trying to get around him.

"Ah, Misa, wait." he said stopping me. "I don't know about Ken, but it's kind of been bothering me about what happened this morning." He admitted. My eyes went wide in shock. That's what it was. He was thinking about that.

"Uh, please, don't misunderstand! I don't know what got into John. I guess he got upset because I said I'd do something that I couldn't do at the last minute."

"Oh, is that what it was? It still seems I don't know a lot about you. Although, I did hear the rumors about him liking you for a long time, but I didn't know it was to that degree."

You're telling me...

"That's your business though. I shouldn't ask more about it. I'll see you around."

Sano seemed more concerned about it than Ken did. And he asked me about it. Ken didn't ask or seem concerned. Maybe he doesn't care about things like that. But if Ken really did like me, then it should bother him at least a little...

Wait, what am I thinking? We're not even together. So, it shouldn't bother me. That's probably why it didn't bother him. Maybe...

29

"Hey, Misa, you're headed—what's wrong?" Katie showed up at my locker at a bad time. I quickly tried to stuff a paper in the closest closed thing I could find.

"Y-yeah, I just have to go get Ken."

"What's that?" She pointed to the paper I was trying to hide.

"This? I-it's nothing."

"Is that a note? From whom? You have to let me see." I tried blocking her, but she still managed to get it.

"No, Katie. Don't read it."

"What is this?" Her playful look was gone, and I could see her blood begin to boil.

"I don't know. I just found it shoved in my locker."

"It says *whore* in big letters. Who wrote this!?"

"I don't know!" I said again, shoving the note in my pocket. "It's nothing. People are just misunderstanding."

"Misa this is not a misunderstanding. Why would someone do that?"

"Well, there are a lot of girls who like Ken, and with what happened this morning, not to mention the Sano thing that happened a while ago, it's no surprise."

"I bet it was Jennifer." She came to her conclusion.

"She's not even here today." I reminded her.

"Yes, she is. I just saw her in the other hallway talking with someone by the library." I didn't see her in class at all, but if Katie saw her, then maybe I just missed her.

"I have to go," I said.

"Misa, you're going to have to do something about her. Because if you don't, I will." That wasn't a simple statement, that was a warning.

"Katie, just hold off for now. I don't know why, but I don't think she did it. She wouldn't sink this low. Just leave it alone for now, please?" She looked at me for a minute before she answered.

"Okay, Misa. But if something else happens, I'm not stopping."

"Thanks." I said to my best friend as I walked away. She's always there for me whatever the issue may be.

I wished these issues stopped coming up. I told Ken I'd help him after school, so I went to find him quickly, so I won't have the chance of running into anything or anyone else today.

"Hey, you ready? Let's go." I saw him at his locker, and I just grabbed his things.

"Whoa, what's the rush for?" He asked.

"Rush? There's no rush. I thought you'd want to get home so you can work on your project." I said.

"Well, that is my plan for today, but I have to wait for Sano and Eden first. I figure since we're all going to the same place, it's better to just go at the same time."

"Oh, right." I stopped moving. They wouldn't need to go separately like I did when I was going to Sano's house. But now I'll be with both him and Ken. I wonder if Sano is still thinking about it. He said it wasn't his business, but I know he wouldn't just leave it at that. I'm already on edge and don't want to find out if he wants to make it his business or not.

"Um, hey, since you got two other people coming, could one of them just hold your stuff? I need to hurry home, and I'm sure they wouldn't mind."

"Well, that should be fine, but what's with the urgency to get home?"

"I-I just need to get home. Is that such a crime? I'll help you next time when there aren't many people surrounding you." I put his things back down next to him and walked away.

Walking home with those two would definitely be a bad idea. My school is big, but gossip is bigger. Since Ken has a lot of fans, this time it won't go away so easily. I just wonder who wrote that note. It has to be someone who feels strongly about this.

Jennifer must have come in late, and with the number of people she knows, she has to have heard about it. The note was handwritten, and I've seen her writing before in class. This doesn't look like her writing, so I can't send Katie out on an assassination mission just yet.

I tried to spend the rest of my day in my room avoiding the lower level at all costs. They stayed in one spot for the most part for Ken. I heard laughter and them joking around. They must be enjoying themselves. It's the last day they'll be hanging around each other like this since they are finishing today. They don't really have much to worry them.

This time, I think it's just me that's the center of the gossip, and it's not bothering Ken at all. I wonder if he saw that note I got, would he care? With the different rumors that have started since all of this began, I can understand why no one knows what's really going on. And for them to know, I'd have to tell them what's really happening between all of us. I have to let them know that we're all friends, but I'm only interested in one being more. But the answer to that is what everyone wants.

Sano is nice and considerate and doesn't have a problem with anything I do no matter how much I messed up. He also stood up for me at the park when Jenny was trying to get in my face even when he wasn't sure what was going on.

Ken can joke a lot. But he's also nice and can be considerate. He's always full of energy and doesn't have a problem with helping me do things. He didn't even show any signs of anger when he got hurt since he was out looking for my phone, and made Jayson come back here to bring him just because he wanted to see if I was all right after Jenny blew up at me. He's always doing too much when it comes to me, but he's yet to say something about what was done earlier.

"Oh Mimi." Without noticing, it got really quiet downstairs except for the sound of Ken calling up to me. I had no choice but to go downstairs to see what he wanted.

"What is it?" I asked.

"We're finally done building our masterpiece!" He said, but didn't continue. I looked around and didn't even see it.

"Where is it?"

"It's outside. Did some spray paint touch up and its drying." He stated.

"Is that all you called me for?"

"Aren't you happy for me?" He gave me his sad face.

I just sighed. "Yes, congratulations. Job well done. You guys are the greatest rocket builders ever."

"Hmm, that didn't sound very sincere. But I'll take it!"

"If that's all, I'm headed back upstairs." I turned to leave.

"Wait. You've been in your room this whole time, so I know you haven't eaten yet. I haven't either. Since I can't move much, why not assist me in making something really tasty?"

"And what do you want that's really tasty?"

"Pancakes!" He said like a happy eight-year-old.

"Pancakes?"

"Yes."

"You do know it's seven at night, right?" I reminded him of the time.

"Yes, I am aware of what time it is. But are you aware of such a thing called breakfast for dinner?"

"Well, yeah. But it's still…" I couldn't think of a good argument.

"It's still food. Who made it a law that it had to be eaten only in the morning? I think if it's meant to be eaten, then it can be eaten at any time. So, how's bout it?"

"Fine, I guess." I didn't want to fight with him about it.

"Alright! Can never go wrong with pancakes. And what better pancakes then homemade ones."

"Wait you want to make them from like, scratch? We have a box in the cabinet."

"Can't get any better than scratch," he said.

"I don't know anything about making pancakes, so how do you expect me to make them from scratch?"

"It's not that much different from the box mix. Don't worry, I'll be helping you. From the chair."

'From the chair' he says. That pretty much means it's all me. The last thing I want right now is to try cooking something new.

"This will be really simple. I've made these plenty of times. It doesn't need many ingredients either. How about I take care of the mixing, and you can do the making?" Ken suggested. I agreed with that since there's a less likely chance, I'll add something wrong.

I pulled out the ingredients and utensils he asked for. I watched as he started mixing as if he came up with this recipe on his own. He didn't use any instructions, or actual measuring spoons.

"Shall I narrate as I go?" He asked as he saw me just staring at him.

"Why do you always need to separate the flour and milk and stuff?"

"Well, in most dishes, mixing dry ingredients and wet separately helps in a lot of ways. It prevents bad lumping, easier for things to blend well, and just helps you attend to all the ingredients for a better-quality taste." He sounds like he should be on a cooking show. He even looks like he is enjoying himself. "Alright, now we just need a pan nice and greased. What's wrong?" He looked at me.

"You're enjoying this a lot," I told him.

"You think so?" He stopped and thought about it. "I guess doing this, it would remind me of the only thing I always enjoyed doing with my father growing up. He'd actually take the time to make these with me. But we haven't done that in quite a while."

"What made you want them all of a sudden?"

"I don't know. Just felt like a day to have pancakes."

"And what exactly made today a pancake day?"

"Do you really want to know?" He asked.

"I mean, I asked, so yeah."

"Well, to keep a story short and sweet, my father and I normally made pancakes to help us relax when we had a lot on our minds." I couldn't help but be taken by surprise. For him to be saying that means something has been bothering him enough to make him need to do some relaxing technique like this.

"W-what's on your mind?" I asked.

"Oh, this and that." He answered.

"What's up with that reply? That's not an answer."

"It is an answer. Just not well explained."

"If you never intended to say anything, why did you say something at all?"

"You asked me why I felt like pancakes, and I told you. You were one who wanted further details of another topic."

"Well sorry for wanting to know what's going on with you." I said getting a little more irritated than I wanted.

"I think you're the one that has something to talk about. You've been strange all day." He said reading me.

"How have I been acting strange? I'm all right. There's nothing wrong with me." I paused for a second. "You're the one that has the problem."

"Why do you say that?" He looked confused.

"Because you say you like me, but you don't have any problem with seeing another guy kiss me." I finally said it out loud. Ken stayed quiet. I was staring at him, and he was staring at the pancake batter. "You know what, forget I said anything. You can finish your own pancakes," I said walking out. But he extended his arm out in front of me.

"So, what kind of reaction were you expecting from me?" He asked.

"What?"

"You were looking for some kind of outburst from me about that, right?"

"I…" the words couldn't come out.

"Shouldn't that leave me to think that it would mean something to you if I did act out in jealousy?"

"W-what are you trying to say?"

"Why would you want me to be upset about that?" He looked at me for an answer, but I looked away struggling for one.

"Y-you said you like me, so wouldn't something like that cause for you to get, like, upset, or something?"

"Yes, that's normally an appropriate response to what happened, but for someone who doesn't have any interest in me, it shouldn't matter to them one way or another if I reacted to the matter or not, right? But for you to want something to happen, what should that lead me to think about you and your feelings toward me?"

I turned back to him, and he was staring at me. Was he asking if he actually mattered to me or not?

Why did I want him to be upset by that kiss? And why did I get upset because he didn't? Sano actually asked me about the situation and wanted to know about it, but that only made me want to hear Ken's reaction more. I wanted Ken's reaction more... is it really because he matters that much to me now?

"Well?" Ken was waiting for a reply.

I was too busy trying to end this inner battle, I skipped this important detail. Every time I became aware of what he was doing for me, I came to like it. I like all the things he's done to try to keep me around even if I didn't understand why.

And when I was taken away by John and he didn't say anything, it bothered me because I was waiting for him to get upset and wanted him to come to me because I liked when he came to me. Because... I like him.

"I- I don't know." I walked out not wanting to finish this conversation and went upstairs to my room.

I can't believe I didn't realize this sooner. I've started liking Ken. When did the crossover happen? At first, he was just a rich, perverted stranger to me. But now, well, take away the stranger part, and replace it with...

"Misa."

I looked and saw Ken in my doorway.

"For someone who's injured, you managed to get up the stairs quickly."

"Yeah, and I probably shouldn't have chosen the quicker method, but that's beside the point," he said. I can see he wants to pick up where I cut it off.

"Shouldn't you be making your pancakes?"

"Oh, I will, but I just want to confirm something."

"W-what do you want to confirm?" I looked at him. He looked at me with his mischievous smile.

"You wanted me to flip out today because you know how I feel towards you. But when you saw that I didn't, you felt hurt because I seemed calm. And why exactly would you feel upset?" I didn't answer that. "It's because you like the attention I give you, and that's because you've started liking me. Am I right?" Leave it to Ken to hit the nail on the head.

"I don't want to answer that." I said.

"And why not?"

"Because I don't. You can't make me answer anything."

"You're right. I can't. But you know, since you didn't instantly reject me like you used to, I've already gotten what I wanted." He said. Which is something I didn't consider. Then he turned from my door but stopped. I glanced to see what he was doing.

He was touching his leg.

"W-what's wrong?" I asked him.

"Well, it appears I've overdone it for one day."

"Did something happen?"

"Not sure, but I may need to have another checkup. I might've loosened some stitching." I gasped.

"What did you do? Are you okay?" I walked toward him without thinking.

"I'm okay. Now that is."

"What?" I asked. He grabbed me by my arms and pushed me against the wall. Now I'm back in a position I've seen far too many times. Face to face with the most mysterious guy in the world.

"You tricked me!" I told him.

"I had no other choice. I can't very well move how I want to now can I?" He moved to be directly in front of me without putting much pressure on his injured leg. I couldn't escape.

"Oh, this is low."

"Low? What do you mean? I'm only standing in way that makes your only exit a risk for hurting me more, and I know you wouldn't do that. But that isn't a low." He tried acting innocent.

"Now that we've gotten to this point, how about we address that whole thing that happened."

"W-what thing?"

"You and that guy. He's been around before, but I don't exactly know who he is yet." He stated.

"His name is John and I've known him for a few years." I simply put it.

"*And*?" He wanted more.

"And… he's liked me for a long time, but doesn't know the meaning of no."

"Ah, I see. So, you have your own Jenny as well."

"I-I guess you can say that." I never thought of it like that…

"I don't know if I like these odds," he said.

"What odds? There are no odds with him. And other than him, you're the only one that likes me."

"So, you're still one sided with Sano?" My eyes widened when he said that. "Don't think I haven't been keeping tabs about that. But I know that he wouldn't try anything like this John guy. He has guts I tell you. To do that in front of the class and me." His voice was low. It was finally there. The look of jealousy in his eye. "I was actually telling myself that didn't really happen. I repeated it over and over again. And when I finally got it out of my mind, you brought it up again downstairs." He admitted. He wasn't just jealous. He was overly jealous.

"Well, you need not worry about him. I don't like him in that way."

"He's really serious about you. It makes me feel like I need to do more." He started moving in closer to me. I wanted to move back, but I had nowhere to go.

"You can't run away. I think I should get a little sympathy for witnessing something so heart breaking."

"And what do you want from me?" I asked afraid of the answer.

"For you to kiss me."

"What?"

"You didn't like what John did, and I didn't like what John did, so the best way to rid what he's done would be to override it, no?" The look in his eye tells me he's serious. The smirk on his face tells me he's enjoying this. He seriously enjoys putting me in these situations.

I looked away. I thought about the first time I was supposed to kiss Ken, and how that went. If I could, I would reverse time far enough before John kissed me to stop that from ever happening. But since I can't, I either have to live with it, or… *override it.*

I looked to Ken who was waiting. The time has come again for me to kiss him. The racing in my chest started. It's been a while since the first time we did it. Back then, I hardly knew him. Now, I know a little more about him and my feelings have changed. If I do this, that will mean I've admitted that. If I did that, then all this confusion could be over. That makes the most sense. So why aren't I moving in? I looked back down to prepare myself. Then I looked at his leg and saw something on his pant leg where his cut is.

"Is that blood? W-were you serious when you said you loosened your stitching?" He looked down.

"Well, I wasn't exactly lying, but I didn't think I actually did either."

"You need to have this looked at! How did you manage to do this?"

"I would think since I just got this not even three days ago, it probably hasn't even started healing much."

"Doesn't it hurt?" I asked. He thought about it for a second.

"I've been feeling the same pain since after I got the stitching. I can hardly feel anything there."

"So, you've been in pain this whole time and hurting yourself more doing all this moving? What's wrong with you? You need to call someone right now to have them take you to the doctor and check your cut in case it's opened or infected or something."

"That would mean my departure. But, if Mimi is so concerned about it, I guess that would be best." He said. Then he finally moved out of my way.

I can't believe he's been hurting this entire time. And I didn't notice. And I can't believe I'm about to say this, but Jenny was right. She was able to see that he wasn't feeling good. I should've known that after having a blade dig into him that deep that he wasn't okay. I have to make sure that he gets looked at, and didn't do any additional damage.

Ken called Jayson to get him, and he was here in the blink of an eye and took Ken back home and examined again. I went to school the next day by myself.

30

Ken was told to stay home for at least a week, or until he gets his stitches taken out. He told me his doctor didn't want him to go to school, but he persisted anyway. I hope he'll learn that always being persistent will get him nowhere. Maybe now he'll stay put and start to actually get better.

"Misa." I was going to my locker when I heard Katie's voice from behind me.

"It's rare I see you before class," I said.

"Well, with what's going on, I just want to keep an eye on you."

"It's not that bad. Maybe it's already forgotten."

"I don't know, that stirred up kind of quick yesterday. Where is Ken anyway?"

"He went back home. He isn't coming back around until his leg gets better."

"Really? Did something happen?"

"He just over did it yesterday." I don't really want to explain everything to her about yesterday just yet.

Thinking about what we talked about. It finally made me realize that the weird feeling I was getting lately was more than the usual uncomfortable feeling I used to get.

"Well, hello there." Just as me and Katie turned the corner, we were cut off by Jennifer.

"I hope you're having a good start of the day?"

"Is there something you want?" I asked her.

"Oh, not much. Just wanted to let you know that Ken will be in good care."

"And you needed to tell me this now because?"

"Thought I should tell you as soon as possible. Don't want you to be worrying too much. Then again, you probably aren't worried that much since you've gotten your hands filled with other things... or should I say people." She said hinting at what happened yesterday. "But don't worry, Jenny has already been so kind assisting him with anything he needs. He's being treated with great care. Much better care than you could give. I should thank you for having him come back. He'll start to heal properly now that he's away from you."

"Alright, I think I've have just about enough of you." Katie finally spoke up.

"Excuse me?"

"You really need to lay off. You're always talking so highly of yourselves. Just because you sucked your way up to where you are now, doesn't make you at all important." Katie continued.

"Um, this is a conversation between me and her," Jennifer said rolling her eyes.

"Really? Couldn't tell by the way you came and interrupted our conversation. You're nothing special. You're just an instigator and a sidekick. Always trying to start a problem so your precious sister can have what she wants."

"Just like a nobody to step into something that they could never be a part of." I was pretty sure I saw Katie's last good nerve twitch as Jennifer said that. She took a step toward Jennifer.

"Exactly who'd want to be a part of your pathetic world? I find where I am way better than trying to be a part of such sad people like you." Katie poked her in the chest hard enough to make her take a step back. Jennifer was taken aback as she put her hand to her chest.

"Katie, it isn't worth the trouble." I tried calming her.

"You're right, it isn't. I'd rather talk to the person that's actually important in this situation. And you are far from important. Come on, let's go," Katie said. We walked off, leaving her there. Katie purposely bumped into her as she passed. Hard.

"Was that necessary?" I asked.

"I didn't do anything unnecessary. I just said the truth. And you can't tell me it wasn't." I couldn't say anything since I couldn't deny it.

"Although, he probably is better off there. They have all he could need in case something happened." I thought.

"Are you still so worried about your little Ken?"

"It's not like that. I, I can't help that I feel bad about him being hurt."

"Yeah, and because you felt bad and stayed home on Sunday, this situation has happened."

"What was I supposed to do? He needed help and I couldn't leave him there by himself while I did other things that weren't absolute needs to do."

"Sounds like you guys have gotten close."

"Close is a bit much. It's just that he's been around for a while now, I've gotten used to him."

"You mean you've gotten to know him, and you've started to like him."

"That's..."

"Admit it, Misa. You can't make excuses forever. It was bound to happen since you never told him you didn't like him, and you wanted him out. You were always saying what you thought was right, but that was just because you didn't want to think you would like him since you liked Sano."

"I... I guess you're right." I felt defeated. I couldn't deny it anymore.

"So, now what are you going to do?"

"I don't know. I mean, is Sano really an option? He's never told me that he liked me or showed interest in me in that way. It's still... one sided." I said repeating how Ken called it.

"Should you just leave it at that? I mean, Sano might like you. He just never said it."

"How am I supposed to know?"

"Well, sometimes you have to do things on your own. You may have to ask him."

"Me? You want me to go up to him and ask him if he's into me?"

"Not in those words exactly, but yeah. Who says the guy always needs to do it? He might even be hiding it because Ken is here."

"Even so, I think I should wait on that. I just figured this out, so I'd like to see if this is real or not."

"I guess that's not a bad option. Once you've finalized where your heart is, all the headaches will be over."

"I'd like that to happen," I sighed. We entered the classroom, and all eyes went in our direction.

"Guess the situation is still a buzz." I said to Katie.

"Let's just go to our seats." We headed for our chairs, and someone stuck their foot out, making me trip.

"Oh sorry, accidents happen, right?" The girl said. I didn't say anything and went to my chair. Class was about to start, and the teacher showed up at his usual time.

"My, so many smiling faces today," he said sarcastically.

"Oh, Miss Macky, is Masidone not here today?"

"Um, he won't be here for a few days."

"Ah, must be that injury he got, right? What happened to him anyway?"

"He uh, got hit by a shoe," I said repeating what he said to his teacher.

"A shoe? What kind of damage can a shoe make?"

"It's a long story."

"I heard she's the cause of it," I heard someone behind me say.

"First, she's messing around behind his back, now she's hurting him."

"Some 'fiancé'." She emphasized.

"That's enough of that," Mr. Hallens said. Things weren't going as well as I thought. They still aren't over that kiss scene yesterday. These girls must be a part of Ken's fan club. To think he could have easily gone for anyone here, but he insisted on staying around me.

"Sorry, I'm late." I looked to the door and saw Jennifer coming in. She came in and went to her seat, completely ignoring me. She must not be over what happened earlier.

I felt things were getting out of hand. All throughout the day, there have been comments here and there about me and even a few people came up to me and asked what my real relationship with Ken is. I didn't answer them for more than one reason, but the main one was I still don't know yet. Even though Ken figured out something was different with me, I didn't confirm it with him, so nothing has really changed between us. Now I can't do anything until he gets back.

"Hey." I was at my locker when Sano approached me.

"H-hey, what's up?" I wasn't ready to see him. There was more decoration in the 'whore' and 'cheater' category someone left, and I was still getting rid of it. He looked, but I don't think he noticed.

"So, I'm sure Ken told you we finished building the rocket."

"Yeah. You all finished it yesterday. You all are good. I could never do that. It almost looks real."

"Thanks, but It's nothing like a real one. We left it at your house because we had to paint another part of it, and it needed to dry before we moved it. I was wondering, if it were okay, if I could come by to get it since Ken can't bring it in."

"Um, yeah, that's no problem."

"Alright, I have to do something before I go, so I can be there in like an hour."

"Okay, that's fine." He walked away after that. That project date must have changed or something. He seemed like he really needed to get it. I thought he was going to ask about everything that's going on, but he didn't.

He seems like he just wants to make sure he's able to turn in the project, which I can understand since it's worth so much of their grade.

I went home and waited around for Sano to show up. I didn't want to touch the rocket in fear of breaking something; but having it ready for him to go would be better than making him go get it. I went to go grab it when I heard a knock on the door. He must be here already.

"Oh, Katie?" I said answering.

"Hi, yeah, I have something I have to tell you, but first, I really have to go to the bathroom." She said on a mad dash up the stairs.

I'm not sure what just happened, but I just closed the door and went back to get the rocket. I went out back and saw it lying on the cardboard on the grass. I tried lifting it up, but it was a lot heavier than I thought. They worked way too hard on it for days for me to break it. Leaving it there for him to get seemed like a better idea, so I went back into the living room when I heard another knock on the door. This time it was actually Sano.

"Hi," I said letting him in. But he didn't say anything.

"Something wrong?" I asked him. He was quiet and unusually serious looking.

"I came to get the rocket, but I also came because I have something else, I want to say." He admitted.

"What is it?"

"I don't want to take too long, so I'll keep it short. This situation that's happening at school is really bothering me. And I know it has to be upsetting you with all the rumors and people harassing you. I saw all the notes someone is putting on your locker." He told me.

So, he did see it!

"I mean, this is kind of surprising since this has never happened to me before." I told him.

"It's because Ken has a lot of admirers and have since he first got to the school. Since he made that statement about being your fiancé, they kept their distance, but now that they're thinking something is up, it's all coming out." He explained.

"Since Ken isn't here either to help clear the air, this could last a while. That's also why I didn't want to say this at school and cause more of an issue for you, but Misa..."

I think my heart skipped a beat or two as he looked at me more intensely. "I don't know when it started, but lately I've been thinking more about you and everything. Those girls, John kissing you, the school situation, it's all been so bothersome to me because I still don't know a lot about you and how this is all happening. And I guess maybe that's because I've started liking you more than just a friend and I want to help you."

31

"I didn't want to tell you this at school, but I did want to tell you. I just wanted to let you know that if you have any problems with anything, you can ask me, or just tell me about it. I know things have been hard on you recently, so I want to help you like you were trying to help me. Before things got out of hand." The hazel eyes I studied for years were steady as he spoke. The room was quiet while his words echoed in my head. I was speechless.

"I, um..."

"I guess you weren't expecting to hear this from me, so I understand that you wouldn't be able to respond to it. But do take it into consideration." I still couldn't find the proper way to respond. I just stood there hoping he couldn't hear how hard my heart had started pounding.

"Is it okay if I go get the rocket?" I just nodded my head. I watched him go to the kitchen and heard the back door open. Within that same minute, I heard the door open again and he came back to the front. "Guess I'll see you around. Thanks for letting me stop by."

"N-no problem." I watched him carry out the rocket as I slowly closed the door.

"What... was that?" I turned quickly and saw Katie coming down. "Misa, what exactly did I just witness?"

"Katie, you did come, didn't you?"

"Yeah, had to use the bathroom and it seems I almost interrupted something big." She pointed to the door. "Did Sano just come here and tell you he likes you? Like, like you like you, kind of like?"

"I, I think he did."

"Did you, at all, know that he was going to do that?"

"No! I thought he was just coming to pick up the rocket. I never knew he had those feelings. I mean, he has asked about what was going on but wouldn't press about it like he wanted to know, but not know."

"Well clearly, he wants you to know. What are you going to do about what he said?" Katie asked me.

"I don't know. I knew he liked me as a friend, but I didn't think anything more than that."

"Why not? I mean it seems he trusts you. He let you in his house and everything. Then when he found out that you knew he wasn't honest about things he said, he really wanted to clear the air about that so you wouldn't think he was a bad guy."

"I guess you're right."

"And it sounds like he knows about Jennifer and Jenny. How does he know about them anyway? I mean, yeah Jennifer is in our class, but he said girls like he knows Jenny."

"Actually, we had a run-in with them when we met up Saturday."

"You did? And you didn't tell me? Something happened, right? That's the only reason you wouldn't. What was it?" Katie had that look in her eye. I wouldn't be able to get out of this conversation without telling her, so I told her what happened when those two came and started trouble when we were at the park.

"So that's why Ken had come back early. I knew it had to be a reason for it. And that also explains her behavior today. Why didn't you tell me?"

"I didn't want you to do anything rash."

"Well, good luck with that, because now I really do believe she was the one that left the stuff at your locker. She's trying to make you out to be the bad guy and a laughingstock so she can try to trick Ken and get him back to that other girl."

"I don't know about that." I still didn't want to believe it.

"Oh! And speaking of her, that thing I had to tell you is about her. After I got done talking with Eden after school today, I passed by Jennifer on my way home. She was sitting outside talking on the phone to someone. I think it was that sister of hers. She was telling her about what was happening. And then she said she was going to tell her mother about everything."

"Her mother?"

"Yeah. Have you ever met her mother?"

"No, I haven't, but why should that be such a big deal?"

"Misa, think about it. Those two weren't made in a lab with that behavior. They had to have gotten it from someone. Just think what she'd do if she knows about the girl that's keeping Ken away from Jenny."

"Yeah, I didn't think about that."

"You better be careful. They're already living in his house. They can't get any closer to the goal than that. Even though Ken has been staying here, who knows what is being plotted there without anyone around to know."

"Alright, alright I get it. What am I supposed to do?" The thought of someone who was both Jenny and Jennifer combined is something that nearly frightened me.

"You just have to try to stay on their good side," she said.

"How am I going to do that? Those girls don't like me. Just me being around is enough to stay permanently on their bad side."

"I don't think you really need to worry about them as much as you should worry about the adults. You don't need to befriend those two, you need to impress the higher ups."

"And how will I do that?"

"Easy, you just have to stay around Ken more."

"And how am I going to do that now that he isn't around?"

"That's also easy, and the best part of this master plan. You make a trip to his house to see how he's doing and show them that you're more than the two-timing whore they think."

"Okay, ignoring that last comment, what? I can't do that."

"Why not?"

"That's like stepping foot in a lion's den with meat around my neck. That's all the possibility to do who knows what to me."

"But I think that would be a perfect idea. Showing his father how capable you can be in situations like this."

"He just left because he was overworking himself because of me."

"I didn't mean go today. And he wouldn't be doing anything. He'd stay in bed while you bring him food and the remote and all that good stuff. He'd love it."

"I don't know…"

"You have to make the first move before the other team strikes. Once this mother starts coming around, it may be over for you."

"B-but how would I even get there? Do you have any idea how far they live?"

"Right. Well, there isn't anybody you could call for a ride?"

"Uh, well…" I thought about it, and the first person to pop into my head was Jayson. He'd do anything if it involved Ken. And he would probably welcome this idea. "I don't know if I should."

"Misa, if you really did start liking him, and you feel responsible for his injury, then you should at least do this."

"But how am I going to be able to do anything with them there? They'd definitely get in the way."

"Not if they aren't home." She said a little too mischievously.

"How do you expect me to know if they're there or not?"

"Because I also heard that they would be going out of town Thursday for someone's wedding and wouldn't be back until Saturday." "Exactly how long were you listening to her conversation?"

"Oh, just a few minutes. Maybe thirty."

"You were listening to her conversation for thirty minutes?"

"Hey, she had it coming. She's lucky that's all I did now that I know what they've been doing." She wasn't over how Jennifer acted earlier, and knowing the harassment they did at the park, she's definitely not going to let it go. I can't believe she got all that while listening to her conversation. Right down to even knowing if they'll be home or not to bother me. If they really are going to be gone, then that does give me the opportunity to go there and help him while he's still letting his leg heal.

"It's not that I wouldn't want to do this. It's just going to his house and everything. Would it really be okay? What if his father doesn't like unexpected guests? And worst of all. What if that woman is there?"

"Even better to show that you are more than what they think. They'd never expect that you would go out of your way to go there. It would impress them big time."

"I guess I could see about this. But now what am I to do with what Sano just told me?"

"Well, do you still like him?"

"Do I still like him?"

"Yeah, do you still feel the same way you did before all this happened?"

"Uh, well," I paused for a moment. "I don't know. Lately, even though we've been around each other, and he has been kind and nice and everything…"

"So, you're telling me, after all the dreaming and talks of fate, you're not into him anymore?"

"No, that's not it. I mean, it could just be with Ken being around and he kept being on the mind just as much…"

"You pushed your feelings aside for Sano, and now you have new ones replacing those."

"Well, uh, I guess that's what happened?"

"Does Ken know?"

"Maybe. I didn't tell him though."

"Well don't tell him." she demanded.

"Don't?"

"Yeah don't. Because if you do, and somehow those pushed feelings for Sano come back, then you'll be in big trouble and back at square one. Just see what happens with this Ken plan."

"Okay then. I guess I can think about it. Is this what all girls who can't choose who they want to be with have to go through?"

"The ones that actually care for who they want to be with. Unless you do want to take them both for a spin."

"No, I'm not dating multiple people at the same time. This is already too much trouble. Besides, did you forget they're brothers? This is already weird enough."

"Not full brothers though," She reminded me like that made a difference, "but it's probably best to ditch the hots for both of them."

"Excuse me for not knowing they were related." I told her. I still can't believe that it turned out to be like that. The cool and calm Sano and the hyperactive Ken are brothers.

"I still want to know why Sano would tell you that when he knows Ken likes you." She wondered. I was wondering that too.

"Well, you can't control emotions."

"You're right, I guess. Don't let that Jennifer hear about this. If she's bringing her mother in this now, that means they're really trying to get you out of the picture and make Ken's father see that he should just stay home and accept Jenny." Katie said.

"He doesn't even like her."

"But just like with you, eventually she could persuade him." She had a point I didn't consider. He's always saying that he doesn't like her, but I didn't really like him at first either. He's known her longer. With them together like this, maybe she could somehow change him.

"Misa?" Katie called me.

"I-I'll go." I told her.

"You will?"

"Yeah. I'll go Friday after school. I know someone who could pick me up." I said. That is, assuming Jayson really will go along with this.

"So, you will go?"

"Yeah. I'll get his assignments he missed so I can seem like I actually have a reason to be there."

"That's the spirit. Maybe get some kind of get-well package too."

"You've really put some thought into this." I said. She listened to one conversation and got all of this from it.

"You like Ken. I approve of Ken. You're always saying you don't know what to do, well here it is. Exactly what to do and how to do it. I expect good results." She said with confidence. Katie, my best friend, is always looking out for me and helping me in my times of need. I couldn't ask for a better friend.

I never thought I'd find myself going to Ken's house on my own. No real reason to go other than to see him. This could be my chance to see Ken in his own home and how he lives there. Here, he doesn't do much. But what about when he's in his own house? I finally get to see how he really is being at his home. This could probably be a good trip after all.

Going to Ken's classes to get his homework wasn't the hard part. Doing it without Sano knowing was a challenge. I managed to get Ken's schedule to see where his classes were, and Sano was pretty much in all his classes when I went to find them. I had no idea they were in such classes together. There's no way I can get to them without him seeing and noticing what I'm doing. I'll have to go after school to avoid him. Talking to him now after what he said is going to be really awkward.

"Did you find his classes?" Katie asked me when I was headed out.

"Yeah, I'll go tomorrow to get his work. I knew he had some tough classes, but I've never even seen these classes."

"Well, not everyone can get into them, or would want to. I heard those AP classes were really hard." She said. Ken never has any problems with any class he has. If our history class wasn't required, he probably would be in something better than that.

"Oh, hey, look who's coming." Katie tilted her head toward the direction she saw John coming.

"Misa." He came up to me a lot calmer than he normally does. "I haven't forgotten what I did the other day. And I want to say I'm sorry about forcing myself on you. It must have cause you a lot of trouble."

"Gee, what gave you that idea?" Katie said smartly.

"I know the people around here have started more rumors about you because of it. But I... I don't regret doing it!" He admitted, "I've always wanted to be with you, Misa. Once I saw Ken and then Sano getting closer to you, I saw my chances slipping further and further away and began acting rash. But now I really see there are no chances. I just want to let you know that I will always be on your side no matter what you choose to do." I could see the hurt in his eyes, but more determination than ever.

"I'm sorry John, but I'm sure you'll make some lucky girl happy one day. Just give it some time and you'll be able to find someone ten times greater than me." I tried comforting him.

"Aw, I doubt that'll happen. If it weren't for you and when you saved me back during swim week in gym class, I probably wouldn't be here today."

That day back when we were freshmen. Back when he was quiet as a mouse and hadn't quite hit puberty yet. No one paid any attention to him, and he was always by himself. So, when the teacher stepped out and he slipped into the pool and didn't know how to swim, I jumped in to save him since no one else did.

"It was because of that day, that you became the person I always wanted to be with. But I see that won't happen." John said.

"We can always stay friends. If you don't try what you did the other day again."

"Of course! And don't worry, I'll try to change the rumors that have been going around and stop the person that's been tampering with your locker."

"Wait, you know about that?"

"Yeah, I was passing by and saw some people hanging around your locker, but I didn't know what they were doing until I passed back by and saw those hurtful words and signs."

"Did you see any of their faces?" Katie beat me to asking.

"Well, I know it was three of them. And I'm not sure, but I think one of them was that new girl that came a few weeks ago."

"I told you that Jennifer was the one doing this!" Katie walked off.

"Where are you going?"

"To find that girl."

"You can't just go up to her like that."

"And why not?" Katie asked, not understanding.

"Because you just can't. She probably isn't here now anyway."

"Actually, I saw her talking with Sano just now." John said.

"With Sano? Why would she be talking with him?" I asked.

"I thought he didn't exactly like them for how she's been treating you." Katie said.

"Did you hear them talking at all?" I asked John.

"They weren't saying much when I was passing. But it seemed like it was serious."

"Serious?"

"You think he confronted her?" Katie thought.

"I don't know. He said he was upset about it, but I didn't think he'd actually say something to her." I thought. Was it because he told me he liked me that he finally talked to her?

"You can't let that bother you Misa. You have a plan remember?" Katie reminded me. But I couldn't help but want to know why he would go out of his way to talk to her.

Just as we stopped talking, we saw someone passing by at the end of the hallway.

"Isn't that her?" Katie said. It was Jennifer. She was going down the other hallway and fast. "Didn't she seem…"

"Upset?" I finished for her. Did Sano say something to her to make her that upset?

"We should go." Katie suggested.

"Wait. I have a favor to ask." I said to John. "Do you think you could keep a listening ear out for those two about anything that may sound important?"

"Misa, you sure about that?" Katie asked concerned. I know getting John involved in this is risky, but something about the calmness he's showing is giving me a reason to ask.

John just cheerfully replied, "Hey, getting information is what I do best. You can count on me!"

For all we know, it could be nothing, so I don't want to directly ask Sano, and I know I'd get nothing from her, so this is my only option right now. I can't ask him anything right now while I have my Ken plan. But for someone like Jennifer to actually run off like that. What was said to her?

When Thursday rolled around, sure enough, Jennifer wasn't at school. She must be gone for that wedding. I went around school to get Ken's work. It seemed that someone had already got it for him. But some of his classes had additional assignments, so I got those.

I called Jayson to ask him if it was okay to go there. He was so excited to know I wanted to do it. I could see his reaction through the phone. He said he could be here to get me right after school was over. I'm starting to feel a little nervous about this. Even though it's only been a few days since he left, it's going to be weird to see him again at his home…

"Are you ready for this?" Katie asked more pumped up about it than I was.

"As ready as I can be. I told him to meet me outside of the store up the street. So, I'll head there."

"You've been staring at your locker for some time now. Did someone else put something on it?" She scanned the inside looking to see if I was hiding anything.

"No, not really. I don't know what John did, but a lot of the commotion has kind of died down."

"No matter how crazy he is, people will still listen to him if he has something to say."

"That is true." I said. I got a few judging looks from some girls I remember seeing from Ken's classes. But no notes or signs on my locker, so I was able to breathe easily from that.

"Guess I'll get going." I closed my locker and threw my book bag over my shoulder. The harder impact on my back reminded me I had something in there for Ken aside homework that I didn't tell Katie I got.

"Alright. If it gets too late, you can come crash at my house again, but you better tell me anything that happens." She said like a concerned parent. She's never been around Ken as much as I have. What she doesn't know is that anything could happen.

I headed to the store where I said we'd meet. I was looking around for expensive cars when I saw the dark blue car with the jaguar on the front with a tall man dressed in black with hair that's blowing a little too much in the wind leaning against the driver's door. If I didn't know who he was, I would've thought he was posing for a magazine. He lifted the sunglasses he had on with a big smile when he saw me and called out.

"Oh! Misaky!" He waved me over to him.

"Sorry for having you come out here." I said when I reached him.

"Oh Misaky, this is probably one of the sweetest things I could be a part of. For you to want to come and check on Kenny-kens is the best thing you could do. He's going to be so happy to see you."

"You didn't tell him I was coming?"

"Of course I didn't. I want this to be a surprise. He's been so distant. I don't know what's on his mind. But seeing you will surely bring his spirits up. And the other two girls aren't there. They left yesterday for a wedding they were invited to. You don't have to worry about Mama Baker either. Did you time this well or what?"

"I guess I just got lucky," I said. Lucky that Katie managed to hear Jennifer's conversation about everything making this easier to plan out... but he doesn't need to know that.

We got in his car, and he started the drive to the undiscovered land known as the Masidone mansion. It felt a little longer than the first time. Maybe because I'm going without Ken with us. That's because he's already there and has no idea that I'm on my way.

After the long drive, and a lot of silent deep breathing exercises, we finally arrived. Even though it was a bit cloudy and grey here, the house still looks so beautiful, like a high quality black and white picture. The wind was blowing making the grass move and dance around the yard decorations.

It was quiet, but our footsteps echoed louder as we approached the double doors with the large scripted 'M.' Jayson put in a passcode and unlocked the door. Sadly, there was no maid performance this time.

"He's in his room, Misaky. I'll take you there." He said.

I followed him up the right grand staircase to the upper level of the house. Looking back down from here gave a wonderful overview of the entrance room. The lights were on in their chandelier making what could've been a dark grey room shine brightly in every corner, bringing the house alive on cloudy day such as this. He took us down the hall passing a couple doors before he stopped at one on the left.

"Kenny-kens," he said knocking on the door, "you have a visitor to see you. Can we come in?" There was a bit of silence before I heard muffled movements from a bed.

"A visitor? Sure, the door is unlocked." I heard Ken speaking from the other side. I looked at his door wondering what kind of expression or reaction I should expect to see. Jayson opened the door and walked in.

"You'll never guess who's here to see you." He said as I slowly trailed in behind him.

I've been in his house before and toured the whole place, but didn't go to Ken's room then. I could feel my heart rate slowly increasing. It felt like I was intruding on private property. I didn't look up right away, but when I did and saw Ken in my line of sight, he was sitting up on his bed extremely surprised.

"She wanted to see how you were doing and asked to come by," Jayson explained enjoying his successful surprise.

"I see. So, this is what you weren't telling me yesterday, and why you had to leave earlier." He shook his head as he started understanding everything.

"I wanted to surprise you. She called yesterday to see if it was okay. I thought it was so sweet that she wanted to do this, and I knew you'd be happy to see her." I was looking at Ken who still seemed more shocked than happy.

"Well, it certainly is a surprise. I had no idea Mimi missed me so much." Ken finally relaxed his face and smiled.

"I- I just brought you your work," I said showing him my book bag.

"I'll leave you two for now. Let me know if you need anything." Jayson walked out and closed the door. I was in Ken's home. In Ken's room. Left alone with just Ken. It couldn't get any more awkward than this.

"You are allowed to move," he said. But I still wasn't sure if I should. It was so big.

Everything was neatly put away in its place, making it look even bigger. It's nothing like how he keeps his room at my house. His desk and bed were by the window. His TV was on the other side next to a door that I think was a bathroom. He has his own bathroom in his room.

"Are you giving my room an examination?"

I came back to my senses. "I was just looking. Anyway, here." I went over to his bedside to hand him his papers.

"Ah, thanks. I should've known they would have assigned extra work." He said looking everything over. I slowly backed away from his bed not wanting to be too close, but even though he wasn't looking, I think he noticed. "You really came all the way here just to give me a couple pieces of paper?" He asked in suspicion.

"What's wrong with wanting to give you your work you were missing? I would've thought an A+ student like you would want to make sure he'd have all his work done."

"So, I can't have the wonderful thought of you coming here to see me and how I was doing?" He pouted.

"No, you can't." I paused for a moment, "But since I'm here, I guess I can ask how you are doing."

"Well, since I've been under constant surveillance, I've managed to get a lot of rest." He said.

"Have you been lying in bed this whole time?"

"It was the only way they thought I wouldn't hurt myself again.

Now any time I'm away from my bed for more than ten minutes, someone is going to come knocking on my door to see what I'm doing." He told me. It sounds more like he's on lock down.

"Is this the first time you've ever gotten hurt?" I had to ask.

"I've gotten cuts and a few bruises here and there before, but never needed any stitching, so I guess that's why they're overreacting." He's never seriously hurt himself before. But because he's been around me, he has.

"It's not so bad. Other than always being worried about, and the repeated, 'are you doing okay' question, it's not such a bad situation. I mean because of it, Mimi came all the way here to see me." He looked at me like a happy child. He was being taken really good care of here. Suddenly, that reminded me of what Jennifer had said before.

"But I'm sure you've been getting a lot of attention here already. I heard Jenny has been taking really good care of you this whole time." I don't know why I brought her up. I thought about what she said at the park and how she knew he wasn't actually as okay as he said he was, and what she could've been doing to make sure he was getting better.

"Did you hear that from Jennifer?" He asked. I looked away from him and stayed quiet.

"Has she been saying things to you again?"

"She thought I was worried about you, so she told me that you were being taken good care of."

"Misa, I don't know what's been going on at school. When I left, I saw there were other people making a big deal out of what happened, and I don't know if it's still a problem. I asked her if she's been up to anything, but of course she wouldn't say it. So, I want to ask you. Has she been causing you any trouble at school?"

He seemed concerned about it. I couldn't tell him she was the one who has been the cause of the problems. "She really hasn't said much to me after she told me that. So, I'm not really sure what she's been doing." It isn't really a lie, so he shouldn't question that.

"She's been acting strange, and I was wondering if it had anything to do with you or how things have been turning out." He said. She's probably still bothered by whatever was said when she was talking with Sano. That conversation is still a mystery to me. I didn't want to keep talking about her or whatever it is she's up to, so I changed the subject.

"Are you still feeling a lot of pain in your leg?"

"Hm, not as much. With lying in bed all day, it's feeling better," he said rubbing his hand over it.

"That's good then. It's not every day you are the one that isn't able to do something."

"It's taken me by surprise also. This is the longest I've even stayed in one place. I haven't even been able to get my own food and water."

"It's because when people get hurt like this, they're supposed to stay still, and have someone help them when it's needed." I said like he didn't know that.

"So, if I stay like this, you'll be there to help me?" He asked.

"It's only a cut. It won't last forever, so I don't think you are in any permanent danger... But for now, I guess I can help you." I said softly. Ken looked at me for a moment without saying anything.

"What?" I asked.

"Oh nothing. It's just that you seem different today is all."

"H-how am I different?"

"If you can't tell, then it'd ruin the fun of knowing." His spirit must be returning if he's able to joke around like he usually does.

"You're always doing that. There isn't anything different from how I normally act. Are you questioning my reason for coming here? Is it a crime to want to see if the person you caused to get an injury was okay?"

"Are you still blaming yourself for this? I told you I don't blame you for what happened. It was my own careless act that got me like this."

"Even so, I still think this wouldn't have happened if you didn't need to go back out to the rink looking for my phone."

"I did it on my own free will. I wanted to help you look for your phone. You have nothing to worry about."

"Aren't you the least bit upset? Getting hurt and injured being out with me. I'm sure it wouldn't have happened if you were with one of your fans or even Jenny." I started lashing out.

"You have me really wondering what has been happening in my absence," he said.

"You've only been gone four days, but more has been happening lately. And for what? Just so one person can have his little happily ever after. What about me? In my whole life, I've never been in this kind of situation before. Now I have to worry about other girls getting upset and wondering what Jenny and Jenifer plan to do by bringing in their mother..." The words were out before I was able to stop them from coming.

"Did you say their mother?" Ken asked. I didn't come here to start trouble, but I've been so pent up with everything on my mind, I must have lost it after seeing him again.

"What did Jennifer tell you?"

S-she didn't tell me anything. Katie overheard her talking on the phone and told me what she was saying." I explained. He didn't say anything. Just sat there thinking.

"Do you know all of what she was saying?"

"Not really. Katie just told me how she was telling Jenny about me and that they were going to tell their mother about it." In normal situations, that wouldn't sound so bad, but the way Ken is thinking about it, it must mean I'm missing something.

"I don't understand why she would say that" he said.

"Why wouldn't you? It's it a normal thing to want to tell your parents something like this."

"That's not what I mean. What I'm confused about is that I was told their parents passed away."

33

"Passed away? Their parents?"

"Yes, that's what I was told. They passed a few years ago, which is why my father agreed to take them in. But there was still something about it that just wasn't coming together for me. And now that you've said that she mentioned something about a mother, I know there's something I'm missing."

"So, what does that mean?"

"Well, it's nothing that has to do with you," he told me.

But I still wanted to know. "Why would they need to hide their parents?"

"That's what I'd like to figure out. They would never mention them. They always avoid that topic." He said. I wonder why they would hide something like that.

"But again, it's not something you have to worry about." He told me again. "What I'd like to address are the other things you mentioned. Misa, even though this whole situation with me was unexpected for you, I never meant for things to turn out like this," he started, "I know you've been unsure about everything. And at this point, if you want, you can just say you don't want to do this anymore, and it'll all be over." I watched him as he spoke, but I didn't understand.

"I don't want you to continue feeling so troubled because you were forced into something you didn't want to do."

He's telling me I have the option to just be done with him and all of this. All the troubles could just fade away if I were to end this. I could go back to how things used to be. Before that day I saw him coming down the stairs in my house. That's what I wanted for the longest. But for some reason, as I stood here listening to him, something inside my chest tightened when he said that so easily. Is he having second thoughts about me? Would he want to end it? I never know what he is thinking, and for him to just suddenly say this to me...

"Humph!" I folded my arms and looked away from him.

"Misa?"

"You got a lot of nerve you know. Saying that now after all this time."

"I mean, I understand that this is all new for you. It can be a lot to handle for it being a first experience, especially when dealing with me and my particular family. I've been thinking that for a while now. And if your thoughts haven't changed about me, then you can go ahead and call it quits."

"Well, you should know that better than me, right? You're always saying how easy I am to read, and you know what I'm thinking."

"But that doesn't mean I really know. Anyone can take a guess. I'd like to actually hear it instead of always guessing. I already came to the thought that I probably wouldn't see you for another week or two. I never thought you'd actually try to come here just to see me. You risked seeing people you weren't exactly fond of. That didn't cross my mind as something you were going to do." He told me. Guess I shouldn't exactly tell him that I waited till the coast was clear on that.

"So, you not actually telling me what you feel, or thinking is still a mystery to me."

"So, I confuse you as much as you confuse me too, huh? I guess that makes us even. You like to take everything on yourself and never tell me what you're thinking, so I don't know what's going on in your head either." I told him.

"I guess we are even then. But maybe we could change that. A relationship with secrets isn't a good one."

The word 'relationship' caught me by surprise. If I don't plan to take him up on his offer of leaving, then things can lead to that. Was I ready for that? The last time I was with Ken was in my room with him trapping me, waiting for me to kiss him to override what John did. If I hadn't noticed his leg, was I going to do it? That's what a relationship would involve. Was I ready to keep that up with Ken?

"What's that?" Ken had been watching me when he looked down and noticed my still open book bag next to me. Anyone would be confused seeing a large clear plastic bag inside a school book bag. "It's nothing." I moved my bag away.

"Looks like something to me."

"You shouldn't be so nosy and looking into other peoples' things."

"Alright. Your stuff, your business," he said. But I could see his eyes shifting to sneak a peek.

"You can be so childish." I reached into my bag and pulled out what I had.

"Here. I-I didn't know what you liked. When I had my accident that time when I was younger, having my favorite snacks and stuff helped me get through the time easier." I went to the store yesterday after confirming this was happening and bought a small care basket.

Usually, people like getting those things when they're sick or have been injured badly. I couldn't think of what to get someone who could have everything already, so I just grabbed something that has a few different treats in it with a small "get well soon" bear hoping for the best. Handing it to him made me feel kind of embarrassed about it, so I didn't look at him as I passed it off.

"Y-you don't have to take it. You probably have way better stuff, so you don't…" I got distracted by how he was looking at it. He was looking at it like it was a piece of gold.

"So, it is a real thing," he said finally.

"What is?"

"I always saw it in movies, but never had someone bring me this kind of thing before while on bed rest." He made it sound like he was recovering from an illness.

"It's just something we do when we have to stay in bed because we've gotten sick or hurt."

"Since I don't get hurt often, and I haven't really been extremely sick, something like this doesn't come up often for me."

"But didn't you say your father was sick?"

"He doesn't like to express that too much. He rather it not be considered a big deal." I guess that makes sense. He probably doesn't want anyone to find out that he's not in good condition.

Ken was still looking at the basket when I heard a knock on the door.

"It's me, are you both decent in there?" I heard Jayson playfully asked, but I guess I didn't get the joke because I instantly backed away from his bedside.

"You're good for entry." Ken told him, finally setting the basket down.

"I hope you two have been enjoying yourselves. But there seems to be a bit of a problem we've run into." He came in and told us.

"What's the problem?"

"Originally, there was supposed to be a little rain coming our way, however, the wind has been picking up and it's supposed to get pretty bad out there. They're advising people not to leave unless necessary." Jayson said. I looked over to Ken's window and could see the wind was picking up and the clouds grew darker.

"So, what you're saying is…" Ken asks wanting to know what he was getting at.

"Since it's getting late, I don't want something to happen trying to take Misaky back home." I never thought to consider the weather as a problem when coming here.

Just then I felt my pocket vibrate. I looked at it a saw I had three text messages. One was from Katie, and two were from my mom. She must be worried about this weather.

"So, Misaky, this is a very safe house. We have plenty of spare space, and I know this might be an inconvenience for you, but for me, night driving in severe weather is something I like to avoid doing. It's Friday and you don't have school tomorrow, so would it be a problem if I asked you to stay the night here?" I was asked to stay here at the Masidone mansion.

Normal people wouldn't give it a second thought, but there were way too many possibilities for something to go wrong being here. Maybe I should go to the place where my parents are staying. It shouldn't be too far from here. A whole lot closer than trying to take me home.

"I think Misa's parents are in one of the apartments complexes a few miles down by the company." Ken said since I hadn't said anything.

"Oh, that's right. Would you rather go there Misaky? I can go that far." Jayson asked.

I looked at Ken. I wondered was he thinking I wouldn't want to stay here. Normally, he would welcome this idea. My hesitation is making him unsure.

"I can definitely take you there if that's—"

"I-if it isn't a problem, then I'll stay here." I cut Jayson off to say, "I wouldn't want them to worry about me while they're doing their work. So, if it's not a problem, I could just stay here."

"Really? Well then, I'll prepare the guest room." His spirits lifted almost instantly when I agreed to stay. He walked out and went back down the hallway. After all the time Ken has been at my house, I couldn't just walk out of his place when it's for one night.

"You don't have to force yourself to stay here if you don't want to." Ken said.

"I'm not forcing myself. I want to. I can finally get away from my old routine and see something new. And I wouldn't want to put Jay in any harm because of me. What, you don't want your precious Mimi here?" I didn't want him to think I was forcing myself, so I tried teasing him.

"That's not it at all. It's just that you seemed a bit uncertain about it, but maybe I was wrong." He smiled and said, "All I know now is that it's been established that you're staying here with me." He suddenly reached for me with strength I didn't know he had and pulled me down to his bed. "And you're in my territory now, so let's get comfortable." I don't know if it was from the way he was looking at me, or the way he held me down on his bed with him that made me feel really embarrassed, but I immediately got up and stood away.

"I-I think visiting hours are over," I said, and I walked away toward the door.

"Misa," He called to me. "Thanks for the gift. Just having it has made me feel a lot better." He looked at me with a big warm smile.

"N-no problem." I didn't look directly at him.

"The room Jay is probably getting ready is back down the hallway. So just go that way and you'll run right into him." He said. I reached for the door and slowly opened it.

Leaving the closed space with just Ken, the air felt different walking back down the hallway looking for the room Jayson could be in.

I noticed a door that was closed, now open, and sure enough I saw Jayson already in the room.

"Oh, Misaky, you'll be staying here." He said. I walked in and it was just as big as Ken's, but it didn't have as much as his room did. There was just a bed, TV, and dresser with few decorations. The back wall was mostly window, giving such a good view of everything outside in the backyard. I could see it was getting darker and windier. I saw flashes of lightning and heavy rain was pouring.

"This room doesn't have its own bathroom, so if you need to go, the bathroom is right across the hall here. If you need anything from me, there is a pager right here on the wall. At this time of day, the line is directed straight to my pager, so you can use it whenever you want." He showed me an intercom by the door. I was still looking around. Everything was just more than I was used to. The bed was twice the size of mine, the TV had to be fifty plus inches big, and a pager just to get a hold of someone in the same house? It was unbelievable.

"Excuse me." I looked to the door and saw a lady standing there.

"Everything has been done for the day. And with the absence of Mrs. Baker and the Jamison sisters, should I hold off on dinner until requested?" She asked. Then she glanced over at me. "Oh! We have a guest today. My apologies for interrupting anything."

"Oh, it's fine. And you know what, how would you like to have some fun cooking in the kitchen with me again?" Jayson asked me.

"Uh, sure."

"Well then, you don't have to worry about dinner for tonight," he told her.

"Alright, I'll be on my way then." She smiled and walked away.

"Well, Misaky, it's about that time we had that lovely thing called dinner anyway. Are you ready?"

"Yeah, but do you mind if I call my mom? She texted me earlier and I'd like to let her know that everything is okay with me."

"Oh sure, sure. Not a problem. I'll head down to the kitchen. Just come when you're ready." He walked out and I was left alone in this room.

I first messaged Katie back. She was worried if I made it and if she had to make any special trips. I told her that I had to stay here because of the weather. And that had her instantly texting back not expecting that. I was still shocked about it too, but I didn't want to take long talking about it with her.

I called my mom who was worried about the weather back home. I couldn't exactly tell her about it since I wasn't there. I wasn't sure if I should tell her that I was stuck at Ken's house overnight. But she's the one that wants things between me and Ken to work out the most.

Telling her I had to stay at their palace for a night shouldn't be a problem. So, I told her everything about Ken getting hurt and why I came here anyway.

"Well, Misa, it seems I owe a lot to those people," she said. "I feel you've been growing since Ken has come around." She started her 'my-daughter-is-growing-up' speech and I had to listen to it. But then she started something else. "And you know, your father told me about his time at the house when he was off. It seems that you and that kid you were interested in at the beginning of this have been getting close."

"Um, I-it's not how it seems." I tried to tell her.

"Misa, these two seem like they are both good boys. I know from the beginning you liked that one, but I'm glad that you and Ken have been getting to know each other this whole time. You probably feel you're in a tough spot if you did actually start to like Ken." My mother's 'mother's intuition' was too good.

"I just want to let you know, it was such a surprise when I heard that Mr. Masidone asked for you to meet with his son and get to know him for this whole thing. It felt like such an honor that he would even care to look us up, but I also want you to really think about it. You are still young, and still have options, but if you feel you know what you want, then I want you to know I will be okay with whether you actually stay with Ken or not. Working for this company has already shown me new things, and I know you probably have been introduced to even greater things, so just take your time and think about it, because I'm sure both those boys want what's best for you."

My mom talked for a bit more and after that we hung up. Talking with her made me feel a little better somehow. She wanted most for this to happen, but knowing she'd still be okay with me if I decided against Ken kind of made me feel at ease. That's the second time I've been told it's okay not to go with Ken. Should I take that as a sign? What's the worst that could come from being with Ken? Do I really need to take more time making my choice?

34

"Is everything okay with Mama Macky?" Jayson asked me when I finally went down to the kitchen.

"Um, yeah. Everything is fine."

"Did something not go well?"

"No, we just talked about some things. She was concerned about the weather and stuff."

"Did you tell her you were here? She didn't mind, did she?"

"No, she didn't. She thought it was for the best also. She didn't want to put you in any danger getting me back home."

"Oh, I knew she was just as sweet as you are. I believe I met her once when she went to Papa Masy's office to talk about the arrangement. You look just like her. And she seemed so thrilled about this. I knew right from then that you would be a good pick for Kenny-kens. Ever since you came around, he's been able to experience more and see things outside of these walls. I used to think that he wasn't meant to stay in this kind of life. He's always liked to venture out. I believe that part of him he got from his mother. She's also free spirited like him."

He was talking about Ken's real mother. I've only seen his stepmom. I've never seen his real mother before. I wonder what she is like. It seems he got his brain and fast thinking from his father, but what does he and his mother share? There's still so much to know about him and where he comes from. Living separately from your real mother and forced to like another woman that supposed to take her place can really be hard.

I wonder how Ken would have turned out if he were like Sano and chose to live with his mother. If he did that, would he be the same? Would I have still met him? Or would I even have liked that Ken? What about him actually made me start to like him anyway? He hasn't really changed much since he first came around. But now, there's a different feeling I have.

I pushed my thoughts aside while we finished making dinner. We made chicken alfredo, which is something I've never tried making before, but came out well once again because of Jayson's help. I asked if his father was here, but he said he doesn't get in until really late sometimes, so we made him something and wrapped it up. Jayson suggested that I be the one to take Ken's plate to him. I had his plate in my hand, and I knocked on his door.

"I-it's me." It was weird somehow to be saying that at his door.

"Is this one of those late-night visits I always saw on TV too?" I heard him say.

"No, it isn't. I brought your food."

"Oh, I prefer the late-night visit, but this will do too." He said. I opened the door to his room. He was still in his bed, but on his laptop.

"I was told that you and Jay made today's meal?" He asked looking at what I had.

"If you don't want it, then I can take it back."

"Hey, let's not get carried away now. I didn't say I didn't want it. I was just confirming the bit of info I was told."

"Well yes, we made it. Here you go." I handed him his plate of food. He looked at it with disappointment.

"What's wrong with it?"

"Oh, nothing is wrong with it. I just had a different image of how you were to come in happily bringing me my food wearing a cute apron and offering to feed me." He said lost in his crazy fantasy.

"Not even if you broke your arms would I do that."

"So, mean to the weak and vulnerable."

"You are not weak, nor are you vulnerable. If you were able to do all you did when you first got hurt, then days later after you've been resting, you should have even more strength than when you were going on your jealous rampage."

"Ah, that," he said thinking about it, "I guess I was a bit bothered then."

A bit, he says. "I don't think 'a bit' describes it. You cornered me with the look of death in your eye."

"Normally, I'm able to control my emotions, but I guess something like that doesn't really come up for me. I'm not used to the feeling of seeing someone I actually like, be with someone else like that." I felt my face get warm when he said that. He can say those things with no problem.

"It really isn't my place to do or say anything since we aren't actually together anyway." So that's why he didn't really do anything. Even though he says he likes me, he knows it wouldn't be right for him to flip completely out when we aren't even together.

"I-if it bothered you, you could've just said something instead of holding it in and hurting yourself in the end." I told him.

"Well then, I'll keep that in consideration if someone tries to come between us again." He seemed kind of happy. He doesn't have any idea of what I've been thinking the past hour that has me wondering about that smile he always gives.

"Something wrong?" He asked.

"Nothing. Just that smile of yours is creepy." He looked confused as I was going to leave. I hadn't actually considered what I was going to do next. I came here to see Ken, so should I just leave already?

"Misa," he called out to me, "You know how you were supposed to give me sympathy that day?"

My eyes grew not expecting for him to ask about that. "W-what about that?"

"*Well…*" He started. I did not like how he said that 'well.' "Since you didn't really do anything, how would you like to honor that now by accompanying me for tonight's dinner?"

I was expecting that sentence to go several different ways. Not one of them ending with him asking me to eat with him in his room. I had thought about going to the room I was staying in not sure if it would've been all right to be with him.

"F-fine." He looked at bit surprised when I agreed so easily, but then he just smiled again.

"Great! I'll be waiting." He said. He was right about what he said earlier. My behavior was kind of different today. Something about being here with Ken just makes things seem… different.

The night was long. The storm was loud, but didn't bother us in the safe walls of that incredible house as I got a bit too comfortable being there. Waking up in the world's softest bed confirmed that.

It was so comfortable; I didn't want to leave it. I just wanted to make it all mine. But I knew I needed to go back home. I glanced up from the bed and stared at the window and saw a bright sunrise. Nothing like it was yesterday. I saw a few branches scattered on the lawn as remains from the storm.

I got out of bed and went to get a full view. I felt what I was wearing and forgot that Jayson got me something to sleep in. When I first met him, he seemed like a more flamboyant Ken, but after being around him, he just seems like a really nice guy that cares.

The way he cares for Ken and is always so full of energy, I would be surprised if some of that didn't rub off on Ken over all the years, they've been around each other. I was lost in my own thoughts when I heard my phone vibrate. I looked and saw it was a text from Ken. He sent me a good morning message. Normally he comes to my room to wake me up, but he isn't really supposed to leave his bed, so this was the best he could do. I sent '*morning*' back to him.

Yesterday, I went to eat with him in his room. We watched some show he had on and made random conversation. It felt like the first time I've just hung out with him like that. Even though I had other things I wanted to ask him, I didn't bother with it and ruin the relaxed mood we finally seemed to have.

But today's mood doesn't seem like it'll be the same. I looked again at my phone and saw another text. But it wasn't from Ken. It was from Sano. I had been avoiding him again since he told me he liked me. I didn't know what to do since I was busy with Ken. I haven't even seen him around since Thursday. I wasn't sure if I should read the message, but I was curious what he wanted to say to me so early in the morning. I opened it and was about to read it when I heard a knock on the door. It was probably Jayson wondering if I was awake or not. I went to open the door and wanted to close it just as fast when I saw it wasn't Jayson who stood on the other side.

"M-Mr. Masidone!"

"Well good morning to you too Miss Macky. I hope you have been enjoying your stay here. I heard you came for a visit, and due to the weather, you stayed overnight."

"Y-yes. The weather was bad, so Jayson thought it was better if I stayed here."

"Right. He told me that when I got in. But what he didn't tell me was that we were having a guest at all." I couldn't tell if he was upset about that or not.

"S-sorry, I didn't tell you that I was coming. It was kind of a last-minute decision. I had just got curious on how Ken was doing and wanted to bring him his work he was missing." He started laughing when I explained myself.

"No need to get so defensive. You did nothing wrong," he said.

"It just touched me that you went through the trouble to see my boy. You must feel responsible for his incident. Which is also something I was unaware of when it happened."

"T-that. I'm sorry about that too. Because we were out skating and suddenly things took a turn for the worst."

"I've already heard the story from Ken. He said you felt responsible for what happened, but it wasn't your fault." He said. He didn't seem upset about anything, so why was he bringing it up?

"It seems you two have been getting close these days."

"Um, yeah. I guess you could say that."

"So, is it safe to assume that you have made that decision we talked about?"

"Decision?" I repeated. I traced my memory and remembered he was talking about me choosing between Ken and Sano. And if I didn't, he'd do it for me.

"I uh, well…"

"Oh? You haven't decided yet?" He asked.

"Um, well I…" I trailed off. I didn't want to say the wrong thing to him. I didn't prepare to run into him this soon. Luckily, a distraction couldn't have come at a better time. Too bad it wasn't a distraction I wanted.

Actually, having that storm come back and blowing the whole mansion away would have been a better distraction then hearing a "Welcome back, Mrs. Baker." Mr. Masidone turned from the door to see her. The ledge looking downstairs wasn't out of view for him, so he could see her from there walking in.

"You returned earlier than you said. Did you enjoy your trip?" He asked her.

"It was very lovely. Those two couldn't have been a better match." I heard her say. Her voice sounded like it was getting closer. Closer toward my direction. Mr. Masidone turned as if following something up the stairs.

"Did you know we were having a guest?" He asked Mrs. Baker.

"No, I didn't. We have a guest. Oh?" She said when she looked at me. "Well, hello there, Misa."

"H-hi."

At this point, jumping out of the window seemed like the greatest idea I could think of.

"To what do we owe this lovely visit?" She asked.

"It seems she was worried about Ken."

"Really now? And you decided to pay him a visit?"

"Y-yeah." I said.

"I thought I told you about that timid behavior. No need to be so stiff," Mr. Masidone said jokingly. But the amount of pressure I was getting was beyond timid behavior. Both Mr. Masidone and Mrs. Baker stood before me!

And wouldn't you know it, things just got worse.

"I have to go check to make sure Kenny is doing okay. I haven't seen him in over three days!" The voice along with footsteps came up the stairs very quickly. The harsh steps suddenly stopped when they reached the top. "Is there something wrong?"

"Not at all. I was just saying hello to our guest." Mrs. Baker said. I felt a cold sweat coming. I tried ever so slowly to back up to hit that window idea, but I was spotted by them. The loud gasp Jenny released overtook the hallway.

"You?!"

"Why is she here?" Jennifer asked.

"Now, girls, that's no way to treat our guest. She came by to check on Little Kenneth." Mrs. Baker explained.

"Really? So, she was here while I was gone?!" Jenny said not hiding her anger.

"She came by yesterday, but due to the weather we had, she needed to stay for the night." Mr. Masidone said. I looked over at Jennifer and noticed her facial expression changing.

"Well, isn't that nice. You, visiting Ken while he's home and forced to take bed rest because of his injury. I thought you guys were cute at school, but you even came here too. And to think I was thinking you didn't like him anymore after what happened in school earlier this week with that kiss from that other guy." Jennifer said.

I'm finished.

"Kiss? Other guy? Have I been left in the dark about something?" Mr. Masidone asked.

"Uh, I-it's not what you think." I said.

"You sure? He seemed to be really into you. I was shocked and almost didn't want to believe it until I kept hearing it around school." She continued to talk. I didn't know what to say. I almost felt short of breath. The thought of fainting was good too.

"There's someone else other than Sano?" Mr. Masidone asked.

"No! It's not like that! It's a huge misunderstanding!" I told them.

"You know, you're really something else." Jenny had a look of disgust.

"Jenny, I just told you. You can't be rude to Misa. She is our guest here. Show her some respect. I'm sure she has an explanation for this misunderstanding, right?" Mrs. Baker looked back to me and waited for an answer.

"John, uh, he acts first and thinks second. He's a friend that I was supposed to do something with, and then something came up and then he, well…"

"First, you're out with that other guy, and now this. You're too much!" Jenny was still losing her temper.

"Well, well, look who's home! Such a crowd, is there a party I'm missing?" Jayson's lovely voice was music to my ears as he was coming upstairs.

"Mama Baker. My lovely kittens. I see you all have come home safely." He said as he walked toward us. He glanced toward me. And if I were seeing right, he gave a quick little wink. Did he know that things were getting ugly up here? Or maybe…

I glanced down the hallway and saw Ken's door cracked slightly. He must have called him up to help the situation before it got even worse. Ken coming now wouldn't have made it better, so he thought to send him up here to help me. As he always does.

"So, why the crowd here so early? Misaky, I hope you slept wonderfully with that horrible storm. How about we all get ready for a fabulous Saturday morning breakfast?" He suggested.

"No, sorry, I've lost my appetite," Jenny said. Then the two of them headed back downstairs.

"Well now, what's gotten into those two?"

"They're just a bit upset by a misunderstanding that happened," Mrs. Baker started, "But I could see why. Misa seems to be quite the popular girl lately. They're just having trouble trying to understand why she's here when she's been having other boy troubles."

"Now, now. Let's not forget that she's still young and still may be a little perplexed with her current situation." Mr. Masidone said.

"No, I'm not." I surprised myself along with everyone else when I said that.

"Is that right?" Mrs. Baker asked.

"Yes, I'm sure. A misunderstanding happened with someone else and that's it. I know who I like. The one I like is Ken." I told them. And they all heard.

That was it. The words were out, and I couldn't take them back.

"Oh? And are you sure about that, Miss Macky?" Mr. Masidone asked me again, making sure I knew what I was telling him.

"Yes, I am."

What I said, or even the look on their faces when he, Mrs. Baker, and even Jayson exchanged looks, wasn't the thing that made things weird. The weird part was that it didn't feel as wrong to say as I thought it might. It actually felt kind of right. Suddenly, a huge weight was lifted off me. I've made my choice. And I think I'm okay with it.

******

Thank you for reading *My Choice*!

Stay up to date with current and new releases by following Brandy on social media:
Instagram- brandywrites11

Don't miss the next book in the *Choices* series!

From the Choices We Made

******

From the Choices We Made

You never realize how those crazy 'what ifs' can be true until you actually experience them. Like, "What if I got picked to be homecoming queen?" or "What if I won the lottery?" or even, "What if the son of a multibillion-dollar company wants to be with you, but has to compete with his half-brother?"

A few months ago, I never would have thought any of those 'what ifs' could possibly happen. But after Ken Masidone showed up and showed me how that last one was true, I really think anything is possible. Especially after I made it my mission to be with said half-brother, but instead, proclaimed my interest in Ken to both his parents one sunny Saturday morning after being cornered by them and everything kind of just happened.

It was no secret they were thinking things were going to turn out differently. But, even after I told them that I liked Ken, things turned out pretty well. I mean, I didn't get shipped overseas, and Jenny didn't come and try to put me in an early grave.

I told Mr. Masidone what he wanted to know, and he and Mrs. Baker passed a couple looks to each other, and then said okay to my choice in choosing Ken. Ken had finally decided to come out of his room, and he accepted, of course. Jayson got excited for us, Jenny and Jenifer took the walk of shame back home, my parents are extremely happy that everything went according to their plan, and everything is just all honky dory now between everyone. All the tension was gone, and I was actually feeling good about the whole thing while on a romantic getaway to the islands.

However, that was just how last night's dream went. The other night, Katie appeared in it as one of the maids, and took out Jenny and Jennifer with a serving tray.

What really happened at the Masidone mansion after the morning started off downhill, only stayed there. It wasn't anything like how my brain keeps trying to make it seem…

From the Choices We Made

Available on Amazon and other outlets

www.ingramcontent.com/pod-product-compliance
Lightning Source LLC
La Vergne TN
LVHW011248230225
804300LV00007B/71